BEYOND A
REASONABLE
DONUT

Books by Ginger Bolton

SURVIVAL OF THE FRITTERS

GOODBYE CRULLER WORLD

JEALOUSY FILLED DONUTS

BOSTON SCREAM MURDER

BEYOND A REASONABLE DONUT

Published by Kensington Publishing Corp.

BEYOND A REASONABLE DONUT

GINGER BOLTON

KENSINGTON
PUBLISHING CORP.

www.kensingtonbooks.com

KENSINGTON BOOKS are published by

Kensington Publishing Corp.
119 West 40th Street
New York, NY 10018

All Kensington titles, imprints, and distributed lines are available at special quantity discounts for bulk purchases for sales promotion, premiums, fundraising, educational, or institutional use.

Special book excerpts or customized printings can also be created to fit specific needs. For details, write or phone the office of the Kensington Sales Manager: Kensington Publishing Corp., 119 West 40th Street, New York, NY 10018. Attn. Sales Department. Phone: 1-800-221-2647.

The K logo is a trademark of Kensington Publishing Corp.

ISBN-13: 978-1-4967-2559-2 (ebook)
ISBN-10: 1-4967-2559-X (ebook)

ISBN-13: 978-1-4967-2558-5
ISBN-10: 1-4967-2558-1

First Kensington Trade Paperback Printing: June 2021

10 9 8 7 6 5 4 3 2 1

Printed in the United States of America

ACKNOWLEDGMENTS

Thank you to my helpful writer and critiquer friends, including Cathy Astolfo, Alison Bruce, Melodie Campbell, Nancy O'Neill, Joan O'Callaghan, Cam Watts, Krista Davis, Daryl Wood Gerber, Laurie Cass, Kaye George, and Allison Brook.

Sgt. Michael Boothby, Toronto Police Service (Retired) again reminded me kindly that police do and do *not* do certain things and act in certain ways. I'm not sure my characters always obey Mike (or me) but I owe Mike many thanks.

Again, I recommend the Malice Domestic Conference to everyone who loves traditional mysteries and getting together with other writers and readers. The organizers and volunteers deserve our appreciation.

My thanks go to agent John Talbot. Without his help, I wouldn't be having all this fun in the world of Deputy Donut.

It also would not have happened without my editor at Kensington Publishing Corp., John Scognamiglio. I owe you, John.

In fact, I owe all of the staff at Kensington. Carly Sommerstein is in the background making certain that my manuscripts end up as (gasp!) real books. She finds me some amazing copy editors, and I thank them, too. Larissa Ackerman not only helps usher my books out into the real world, she and Michelle Addo coordinate and organize the Kensington CozyClub Mini-Conventions. We might show up in a city near you, and it will be fun for all of us. Thank you, Larissa and Michelle. Kristine Mills designs my covers. I love them! Thank you, Kristine. And Kensington arranged for artist Mary Ann Lasher to paint the pictures that go on those covers. I wish she could see the awe and the smile on my face when I catch my first glimpse of them.

Thank you to my family and friends who understand that writers are people who can't help writing.

And thank you to everyone I've missed, especially readers. Thank you for being willing to believe, as I do, that Deputy Donut actually exists.

Chapter 1

꒓

Maybe I shouldn't have driven our Deputy Donut delivery car to the fairground in Fallingbrook that August morning. The sturdy Ford sedan had been through a lot in its seventy-plus years. With luck, it would survive creeping down this grassy hill even though its springs squeaked with every bump and hollow. I eased it around a grove of spindly trees.

On the passenger side of the wide front seat, Nina pointed ahead. "Emily! Look!"

A village of colorful tents, food trucks, and amusement rides had sprouted up on the flats below us. A jaunty banner fluttered above an opening in the orange plastic fencing surrounding the site. "FAKER'S DOZEN CARNIVAL," Nina read aloud. "GOOD LUCK ON FRIDAY THE THIRTEENTH!" Laughing, she turned toward me. "That sounds like a dare."

I cranked down my window, letting in sunny breezes and the smell of freshly mown grass. "Or a threat."

"Mirrors to break, black cats to cross paths, salt to spill, and ladders to walk under!" Although in her midtwenties, my enthusiastic assistant was bouncing almost more than the car was. "Too bad we'll be selling fritters all day. We could go play with the ladders. I just had a new fourteen-foot-tall one delivered, and now I can safely reach the top of my biggest canvas ever. I walk underneath ladders all the time, and I'm one of the luckiest people in northern Wisconsin, maybe in the whole world! I still can't believe that the Arthur C. Arthurs Gallery is giving me a one-person show."

I was almost as excited as she was about her show at the prestigious art gallery in Madison. "It's not luck," I reminded her. "Did you finish your paintings in time for the movers last night?"

"All but one, so they crated the others and took them away. All I have to do is put the finishing touches on the biggest and, I hope, most expensive one. And don't worry. I scheduled time for the preparations for Samantha and Hooligan's wedding on Wednesday. The florist has already ordered the flowers. We'll decorate the tent Wednesday morning, and then I'll help you, Samantha, and Misty with your hair and makeup before I scoot into my seat to watch you all walk down the aisle. I can hardly wait! Samantha and Hooligan are a perfect couple, and it was sweet of them to ask me to design the flowers."

I steered toward an opening in the fencing. "They're thrilled to have a real artist doing it."

"They're paying me too much."

"I doubt that." I knew that Nina was worth every cent, and she could use the extra funds, besides. She worked full-time at Deputy Donut, but the combination loft apartment and artist's studio she rented had to be expensive, as were art supplies. And she hadn't yet sold many paintings. She'd been saving for that ladder for about a year.

A tall and imposing woman stepped in front of our pretend police car, thrust out her hand, and yelled, "Stop!" Her bright pink, purple, and yellow floral dress, broad-brimmed straw hat, and black sandals might have given the impression that she was a genteel lady on her way to a garden party. Her severe black vest and belligerent stance—inches from our chrome front bumper—ruined the impression. I stopped the car. Now that we were close to the carnival's food stands, I smelled popcorn and candy floss.

The woman studied her clipboard. EVENT MANAGER was embroidered in white letters on the black vest. She had to be Marsha Fitchelder, the organizer of the Faker's Dozen Carnival. She bent down and peered into the car and then looked back and forth from us to her clipboard as if comparing us to the photos on our vendor's application. The hats we'd worn for our carnival identification photographs, imitation police hats with fake fur donuts taking the place of badges, were on our heads. Still, Marsha should be able to see my dark brown, curly hair and Nina's lighter brown, shorter hair beneath the caps. Maybe, since Marsha was in dazzling sunlight and we were inside the car, she couldn't quite make out that my eyes were blue and Nina's were brown, but she should have been able to see Nina's high, sharp cheekbones and her amazingly long eyelashes. And although we weren't standing up, it must have been clear that Nina was tall while I, as Nina liked to tease, could barely see over the old Ford's big steering wheel. I hoped Marsha wasn't going to haul out a scale and make us prove we were the weights we'd claimed to be.

"ID," she demanded.

We handed her our driver's licenses. She stared at them, examined our faces, and gave me a suspicious glare. "You don't look all of thirty-two." Marsha was quick at figuring out ages from birth dates. She must have been doing it all morning.

I thanked her and held out my hand. "I am."

She plopped both licenses into it. "But your assistant looks twenty-six, like she is on her license."

Attempting to ignore Nina's unladylike and very fake coughing fit, I smiled my best customer-relations smile. "We're from Deputy Donut." That should have been apparent from more than our hats. A huge plastic donut with white plastic frosting dotted with tiny lights masquerading as sprinkles was mounted flat on the car's roof where the light bar would be on a real police cruiser. And in case that enormous fake donut didn't make it clear, our Deputy Donut logo, the black silhouette of a cat wearing a rakishly tilted hat like ours, decorated the white front doors of the black car.

Marsha stuck out her lower lip. "You can't drive in here."

I stated what I thought was obvious. "We're exhibitors."

"I know that!" She gestured toward the way we'd come. "You have to park back there in the parking lot."

I checked the rearview mirror. "Back there" was far away, high on that lumpy hill I'd just driven down. And we'd brought large pails of ingredients. I asked politely, "Can we unload first?"

Marsha's face was close to mine. She'd been eating peanuts. "That was supposed to be done last night."

I gripped the wheel more tightly. "The large things were brought then, but—"

Marsha interrupted me. "Today, you carry in whatever you didn't have the foresight to deliver last night."

I pleaded, "Can we unload here, and then leave the car up there on the hill?"

Marsha either growled or cleared her throat. "Not in front of the entrance." She pointed toward my left. "You can take one of the spots over there, but they're reserved for dignitaries, so you'll have to unload quickly and then park where you were supposed to. We open at ten and it's already nine."

She stalked back to the middle of the entryway and stood there with her feet apart, her arms folded, a scowl on her face, and breezes rippling the hem of her flowered dress.

Nina whispered, "Is that her real personality or is that one of the day's faker's dozen pranks, like she's faking being ornery?"

"That would be funny. She's doing a good job of it."

"Who are the dignitaries she's expecting?"

"On Friday the thirteenth? They could be anyone or anything."

"Today is going to be fun." The always-cheerful Nina was not being sarcastic.

Leaving space for about three limos between our donut-topped car and Marsha, I parked in front of a RESERVED sign zip-tied to the orange fencing. I asked Nina, "Wouldn't you rather be at home, painting in your loft?"

"Of course not! If we weren't here today, we'd be serving donuts and coffee at Deputy Donut, and that's always fun. Besides, I have to wait for paint to dry before I add to my"— she made air quotes—"masterpiece." I could tell from the tremor in her voice that she loved that almost-completed masterpiece.

We each carried two heavy pails of fritter batter past Marsha. She was haranguing the driver of a red cube van and didn't seem to notice our polite greetings.

The walk was long, but we finally arrived at a big red-and-white-striped tent decorated with a Deputy Donut banner draped across the front. The banner, created for the Faker's Dozen Carnival, featured the black cat from our logo, horseshoes, four-leaf clovers, and donuts. The night before, my father-in-law and business partner, Tom, had persuaded some of his retired police-officer colleagues to help him and the staff from a rental company wrestle three large deep fryers, a fridge, and three sets of stainless-steel counters and cabinets into our tent. The carnival had provided a capacious sink with hot and cold running water. Nina and I put the batter into the nicely cold fridge and went back for more.

Marsha was not at her station. A windowless black van had appeared between the entryway and our donut car.

I muttered to Nina, "Did that van escape from a morgue parking lot?"

She giggled. "Usually our first-responder friends attend events with their fire trucks, ambulances, and police cruisers, just to be ready. A van from the morgue is carrying preparedness a little far."

I intoned in a sinister voice, "Maybe not on Friday the thirteenth."

We walked around the back of the van. On the other side of our car, Marsha was beside a tiny pink car with MIME MOBILE written in purple on the door.

Marsha shook a finger. "You can't leave your car here!" She wasn't talking to us. She was glowering at a tall, thin woman wearing a black beanie on her fluffy orange hair, a red-and-white-striped T-shirt, pink sandals, and baggy black shorts held up by chartreuse suspenders.

The thin woman turned toward us. She was made up like a sorrowful clown, her face powdery white with a dramatic, downturned red mouth, a red dot on the tip of her nose, and thick black eyelashes painted on her cheeks and forehead. She wore white gloves with red fingernails inked on them. Without a word, she mimicked Marsha's stance and finger-shaking.

I restrained a smile. People who had been heading toward the entryway had gathered around us. They laughed.

Marsha's face reddened. "Don't you shake your finger at me! Move that car."

The mime sidled closer to Marsha, peered down at Marsha's clipboard for a few seconds, and then pretended to hold a clipboard of her own. She ran her gloved finger down the top page of her invisible clipboard, jabbed her finger down on it, looked straight at Nina and me, and pointed two fingers at her eyes and then at us as if to warn she was watching us. Then she made a circle with both hands and planted the circle on her forehead, obviously imitating the donuts on our hats. Holding her stomach with both hands, she bent over and acted like she was laughing uproariously, without the roar.

Our hats were funny, but I didn't think they were that funny.

Marsha clutched her clipboard close to her chest and ordered, "Now move that car!"

The mime made the exaggerated shrug of a person who could do nothing about a tragic situation, patted the car, and motioned with her hands as if outlining an even smaller car.

Marsha balled her free hand into a fist and put it on her hip. "I don't care how small it is. It's in the area designated for dignitaries."

With great exaggeration, the mime cradled an invisible clipboard lovingly against her heart, plunked a fist on a hip, and then thrust her hands into her pockets, turned them inside out, and looked desolated.

The audience clapped. The mime pulled her beanie off and waded into the crowd. Her posture dejected, she held the beanie upside down and pointed into it. Her pockets were still inside-out. People good-naturedly put coins and bills into the hat.

Steaming about as much as the hot dog stand beyond the fence, Marsha stomped back toward the carnival's entryway, probably to ward off more vehicles.

I turned away from the crowd surrounding the mime, opened the donut car's trunk, and asked Nina, "Can we take the rest in one load?"

"Sure. It will save us time." Our arms ended up full, but I managed to slam the trunk, and we carried boxes of donuts we'd made and decorated early that morning to our tent and set the boxes on one of the stainless-steel counters.

I offered Nina the car keys. "Want to drive the car up that hill and park it while I organize here?"

Nina loved driving that car. We all did. "Sure! It can handle that hill just fine." As coltish and bony as a teenager, a very tall one, she bounded away. We were dressed alike in knee-length black shorts, long-sleeved white shirts, and our donut-festooned police caps. We never bothered to coordinate our shoe colors. She was wearing turquoise sneakers. Mine were red.

In order to make change, we'd brought coins from our shop and brand-new bills from the bank. I sorted it all into the lockable cash drawer's compartments, and then I put on a Deputy Donut apron, white with our logo embroidered on the bib. I filled the deep fryers with oil, started them heating, stowed away ingredients we wouldn't need at first, and arranged decorated donuts in a glass-sided display case.

Nina returned. I thanked her for parking the car and asked, "Were Marsha and the mime still putting on a show?"

"No. Turnstiles are blocking the entryway. Marsha and a couple of other people wearing black vests are checking tickets that people bought at the fairground gate where we first drove in, where we showed our vendor's pass. I didn't see the mime, but her car was still beside ours."

When the oil reached the correct temperature, we dropped spoonfuls of fritter batter into it. They were corn fritters, but in honor of the day of luck, fun, pranks, and jokes, we were calling them corny fritters. We were making them small so they'd be easy to eat with fingers, and if people wanted a dozen, they were getting thirteen for the price of twelve. All of the food vendors at the carnival were doing the same thing.

Our timing was good. At precisely ten, I removed the first basket of fritters from the hot oil. A family wanted a baker's dozen. "The regular corny fritters are ready," Nina told them. She looked over at me and the fryers. Fritters bobbed in all three of them. "And the peppercorny and turbo-charged spicy corny fritters will be ready soon. We can dip any of them in granulated or confectioners' sugar." She pointed at the display case. "And we have donuts, too." The family opted for non-spicy, non-sugared corny fritters.

Nina and I got into a rhythm. I made the fritters, put them into paper bags, and set the bags on the sales counter for customers. Nina took care of the money. If she needed to touch food, she pulled on a pair of food-handling gloves.

A couple with their arms around each other wanted turbocharged spicy corny fritters. "What's with the police car out front?" the man asked us.

Did he mean ours, which, unless Nina was playing pranks on me, wasn't exactly out front but was up on the hill? I put their fritters into tiny paper bags. "The one with the donut on top?"

Dimples bracketed the man's grin. "Not that one. I recognize your Deputy Donut car. I mean a real one from the Fallingbrook Police Department. Two officers were talking to one of the people taking tickets."

The woman in line behind the couple explained, "The event manager was yelling at them to tow away a little pink car because it belonged to an exhibitor, not a paying guest. The officers explained that anyone can park outside the area that was rented for the carnival." The woman flapped a hand toward tents and booths around us. "Apparently, the carnival doesn't have jurisdiction outside the orange fence, except for the fairground's main entry where we bought our tickets."

The woman beside her added, "I thought the carnival's manager would blow a gasket, but the police officers were polite and talked her down."

I wasn't surprised. Some of my best friends worked for the Fallingbrook Police. That department had a culture of friendly service dating back to before Tom was a detective and then chief.

Nina made change for the couple at the front of the line. "Did the police have the little pink car towed?"

The man pocketed the change. "No. They apologized and left."

The mime must have been lurking around the side of the tent. She appeared in front of me, pointed at her heart, pretended to lick the index finger of one of the white gloves with the red nails, and made a vertical stroke in the air. I translated the gesture as *Chalk one up for me.*

The people in line laughed, and the mime went through her routine of being nearly inconsolable while she passed her beanie around.

Nina whispered behind her hand to me, "She could be making more than we are."

Maybe she wasn't. People loved our fritters. About midmorning, a pair of cute teens in shorts and red Fallingbrook High T-shirts asked to have their turbo-charged spicy corny fritters dipped in confectioners' sugar. We had brought a large covered plastic bucket of it.

Nina and I searched the cabinets underneath the counters. We looked inside the fridge.

The bucket of sugar wasn't anywhere in our tent.

Chapter 2

We explained to the patiently waiting couple that we must have forgotten to bring confectioners' sugar to the carnival.

"That's okay," the girl told us. "Our fritters don't need to be covered in it."

I could tell that the boy's frown was a fake, even before he grinned and agreed.

I offered, "Would you like us to roll them in granulated sugar instead?"

The girl exclaimed, "Sure!" When she tasted hers, she fanned her face with her free hand. "Whoa, you weren't kidding about spicy." The boy smiled down at her. They headed into the crowd.

Nina appeared as puzzled about the missing sugar as I was.

What could have happened? We'd told the couple that we must have forgotten the confectioners' sugar, but both of us knew we hadn't. Earlier that morning when we'd been ready to leave Deputy Donut, we'd realized that we hadn't packed any. We hadn't wanted to make ourselves late by taking time to scoop some of it into a smaller container. Nina had dashed into our storeroom and grabbed a brand-new bucket. I'd helped her cram the bucket behind the donut car's front passenger seat.

The wrinkles between Nina's eyebrows deepened. "I checked the label when I got it from the storeroom, but when we were unloading the car, I grabbed pails without reading labels." All of the pails were nearly identical—large and made of white plastic.

I hadn't read labels when we were unpacking the car, either, but I had paid attention to them while I stored the ingredients in the tent. I had placed our small container of granulated sugar on the counter near the deep fryers where it would be handy for coating fritters while they were still warm. I suggested, "Maybe we brought it to the tent, and another vendor decided they needed it more than we did." The only things lockable in the tent were the cash drawer and a cabinet big enough for Nina's turquoise and purple hand-woven tote bag and the cute red backpack I carried as a purse.

Nina asked, "Did we lock the car every time we left it?"

"Maybe not." Locking and unlocking the doors and trunk of the old car was more of a procedure than pressing a button on a remote or carrying a key fob toward a car. "When we went back for that last load, we were distracted by Marsha Fitchelder and her argument with the mime. I think we emptied the trunk, but I'm not sure about the space behind the passenger seat, and my arms were full of donut boxes, so I'm not positive that I locked the trunk, let alone the doors."

"Maybe it was still behind the passenger seat when I moved the car. I should have checked."

"I should have, too."

She suggested, "We could cross CONFECTIONERS' SUGAR off our signs."

We'd stockpiled enough fritters for me to take a break. I frowned. "I hate to eliminate one of the variations we're offering here today, and besides, I can't resist a mystery. I'll go look in the car."

"It's pretty far up the hill."

"I'll find it." Still wearing my Deputy Donut hat and apron, I strode to the carnival's entryway.

Marsha and two other ticket-takers stood underneath red umbrellas beside turnstiles. I pushed my way out through the exit closest to Marsha. She was glaring, maybe because the mime's pink car was still in the area she'd earmarked for dignitaries. The morgue-like van was gone. Whoever the dignitaries were, they had not yet taken advantage of the spaces reserved for them. The little pink car was the only vehicle there.

I started up the hill. Vehicles kept arriving. A windowless black van similar to the one that had been next to our car in the area reserved for dignitaries was among the parked cars and trucks glittering in the sunshine. The van I'd seen earlier had been plain black. This one had a website address, printed in red letters, near the bottom of the driver's door.

I didn't take time to read it.

Farther up the hill, a woman was standing next to our Deputy Donut car. Her right hand was on the driver's door.

Most of the people at the carnival on that nearly cloudless day were in shorts and T-shirts. This woman wore a roomy dark green twill shirt over a long, gauzy coral skirt. Instead of making her look bulky, the voluminous clothing accentuated how petite she was. Her wavy hair was tied back in a low ponytail that almost reached her waist. The hair on top of her head was pale, gradually shading darker to chestnut-brown at the tip of her ponytail. As I climbed closer, I realized that the pale hair was blond, not white, and she appeared to be in her midtwenties.

She shaded her eyes with her left hand, leaned down, and peered into the car. People often wanted a better look at our authentically restored sedan.

I called out in a friendly way, "Hello! Would you like to see inside?"

The woman jerked upright as if she'd heard me, but instead of turning my way, she hunched her shoulders and scut- tled behind the donut car. Possibly heading toward a gray car, she disappeared beyond a white pickup truck.

Had the woman done something inside our car? Had she been trying to open the driver's door, or had she been clos- ing it?

The doors and trunk were locked. I unlocked them. The bucket of confectioners' sugar was not in the car, and noth- ing seemed to have been disturbed.

Starting down the hill, I took a better look at the black van. The website address on the door appeared to be for a health organization for veterans. The lettering was level with the sloping ground, but not level with the bottom of the van, as if the sign had been hastily slapped onto the door.

It could have been the van we'd seen next to the donut car earlier.

If so, our missing sugar might be inside it.

As surreptitiously as possible considering that I was wear- ing a fake police cap embellished with a fuzzy donut, I pulled my phone out of my apron pocket and snapped photos of the website and the van's license plate. I slid my phone into my pocket. Still trying to look casual, I eased into the crowd. People walking down the hill chattered about what they hoped to do and eat at the Faker's Dozen Carnival.

Behind me, a man said, "That's quite a hat." I turned around. The man was about my age. He smiled at the donut above the bill of my hat. "Nice."

Although he wasn't hard to look at, I couldn't help glanc- ing beyond him to our donut car farther up the hill. The woman who'd been peering into the car was again beside it. She was looking down toward the carnival, though, and not into the car. As far as I could tell, she wasn't touching the car. Knowing that it was locked and that if I approached her she might disappear again, I paid attention to the man compli- menting my hat. "Thank you. I work for Deputy Donut."

I did not comment on his panama hat or his dressy black slacks and long-sleeved white shirt. They seemed formal for a carnival in the middle of August, especially for someone in his thirties. Maybe he'd worn a long-sleeved shirt for the same reason I did. I'd figured I might be in the sun more than usual that day, and applying sunscreen while preparing food would have been, at the very least, complicated. My shorts, red sneakers, apron, and funny hat kept my white dress shirt from looking as formal as the man's freshly pressed one, however. Maybe he was a dignitary and didn't know about the reserved spots. I could imagine Marsha waiting to see who arrived before deciding who deserved VIP treatment. By then the chosen VIPs would have parked farther away.

I pointed down the hill. "We have donuts and we're making corn fritters at our tent. It's down there in the middle of the food and game booths, before you get to the rides." Beyond colorful tent peaks and brightly lit signs, a Ferris wheel turned.

The man asked, "Are corn fritters a Wisconsin thing?"

"They're one of our Deputy Donut things. Today, in honor of the carnival's jokes and pranks theme, we're calling them corny fritters."

His eyes lingered on my face, probably on the freckles. "Cute. I'll have to stop by."

"Are you new in town?"

"I'm on vacation."

Behind him, a thirtysomething blonde in hot pink shorts and top and a floppy hat asked him, "How long will you be in the area?"

"For another week, but I'd like to stay longer." Again, his eyes lingered on my face.

The blonde began listing things he should see and do around Fallingbrook. They headed together toward Marsha and the other ticket-takers. Pleased by my accidental matchmaking, I detoured to the mime's car, still alone in the row reserved for dignitaries. I tried not to be as obvious in my snooping as the woman in the gauzy coral skirt had been. The mime's car had only two seats. The pail of sugar could have fit, just barely, behind them. If it was there, it was underneath a heap of clothing and blankets. I behaved myself and didn't try the doors. Aware of the ever-vigilant Marsha nearby, I also didn't take pictures.

At the Deputy Donut tent, Nina was serving cream-filled donuts covered with strawberry frosting and shredded coconut to customers. I dropped more fritter batter into bubbling oil and called Tom. He said that with so many of our regular customers attending the carnival, Deputy Donut wasn't busy. He'd send Jocelyn, our assistant who was back from college for the summer, to the carnival with more confectioners' sugar.

"Not on her bike, I hope," I teased.

"She can drive my car."

Jocelyn arrived fifteen minutes later. Wearing her Deputy Donut uniform and grinning, she plunked a container, not an entire bucket, of confectioners' sugar on the table behind us. "Tom told me to stay here long enough for each of us to have a turn looking around the carnival."

I lifted a basket of golden fritters out of the oil. "Which one of you wants to go first?"

"Jocelyn does," Nina said.

Jocelyn returned a half hour later, and Nina took off her hat and apron and went for her own tour. When Jocelyn and I weren't serving customers, we made up lyrics to go with the calliope music coming from the amusement rides. Several tunes were playing at once, so nothing we sang made sense or had a recognizable melody, especially since neither of us was very good at carrying a tune, but we kept singing and making each other laugh.

She looked past me. Her smile widened. "Hey! Welcome!"

I looked up from rolling fritters in a bowl of confectioners' sugar.

Detective Brent Fyne was smiling at Jocelyn and me. Breezes teased his light brown hair, and his gray eyes were warm. He was dressed too casually for work, in jeans, a pale blue T-shirt, and a lightweight jacket. We usually went kayaking together whenever we both had a free afternoon, but I was taking Tuesday and Wednesday off for Samantha's wedding and the fun leading up to it, and might not be able to go kayaking either of those days, so it didn't matter that Brent had a day off when I didn't. I was a little surprised, though, because he hadn't mentioned it to me.

Judging by his attentive expression, he wasn't as relaxed as he was in my living room with my cat on his lap or when we were paddling in our kayaks on a calm lake or stream. I realized that, despite my first impression, he was probably on duty. It was a warm day for a jacket. Maybe he was wearing it to hide a shoulder holster.

Nina bopped into the tent and handed him a sugar-coated turbo-charged spicy corny fritter. "Try this." She gave me a mischievous smile. "It's little and cute and sweet-looking like Emily, but watch out. It's hot."

The tops of my ears flamed. "Heat hot and spicy hot," I warned.

Like all of the fritters we were making that day, it was small. Brent popped it into his mouth. "Wow. You weren't kidding. It's beyond a reasonable donut."

I laughed. "It's a fritter."

Nina tied on an apron. "Emily, it's your turn to wander around the carnival. It's fun! You might as well go with Brent."

"Yes," he said, "if you can, Em."

"She can," Nina told him.

Jocelyn added, "She's supposed to. Tom said."

The tops of my ears burned more. Jocelyn and Nina were certain that Brent and I should be more than friends, but I wasn't ready to date even now, almost seven years after my late husband, Alec, who had been Brent's best friend and also his partner on the police force, had been shot and killed. Brent understood, and although we were close, I suspected he would have felt uncomfortable in a romantic relationship with his best friend's widow.

I took off my hat and apron, picked up a bag of peppercorny fritters to share, and joined Brent in the walkway between food and game booths.

He asked, "What's Dep doing today?"

Tom and I had named our donut and coffee shop after my cat. Due to the donut-like circles on her sides, Alec had christened her Deputy Donut when she was a tiny kitten. "I took her to work this morning. Tom will drop her off in my house after he closes the shop." With food, water, toys, and litter boxes both at home and in the office that Tom and I had designed especially for her at work, Dep would be fine until I returned.

A pair of eleven-year-old twins who occasionally came to Deputy Donut with their mother skipped past us. Behind them, their mother hollered for them to wait. They did.

Brent asked them, "What's the best thing to do in the carnival?"

The boy didn't hesitate. "The rides!"

The girl pointed to the right. "The Friday the Thirteenth tent. You can break mirrors and walk under ladders."

Brent turned to me. "Who can resist that?"

I smiled back at him. "Let's go tempt fate!"

The mother corralled the twins toward the rides.

Brent and I meandered along, savoring the tasty fritters and trying not to bump into each other or anyone else. We finished the fritters and tossed the empty bag into a trash container. Brent asked, "Mind doing a little pretending, playing a role?"

I looked up at him. "What?"

He stared straight ahead. "This." His hand clasped mine.

Suddenly my throat felt funny, like I couldn't breathe. "No," I managed. "I don't mind." Brent was my kayaking partner, my dinner buddy, and one of my cat's favorite people. His watchful detective look had hinted that he was at the carnival because of something connected to work, so maybe that was the reason for his request. I returned the pressure of his hand.

He murmured, "If I tell you to take cover, don't ask, okay? Just do it?"

"Okay." I knew the drill from my few short years with Alec. Police officers did not plan to mix work with social life, but duty sometimes intruded. "Is there anything or anyone I should be looking for?"

"No. Just enjoy the carnival."

After my initial surprise, holding his hand and acting like his date was almost comfortable. We found the Friday the Thirteenth tent and bought our tickets near a sign that said FIRST, THE GOOD LUCK . . .

Inside, we knocked on wood, stroked an obviously fake and rather large rabbit's foot that was still attached to an obviously fake and rather large rabbit, touched a horseshoe mounted with its ends pointing upward to keep the good luck trapped inside its curve, and hunted for plastic four-leaf clovers in a tray of mostly three-leaf clovers. Another tray was full of pennies. The ones lying faceup were the lucky ones, and people who found one got to keep it. Finally, we had a chance to throw coins into a fountain and make a wish. I kept my lucky penny in my shorts pocket and threw a nickel into the fountain. Grinning, Brent flicked his lucky penny into the fountain.

"I'll have good luck all day," I teased. "You won't."

He took my hand again. "Maybe lucky pennies grant bigger wishes when they're thrown into fountains. Do we dare go into the next section of the tent?" It was labeled: AND NOW, THE BAD LUCK.

I pulled him toward it. "Definitely."

Brent investigated a ladder leaning against a wall inside the tent. "It's securely fastened, top and bottom."

I looked up. "And there's no bucket of paint on top about to spill. It's perfectly safe." We let go of each other's hands. Bravely, I walked underneath the ladder first.

We knocked over saltshakers, spilling salt. We opened umbrellas inside. We touched horseshoes mounted with the ends pointing down, letting good luck dribble out. On a track above our heads, a motorized toy black cat puttered back and forth, crossing our path again and again.

Someone had rigged up a way we could break mirrors without cutting anyone. I peered through thick glass into a box. A tiny mirror slid into view. I could see most of my nose in it but couldn't make out the freckles. I pressed a lever. A hammer inside the box slammed into the mirror. The broken pieces fell out of sight, and then Brent got a turn. Shouting with excitement, kids pressed the lever and ran to the back of the line to smash more mirrors.

Rocking empty rocking chairs was popular with smaller kids. Laughing parents told them not to sit in the rocking chairs. A father explained, "They have to be empty when they're rocked to bring us all bad luck."

Brent deadpanned, "And that's what we came for."

The father grinned at us. "Or not."

A sign at the tent's exit suggested going around the tent to the good luck section and starting over to erase the bad luck we'd brought upon ourselves. "Paying admission again?" I asked. "That would be bad luck."

Laughing, Brent squeezed my hand. "Do you have time to check out the rides?"

"I should go back to our tent so Jocelyn can leave to help Tom at Deputy Donut."

"I'll come with you."

"You don't have to." I didn't want Jocelyn and Nina to see us holding hands. They'd be certain they'd succeeded in their matchmaking.

I didn't have to worry. Brent let go of my hand before we were in sight of the tent. And then I missed the comfort of that strong hand. He said goodbye and headed toward the rides.

Jocelyn left. Nina and I were busy but not overwhelmed until midafternoon, when some of our regulars from Deputy Donut showed up. The women who called themselves the Knitpickers joined the back of the line. We waved at them and served the people in front of them.

A magician in a black top hat and a black coat with tails walked along the line of waiting customers. He touched each Knitpicker's hair and handed the surprised ladies green plastic four-leaf clovers he appeared to have pulled from their ears. The Knitpickers laughed, obviously enjoying the attention and the carnival.

I was standing near a deep fryer, which might have been why I thought the magician's black top hat, white wig with its attached beard, and black leather gloves were too hot for the day. Also, his fleshy cheeks and bulbous nose were flushed and shiny with perspiration. It was the first time I'd ever seen a magician carry a briefcase, but I guessed he had to keep his magic paraphernalia handy, and a briefcase went better with the coat and tails than a backpack would have. Besides, the briefcase was black, matching his suit.

Walking like a proud mama, the mime approached the other side of the lineup and mimicked an actual mother who was pushing a baby carriage nearby. The Knitpickers were now in the front of the line, straggled out and no longer standing two-by-two. They turned and watched the mime.

Her orange puffy wig was crooked. She exaggerated a fake tremble as if afraid of the invisible baby in the invisible carriage. Her knees knocked together in a comical way that made her long skinny legs look almost rubbery. The Knitpickers laughed.

The magician handed the Knitpicker closest to our counter a plastic clover. He reached across the counter. His arms were long. He gave me a clover he had supposedly pulled from my ear.

He set his briefcase on the counter. Reaching over it, he extended one black-gloved hand toward Nina's hair.

His other hand was behind his briefcase where I couldn't see it.

Nina yelped and slammed the cash drawer.

Chapter 3

✿

Nina caught the tips of the magician's gloved fingers in the cash drawer.

The magician yanked his hand out. Clasping his briefcase in one hand and a fistful of brand-new five-dollar bills in the other, he sprinted toward the carnival exit.

I shouted, "Stop!"

The mime followed the magician. Nina ducked underneath the tent's rolled-up wall and ran outside. Dodging carnival attendees, she chased the mime and the magician up the pathway between tents and booths.

Cheryl, the Knitpicker in the back of the line, shouted, "I stuck out my foot, but I didn't manage to trip that mime!" About a year before, she had experimented with dating sites and blond-streaked brown hair. Her curls were now almost pure white. She still wore the saucy purple-framed glasses, though, and a brilliantly turquoise shirt printed with red hibiscus flowers and green palm trees. She resembled a slimmed-down Mrs. Claus on a tropical vacation.

She and the other Knitpickers clustered at the counter. Virginia urged me, "You can go after them, Emily. We'll stay here while you're gone."

I leaned forward, but our counter was in my way and I

wasn't tall enough to see much beyond our tent. "I don't think I could catch them. Can you still see them?"

Virginia backed a few steps. "Just the top of Nina's hat. Oops! She disappeared around the far side of that waffle truck."

I phoned Brent. "We've been robbed." I sounded surprisingly unflustered. "A magician took money from our cash drawer. But he also took four-leaf clovers out of our ears, so maybe the robbery was a prank." I answered the question I was certain Brent was about to ask. "It didn't seem like one. He gave us the clovers." Maybe I wasn't as unflustered as I thought. "But he didn't give us back the money. He ran away."

"I'm at the horseshoe pitch, beyond the House of Mirrors." Brent's voice was calm and even. "I'll be right there unless I find him first, and he and I have a little chat."

The "little chat" remark was typical of Brent's cop humor and his way of defusing a situation. I couldn't help feeling better.

Disposable food-handling gloves made it possible for me to cook and serve fritters and also take money and make change. I gave the Knitpickers their fritters. "My detective friend Brent is at the carnival, and he's on his way. Can you stick around and tell him what you saw?"

Cheryl's curls bobbed with her vigorous nod. "We sure can!"

Virginia stared at the spot where the mime had been entertaining the lineup of people waiting for fritters. "That mime was distracting everyone with her antics so the thieving magician could reach into your till."

Cheryl patted her purse. "At least he didn't get my wallet." She showed us the clip attaching her wallet to a strap inside the purse.

Priscilla clutched at her chest. "I'm having palpitations! He was so close! He could have robbed us all!"

Imitating one of the mime's most despondent grimaces, Virginia groaned. "Or worse."

Cheryl bit into her fritter. "These are worth being almost robbed."

The other Knitpickers agreed. They were some of my very favorite Deputy Donut customers. I asked them, "Why are you here? I thought you spent your afternoons knitting."

Cheryl shook her head, causing those curls to bob in a new direction. "Not every afternoon! We sometimes go on outings. This morning in Deputy Donut, Jocelyn told us you were here today, so we decided to check out the carnival. We always enjoy your donuts and fritters, and besides, we missed talking to you and Nina this morning."

"And here's Nina, back already!" Virginia wasn't usually so animated. The robbery must have disturbed the Knitpickers at least as much as it had disturbed me.

Cheryl patted Nina's arm. "Are you okay?"

Between breaths, Nina gasped, "I thought the magician was heading for the parking lot, but he veered toward the Friday the Thirteenth tent. He'd gotten a head start and he was a fast runner for an old guy. I lost track of him. I started to come back here because I didn't want to leave you alone for long, Emily. I was so angry I wasn't exactly thinking straight, but I finally realized that if the magician and mime were working together, I should try to beat the mime to her car and question her there, but before I got to Marsha Fitchelder and her turnstiles, the pink car was already at the top of the hill. It sped toward the entry gates and went out of sight." Nina's face was bright red. She turned toward the Knitpickers. "I'm sorry I left and made you wait longer for your fritters."

Cheryl tossed me a mischievous glance. "We got our fritters, but we have to wait, anyway, for Emily's boyfriend."

I had to protest. "He's not my—"

Cheryl's smile became so large that her rosy cheeks nearly hid her eyes. "My niece is around here somewhere today. She told me she saw you holding hands with him, Emily. Maybe that wasn't you."

Nina's smile was even more mischievous than Cheryl's. "What?"

Priscilla looked to her right and smiled. "Oooh. Here he comes!" She leaned toward me and whispered, "He's gorgeous! He should be your boyfriend."

I just shook my head.

As always watchful, Brent said quietly to Nina and me, "I've called for more officers. Who got the best look at the magician?"

Nina's breathing had slowed, but her face was still red. "I might have. I chased them but didn't catch them."

"Them?" Brent asked.

"There was a mime, too," I told him. I waved my hand to encompass the Knitpickers. "These people saw what happened. They're the knitters who spend nearly every weekday morning in Deputy Donut."

Brent faced them and said in kind tones, "I'll talk to you six first so you can enjoy the rest of the carnival." He turned back toward me and Nina. "Don't go anywhere." He removed a notebook from a jacket pocket and questioned the Knitpickers, one at a time. I made fritters and bagged them. Nina collected money and gave out change.

Brent let the Knitpickers leave. He asked Nina, "Can you take a walk with me and tell me about the magician and the mime? I'd also like you to point out where you last saw them."

Nina left her Deputy Donut hat and apron behind, and she and Brent went off in the direction the magician and the mime had taken. Even without her Deputy Donut hat, Nina was almost as tall as Brent.

The tourist and the woman in the hot pink shorts outfit

and floppy sunhat showed up together. Apparently, my accidental matchmaking had already lasted a few hours. The tourist turned to the woman and offered, "Would you like a fritter, Connie?"

"No, thanks, Alf. I've eaten too much today."

Alf bought a turbo-charged spicy corny fritter, tasted it, gave me a thumbs-up, and told me, "I'll definitely see you at Deputy Donut before my vacation's over."

Connie corrected him. "If he has time. There's so much to see and do around here."

Tucking one of our brochures into his shirt pocket, Alf winked at me. "I'll make time."

They walked away. Alf was dressed more like Brent when Brent was working, while Brent was dressed more like a tourist. I wondered what Alf's profession was. I'd pictured him in an office. Maybe it was an office full of detectives. If Brent was here looking for someone or something, a detective from another town might be, also. That detective probably hadn't expected one of the women attending the carnival to attach herself to him. Maybe, like Brent, Alf was content to look less like a police officer and more like someone on a date.

I kept up with the demand for fritters but was glad we'd brought boxes of donuts. Nina returned, smiling and no longer red-faced.

Brent was right behind her. "Can you spare a few minutes to look around with me, Em, and let me know if you see the magician or the mime? Nina and I didn't spot them."

I left my apron and hat behind, and Brent and I started toward the Friday the Thirteenth tent. I was ready to tuck my hand into his, but he didn't reach for my hand. I shoved both of my hands into the front pockets of my shorts. "If I see the mime and the magician, should I tell you about them and then dive for cover?"

He smiled down at me. "You got it."

We walked up and down the pathways between tents, food trucks, and games. We checked the outsides of the Friday the Thirteenth tent and the House of Mirrors. We met up with a pair of uniformed Fallingbrook police officers, and I described the mime and the magician. The officers went off toward the rides, and Brent and I headed toward the carnival exit. Earning a glower from Marsha, we went out through the turnstiles.

The area reserved for dignitaries was entirely bare of vehicles, but Brent remembered having seen the Mime Mobile there when he arrived. We climbed the hill. Brent had driven his powerful dark gray sports car, not a police car, to the carnival. We sat inside it with the windows open while Brent wrote down my descriptions of the mime and the magician and the way the mime had distracted everyone while the magician snaked his hand into the cash drawer. Knowing I was probably repeating some of Nina's statement, I told him, "A black van was parked on one side of the donut car for a while, and the mime's car was parked on the other side. I didn't find it creepy at the time, but maybe the drivers of those two vehicles blocked my car in order to keep anyone from seeing what they were doing. I'm not sure if the black van belonged to the magician or to someone else, but whoever it was might have stolen a bucket of confectioners' sugar."

Brent looked up from his notebook. "Someone stole a bucket of sugar?"

"I know it sounds strange. We packed a large white plastic bucket of it in the car, but we might not have locked the car every time we took a load to the tent. The sugar disappeared. Nothing else was taken."

"When did this happen?"

"Between nine and about nine thirty this morning."

"You didn't tell me about the possible theft when I showed

up at your tent or while we were walking around together."
He said it in a mild, nonjudgmental tone.

"It didn't seem like a police matter, let alone a detective
matter. It's possible that we misplaced the bucket of sugar, or
it was stolen from our tent, not from our car. I suspect it went
into the mime's car or the black van, but other people could
have taken it." I showed Brent my photos of the van with the
veterans' health website on the door. "This could be the
black van I saw beside the donut car. See the way the lettering
seems to be crooked as if someone carelessly stuck a magnetic sign on the door? It could have been a handy way of
changing the van from plain black to black with advertising,
which I guess someone might do if they wanted a quick dis-
guise."

"Could be. Thanks for getting the plate number. I'd like a
look at that van."

We walked through the entire parking area. There were no
windowless black vans, with or without advertising on their
doors.

Brent asked me to send him my photos of the black van.

I tilted my head back and looked up at his face. "You're
going to a lot of trouble for a small theft. I mean the money
we lost, not the sugar, which we're not certain was stolen."

He was silent for a beat, and I remembered the way he'd
wanted me to act like holding hands with him was normal, as
if he'd come to the carnival as part of his job but didn't want
to appear to be an on-duty police officer.

As I often did when he didn't respond to something I said,
I leaped in to fill the silence. "Did you come to the carnival to
look for someone specific?"

He gave me a rueful nod. "I'm sorry I didn't warn you. We
had reports of a magician picking pockets at fairs in the area.
I didn't expect him to be here, but I wasn't busy, so I thought
I'd check. The last report of him was north of Duluth. Ap-

parently, he travels in a black van with no windows except in front."

"It sounds like we nearly caught him." I thought for a second and then clapped one hand over my mouth.

Brent grinned. "What did you just remember?"

"It's not much, only amusing in a twisted way. I realized why the magician was wearing black leather gloves instead of more normal white cotton gloves on a hot day. Ink or dirt could have rubbed off from money he stole and left marks on white gloves."

Nodding, Brent wrote in his notebook. "Thanks, Em. Of all the descriptions we've had of him, no one else has mentioned black leather gloves."

"Maybe they're a recent addition to his costume. Maybe he gave his white cotton gloves to the mime, and she painted red fingernails on them. Were you looking for the mime, too?"

"This is the first I've heard of the magician working with anyone, but I'll report it to other jurisdictions."

"You didn't expect the pickpocketing magician to be here, but you came anyway?"

"I couldn't resist the Faker's Dozen Carnival and trying my hand at bad luck." His warm smile was contagious.

I heaved a dramatic sigh. "And Nina and I ended up with the bad luck."

He became serious again. "How much do you think he got away with?"

"I saw a few fives in his hand, maybe five or six. Our good luck was that Nina stopped him before he could grab more. The fives were new ones from the bank."

"I suspect that he and his accomplice are far away by now. Let's go talk to the person at the gate."

I walked down the hill with him. At the entryway, Marsha Fitchelder demanded our tickets.

Maybe I should have kept my hat on. I told her, "I'm an exhibitor, from Deputy Donut."

She snapped, "You should have had your hand stamped."

Brent showed her his ticket stub and his badge from the Fallingbrook Police Department. "I'd like to ask you a few questions."

She made a show of inspecting him from head to toe. "Are you finally here to tow that pink car away? It's about time, but you're too late. That mime dashed out of the grounds an hour or more ago. She even had the nerve to jump a fence over there near where her car was parked. Then she threw herself into her car and drove off like some kind of race-car driver." I edged toward the walkway leading to our tent. "Don't you go anywhere," Marsha ordered, "until I check your credentials." Instead of getting out her clipboard of exhibitors' applications, she returned her attention to Brent. "What questions?"

"Was the mime male or female?"

"Female, I think, but it's hard to tell. She was thin. Like a skeleton. And she never said a word."

"Was anyone with her when she left?"

Marsha planted her fists on her hips. "Who leaps over snow fencing?"

Brent seemed to take that as a no. "Did anyone else leave about the same time?"

"Lots of people. We don't check their tickets on the way out, and it's not like everyone has to stay here until we close tonight at nine. They might have other things to do, you know."

Marsha was exasperating, but Brent continued his quiet questions. "Do you know of anyone else who left the carnival without coming through here?"

"How would I know that? I only know about that mime because I saw her do it, right in front of my very own eyes."

Brent studied his notebook. I thought his mouth twitched in an attempt to hide amusement, but he asked in serious tones, "Can you describe the person who drove the pink car?"

"You know, clown face and a silly outfit. A hat she passed around."

Brent wrote down her nonspecific description and politely asked, "Did you see a magician?"

"There are probably at least six of them here today. You mean the one on stilts?"

Brent looked at me.

I answered, "I didn't see stilts. The one I saw had a top hat and tails."

Marsha scoffed, "That probably describes the other five."

I added, "He was carrying a briefcase."

Marsha snapped, "Magicians don't carry briefcases."

I didn't bother to argue.

Brent asked her if she saw who was driving a black van with no windows except in front.

Marsha scowled up toward the hill behind Brent and me. "I hope you don't expect me to remember every single vehicle that parks up there."

I offered, "It was in the dignitaries' lot, on this side of our car with the donut on top for a while when the pink car was on the other side."

"I thought your assistant drove that van. You know, the beanpole with the eyelashes. As far as I can tell, you two have been causing a lot of trouble." She glowered toward Brent. "Bringing police here and all."

I opened my mouth and closed it again. As far as I knew, Marsha was the one who had called the police to tow the pink car away. And I hadn't exactly brought Brent to the carnival. Finally, I managed, "So, you do remember that I'm one of the exhibitors from Deputy Donut."

She pointed her clipboard at me. "Go back to selling donuts."

After the mime had looked at Marsha's clipboard and pretended to read a clipboard of her own, she'd looked straight at Nina and me. At the time, I'd wondered if our Deputy Donut vendor's application was the top sheet on Marsha's clipboard.

Now I could see that it was. With our photos.

Chapter 4

Maybe I was being stubborn, but I wasn't about to obey Marsha and go back to selling donuts—and fritters—until I was certain that Brent had no more questions for me.

He didn't tell me to stay, but he also didn't say I could go.

I was curious. I stayed.

Brent asked Marsha, "May I see your list of exhibitors?"

She clasped her clipboard close to her black vest, hiding our Deputy Donut application. "You got a search warrant?"

"I can get one. A man dressed as a magician was seen taking money from a vendor. Wouldn't you like to help us learn who's been robbing your clients?" He said it encouragingly.

Marsha pointed at me. "Her, probably. She's been nothing but trouble all day." She held her other hand toward a family arriving behind us. "Tickets!" She added, "Please." It didn't sound gracious.

I went through the turnstiles. Brent followed and clasped my shoulder in a big, warm hand. "I'd better go apply for that warrant. See you Wednesday at Samantha and Hooligan's wedding."

I grinned up into his kind and caring face. "Yes, and since you're a detective, I expect you to listen very carefully. The minister is sure to say Hooligan's real first name." Despite our teasing, Hooligan had never told us what it was. Even the wedding invitation had been worded "Samantha Andersen and Hooligan Houlihan."

Smile wrinkles appeared at the corners of Brent's eyes. "Okay, but you'll be in front with the wedding party and I'll be in the congregation. You'll have a better chance at hearing it."

I whispered, "Did you notice the top page of her clipboard?"

Of course he had. Tilting his head, he asked, "Why was your application on top?"

"It can't be in the beginning of the alphabet. Didn't we pass Candy's Apples?"

"And Bill's Bear Claws."

"Maybe we were the first to apply."

He leaned down and spoke almost into my forehead. "Or she put them in order, with the worst troublemakers first."

I batted at his arm. "That must be it."

He gave my shoulder a quick squeeze and went out past Marsha.

I hurried to the Deputy Donut tent. Nina was her friendly self again, talking and laughing with customers.

We were busiest around the supper hour. A rangy man with a ruggedly handsome and tanned face asked for two dozen turbo-charged spicy corny fritters, not rolled in any kind of sugar. He was wearing black jeans, a pale gray and white checked cowboy shirt, a fringed suede vest, a white cowboy hat, and black cowboy boots decorated with glass "rubies" the approximate size of his thumbnails. He took a good look at Nina. "Whoa, were you ever angry when you went tearin' through the carnival grounds!" His drawl sounded real.

Blushing, Nina dipped her head. "We'd been robbed. I was trying to catch the thieves."

The man asked, "Did you succeed?"

"No."

He patted the back of his jeans and leaned toward her. "If I'd had my lasso with me, I'd have caught them and hogtied them for you."

Nina was seldom at a loss for words, but visions of hogtied magicians and mimes must have flustered her. "Um," she began, "um, thank you."

He said admiringly, "You're a fast runner."

She grinned back at him. "I try."

"I'm Rodeo Rod. I'm performing at the rodeo here at the fairground next weekend. Not tonight, tomorrow, and Sunday, but the weekend after this." He stared straight at Nina. "I hope you'll come."

"I . . ." She handed him a bag containing twenty-six fritters. "I might have to work. When I'm not working at Deputy Donut, I have paintings to finish."

"She's an artist," I contributed. "A very good one."

The praise seemed to embarrass Nina. She looked down at the counter. "Not really."

Rodeo Rod drawled, "Well, don't you be frightened of that mime. I don't think she'll come back here after you yelled at her." Carrying his fritters, he left.

Amused by imagining the usually easygoing Nina racing through the carnival and yelling, I asked her, "What did you tell the mime?"

Nina looked down at the open cash drawer. "Something like *Stay away from our tent!* But I was really angry and really loud." She eased the cash drawer shut. "I wish I'd slammed this on that fake magician's entire hand and kept him from going anywhere." She let out a brittle laugh. "Don't worry. I'm not usually so angry."

"I know." I'd been angry, too, but I hadn't worked up enough courage to chase the thieves and yell at them. However, unlike most people, I had a detective on speed dial. He'd been nearby, besides. I teased, "You have a new admirer."

"I don't think so."

"Who else offers to hogtie people for you?"

"That's a definite point in his favor."

"And he must have been over six feet tall, even if he took off his cowboy boots."

"That's another point in his favor." She looked off into space beyond the deep-fried chocolate bar stand across from us. "I don't usually paint portraits, but he had an interesting face."

"He was handsome!"

"Was he? I didn't notice." She turned her attention to customers.

I couldn't help smiling. Maybe I hadn't actually done any matchmaking, but it was fun to witness someone fall for Nina because he'd watched her tear through the carnival shouting at the woman she was chasing.

It was almost dark at nine when the carnival ended. Nina and I didn't have to carry anything besides our personal belongings and the money from the cash drawer, which I stuffed into the bottom of my backpack. We left the unused ingredients in the tent. Tom and his retired police friends were planning to pick up everything that belonged to Deputy Donut and help the rental company load the fryers, counters, cabinets, and fridge into their trucks. The tent rental company would take care of the tent. It would be a long day for Tom, but between closing Deputy Donut at four thirty and returning to the carnival around ten, he would have had a few hours to relax with my mother-in-law, Cindy, at home. Jocelyn, Nina, and I had told him we could open the shop without him in the morning. He'd merely given us a look. He took responsibility seriously. We all did, but he would never get over his police officer sense of duty. He always figured he was there to help others, and that was that.

Marsha and her turnstiles were gone. Nina and I climbed the hill to the donut car. I offered, "Would you like to drive?"

"I was up late last night on my new ladder, putting the finishing touches near the top of my painting, so you might prefer to drive rather than watch me nod off." We tossed our bags, aprons, and hats into the rear seat and clambered into the front. Nina yawned and apologized. "Instead of taking me all the way home, can you let me out at the grocery store? I need milk."

"Sure." When I pulled up outside the store, I asked her, "Would you like me to wait and drive you home?"

"Don't be silly."

I argued, "But you're tired."

"So are you, and I need the walk. It's not far." She slid out of the car, closed the door, and waved at me. She didn't own a car or a bike. She walked nearly everywhere and probably would have said that ten miles wasn't far. Luckily, she lived less than a mile from the store.

I drove to Deputy Donut. Backing the car into its garage in the lot behind the shop, I noticed that Nina hadn't retrieved her hat and apron, which wasn't surprising, but she also hadn't taken her tote bag with her. All of them were in the seat behind mine. She often carried her phone in one of the front pockets of her shorts. I called her. She didn't answer. We usually kept our ringtones turned off while we were at work, and we didn't always remember to turn them on again the minute we stopped working. I left a message that I was returning to the grocery store, and then I pulled the donut car out of the garage and headed south.

I walked up and down every aisle in the store. Nina wasn't there.

I asked the cashier if anyone had been about to buy milk during the past half hour but had noticed that she didn't have her wallet. No one had.

Nina must have realized before she got to the store that she didn't have her tote bag. She usually carried her apartment keys in a pocket, so maybe she'd decided to do without milk and to fetch her tote bag at Deputy Donut the next day. Driving toward her neighborhood, I didn't see her.

Around the corner from her apartment, I caught a glimpse of the rear of a small pink car tucked almost out of sight in an alley lit only by the nearest streetlight. I drove a little farther on and parked. With fresh memories of sugar going missing from our donut car and the magician helping himself to some of our cash, I wasn't about to leave my backpack containing the remainder of the day's earnings behind. I slipped its straps over my shoulders and walked to the pink car.

It was definitely the mime's, with MIME MOBILE on the doors. No one was in its two seats.

The heap of things behind those seats looked smaller than it had the previous time I'd snooped around the car, as if the mime had removed something.

In the gloom I saw a pinch of puffy orange wig sticking out from underneath a blanket.

Could the mime be underneath that blanket? She was tall. Could she have crammed herself into that small space behind the seats?

If she had, or worse, if someone had crammed her there, was she all right?

I shook off my anxiety and tried both doors and the hatch. They were locked. I knocked on the back window.

The blanket didn't move.

I scolded myself. If I'd been trying to sleep underneath a blanket in my car and someone tried the doors and knocked on a window, I wouldn't have moved, either.

Besides, if I awakened her, she might look out, recognize me, and flee Fallingbrook before anyone could question her about her connection to the thieving magician.

Maybe I was the one who needed to flee.

I hurried back to the sidewalk and around the corner of a building. I didn't hear anyone chasing me. Maybe she had left her wig behind and wasn't in the Mime Mobile. Where was she, and why had she blocked an alley with her car?

Many of the nearby shops had apartments above them. The mime could have carried luggage to any one of them and could be staying there for the night.

I ran the rest of the way to the donut car, locked myself in, phoned Brent, and told him what I'd seen, including the wig that might or might not have been on the mime's head. I gave him the addresses of the stores closest to the alley.

"I'll have a look," he promised.

"Do you want me to wait for you?"

"No."

"Thanks. Nina left the tote bag she uses as a purse in my car. I need to take it back to her."

"See you Wednesday." We disconnected.

Nina's loft was above Klassy Kitchens, a kitchen renovation store on Wisconsin Street about ten blocks south of downtown Fallingbrook. I didn't want to leave the recognizable donut car close to the Mime Mobile. I drove around a different block, found a parking space up the street from Klassy Kitchens, and walked the rest of the way.

Nina had her own door at the street. The door was extra-tall and extra-wide to accommodate whatever anyone might need to store in a loft. I pushed the doorbell button. Far above me, a bell rang. Klassy Kitchens had high ceilings, and Nina's second-floor apartment was about one-and-a-half stories up.

No one came to the door. I knocked.

The door wasn't locked.

It wasn't even latched.

With an eerie squeak, it swung open.

It seemed strange that Nina had neither locked nor latched her street door, but maybe she'd received my message and had left the door open for me to bring her bag up to her loft.

Expecting someone to climb the stairs to her apartment instead of running down them herself didn't seem like something Nina would do.

I pushed the door open farther. The stairwell was dark.

I called, "Nina?" I heard a couple of thumps from, I thought, her loft. Resting my hand on the jamb, I leaned in and shouted, "Nina!" She still didn't answer.

I let go of the jamb. My fingers brushed the metal latch plate. It felt cracked and uneven as if someone had tampered with it. Had Nina broken into her own apartment? I took off my backpack, pulled out my phone, and turned on its flashlight. The latch plate was dented.

I straightened and hollered up the stairway, "Nina! I'm coming up!"

I felt for a light switch but didn't find one. Light shined dimly from above, though, and I had my phone's flashlight. I slung the straps of Nina's bag and my backpack over my shoulder. Gripping the handrail with one hand and my phone with the other, I climbed quickly, not quite running, up the wide stairway. On the large landing outside Nina's loft, I tripped over the screwdriver she must have used to pry at the lock downstairs. I kicked the screwdriver aside.

Nina's loft door, another industrial-sized one, was also unlatched. A strip of light crossed from the crack between the jamb and the door to a corner of the otherwise dark landing. The latch plate was scratched and bent. Nina must have used the screwdriver on this lock, too.

"Nina?"

Something scuffled like a dog or a cat playing on the floor. Nina didn't have pets. Chills galloped up and down my spine. I pushed the door open.

Unlike the walls of some lofts where brickwork was exposed, Nina's walls were stark white. Spotlights above the far wall were focused on the masterpiece that Nina was preparing, the final painting for the show in Madison. The painting was the largest one that would probably fit through her doors and stairway, about ten feet tall and even wider than it was tall. It rested on the hardwood floor and came close to the high white ceiling. The painting was gorgeous blues and greens that made me feel like I was diving into a lake surrounded by forested mountains.

It was breathtaking.

The painting wasn't the only thing that took my breath away.

A shiny aluminum ladder was lying at the base of the painting.

A white plastic lid like the one that had been on our bucket of confectioner's sugar was on the floor beside one end of the ladder, and there were splotches of white powder on the floor near the painting and a slightly larger pile of white powder close to the ladder.

A white plastic bucket was lying on its side beyond the screens walling off Nina's sleeping cubby. The corner of the screens hid all but about the lower third of the bucket. It was similar to the one that had been stolen from us.

The scuffling noises were coming from near the bucket. I ran past Nina's kitchenette and screened-off sleeping cubby.

A woman was on her back on the floor behind the sleeping cubby.

Her head was inside the bucket. White powder spilled from the bucket onto the floor and across the woman's shoulders. The woman's feeble squirming was not helping her remove the bucket from her head.

One of her ankles and both of her wrists lay at odd, twisted angles.

She was long and thin like Nina, and she was wearing black shorts and a long-sleeved white shirt like the Deputy Donut uniforms that Nina and I had been wearing all day.

Chapter 5

✥

Barely noticing that the woman on the floor was wearing pink sandals and, last I knew, Nina had been wearing turquoise sneakers, I knelt beside her. "Nina!" My voice echoed in the large hard-surfaced loft.

The original label was partially torn off the bucket, and the word PAINT was scrawled in black marker over it. I eased the bucket off the woman's head. White powder spilled, forming a fine mist that drifted to the back of my throat. Sugar.

I brushed it off the woman's face. Her hair was short like Nina's, and underneath its spotty coating of sugar, it was a similar shade of brown, but this was the mime, not Nina. She must have removed most of her garish makeup, but it had been replaced by a stubborn layer of white powder.

I stabbed a nine and two ones into my phone and set it to speak aloud. My phone made those buzzy ringing sounds that meant the call had not yet been picked up.

Moving the mime could add to her injuries, but if I didn't clear her air passages, she might die.

I knelt behind her and gently pulled her up until she was almost sitting. I wrapped my arms around her. Leaning against me, she was able to hold her head upright. She was still wearing the white gloves. Powdered sugar hid most of the painted-on red fingernails.

A man's voice interrupted my phone's buzzing. "What's your emergency?"

I turned my face toward the phone, blurted my name, and added, "A woman is injured. I need an ambulance."

The 911 dispatcher demanded, "Address?"

"I don't know the exact address. We're in Nina Lapeer's loft above Klassy Kitchens. It's on Wisconsin Street, about ten blocks south of Fallingbrook's town square. Tell them to come to the door to the right of Klassy Kitchens and climb the stairs to the second floor. The doors aren't locked. It's a long stairway. And it's dark."

"Help is on the way. Stay on the line." I heard clicking noises and pictured the console where I'd sat when I worked at 911.

I apologized to the mime. "Sorry, but I have to do this. We need to clear your lungs." I placed one fist beneath the mime's sternum and slapped my fist hard with my other hand. She coughed.

I asked her, "What happened?"

She gasped, obviously trying to speak. Finally, she managed unintelligible syllables followed by words that sounded like, "A die. A seized her." She moved her head as if trying to get away from the lightweight powder clogging her throat and lungs. Supporting her armpits, I leaned her forward. Coughs racked her.

Someone ran up the stairs toward the loft. Nina strode to me and stopped as if she'd run into a wall. "What's happening?"

"Medical emergency." I cocked my head toward my phone. "An ambulance is on the way."

The mime wheezed and coughed.

Standing above us, Nina wrung her hands. She probably didn't know she was making soft, pathetic little moans.

I glanced beyond the ailing mime. The tall sliding glass

door leading to Nina's balcony was pushed to the side, and a huge hole in the screen opened to darkness at the back of the building. "Nina! Was there a hole in your screen door before?"

"What?" She seemed dazed and unable to process the chaos in her loft.

The 911 dispatcher also asked, "What?"

I shouted toward the phone, "I'm talking to Nina. She just came in." I looked up at Nina. "Your door. Was it open like that when you left this morning?"

Nina stared toward her balcony and shook her head as if to clear it. "The door was locked, and there was no hole in the screen." She grabbed her tote bag and my backpack off the floor and threw them onto a chair beside the sliding glass door.

I didn't remember dropping our bags, but I did remember the noises I'd heard as I was climbing the stairs. "If someone opened the glass door, why didn't they open the screen door, too? Why did they break through it?"

"The glass door slides easily, but the screen sticks." Nina stooped, nudged the screen onto its track, slid it open, and went out onto her balcony. She had walked through some of the powdered sugar that I'd spilled from the bucket, and one of her shoes tracked it outside. The only light on her balcony came from inside the loft, and I couldn't see what she was doing. I heard metallic clinks and clanks, like chains rattling.

I called, "Nina, are you okay?"

"Yes." Almost as pale as the powdered mime, Nina came inside. "My . . . my fire escape ladder. It's made of chains and metal rungs and folds up." She revolved her hands around each other as if rolling up an ungainly bunch of chains. "I keep it under the Adirondack chair out there for emergencies. It was unrolled and hooked over the railing. It was still swinging, and I thought I heard footsteps, like someone running away down the alley behind the building. I pulled the ladder up and put it where it belongs so no one can climb up and get in."

I tried not to show my dismay. I suspected we were dealing with a crime. Nina should not have walked through the sugar and should not have touched her escape ladder. Or the screen door. I had already disturbed, quite justifiably, crucial evidence while trying to save the mime. Powdered sugar was gluing my sweaty knees and shins to Nina's hard maple floor. I told Nina, "I'd like to immobilize her wrists and one of her ankles. Can you find six things like long-handled spoons that can act as splints?"

She headed toward her kitchenette. "Okay."

I added, "And three towels or rags to tie around them."

Nina was upset, so I didn't want to reveal the thoughts tumbling and colliding in my brain while I supported the wheezing mime with one arm and rubbed her back with my free hand.

I was sure that the mime had broken into Nina's stairway and loft and had carried the bucket of sugar up the ladder that was now lying next to Nina's painting. The mime must have been near the top when she, the ladder, and the bucket crashed to the floor.

This could not have been entirely an accident. A spill of sugar near the ladder showed where the open bucket must have landed. When I found the mime, her head had been about ten feet from that spot, and her feet had been even farther. If she had somehow landed with her head inside the bucket and had slithered away on her own power, she would have made a trail of sugar, and she might have wriggled away from the bucket. Neither of those things had happened.

Except for the lower third of the bucket, she'd been out of sight of the apartment's front door, as if someone had dragged her there to hide what he or she planned next. The mime's broken wrists and ankle would have prevented her from moving much, giving her attacker the opportunity to carry the mostly full bucket to her and shove it over her head. And then her attacker must have held her down and prevented her from escaping.

If I hadn't yelled up the stairwell, the attacker probably would have stayed until the mime stopped moving. But I had yelled, and the attacker must have panicked at possibly being caught. He must have opened Nina's sliding glass door, broken out through the screen, found Nina's fire escape ladder, and fled down it.

I called toward my phone, "Hello, 911? Please send police to the same address. Detective Brent Fyne might be nearby. Please ask him to come here, too."

"Okay, Ms. Westhill." Many of the emergency dispatchers in this part of Wisconsin remembered me or had heard of me, knew that I was Alec's widow, that Tom was my father-in-law, and that Brent had been Alec's best friend. Because of Alec, they would do nearly anything for me. Besides, everyone associated with law enforcement in Fallingbrook admired and respected Brent and Tom.

Nina ran to me and placed two wooden spoons, a stainless-steel serving spoon, its matching slotted spoon, a spatula, and a long fork plus three pretty scarves that looked like silk on the floor. Tears welled in her eyes. "Why is she here? And why are you . . . *you* didn't break into my apartment, did you, Emily?"

"I don't know why she's here, and I didn't break in. Your street and loft doors were open."

Nina waved toward her balcony. "Someone broke out."

"It looks that way. Do you want to splint her wrists and ankle, or would you rather hold her upright while I tie on makeshift splints?"

"I'll hold her up."

Coughing violently, the mime shook her head.

Nina knelt behind the mime and slipped one arm around her. The mime cringed away as if she thought she would be more comfortable lying down. I suspected that even if she lay on one side, she would find breathing more difficult than she would with one of us supporting her.

Apologizing for hurting her more, I removed the sandal from the mime's injured foot.

Nina asked, "Is she going to be okay?"

"I hope so." I splinted the mime's injured ankle with two long-handled wooden spoons, one on each side, wound a scarf around it all, and tied it. "She's the mime who was at the carnival."

Nina nodded. "I thought so." She looked up at her painting. "How did powdered sugar splash all the way to the top of my painting? There's like a waterfall of it right down the middle. It's like someone climbed the ladder and threw sugar by the handful at the painting."

"Is the ladder on the floor the new ladder you told me about this morning?"

"Yes. It was delivered last week."

I left the mime's white cotton gloves on her hands and cupped her palms around the outsides of the stainless-steel spoons' bowls, and then tied scarves around her wrists and the long handles of the spoons. My splinting was far from professional, and the mime's coughing made it even harder. I asked Nina, "Where was your ladder when you left for work this morning?"

"Propped up near the center of the painting." Nina rubbed the mime's back. "Do you think it's our missing sugar, Emily?"

"It must be, but why did she take it? To break into a random apartment and bring a bucket of confectioners' sugar into it?"

"And climb a ladder and throw sugar right onto my painting?" Nina was nearly wailing. "The paint wasn't dry. I don't know how I'll clean the sugar off it in time for the show."

Wide-eyed, the mime wheezed, coughed, and seemed to

try to pull away from the sugar that had to be coating the insides of her lungs.

I stared at the ladder as if it could tell me what happened.

Maybe it could. There was a black scuff near the base of one of its legs. I asked Nina, "Was that black mark on the leg of the ladder the last time you looked?"

"I don't think so." The soles of Nina's sneakers were white, my soles were red, and the mime's were tan. Had someone wearing black soles kicked the base of the ladder when the mime was near the top? I immediately pictured the mime's apparent accomplice, the magician, who could have been wearing black shoes to match his jacket, top hat, gloves, and briefcase.

Finally, I heard sirens. It felt like an hour since I'd phoned 911, but it must have been less than five minutes.

I asked Nina, "Did you get my message?"

"About my bag? Yes." With apparent difficulty, Nina managed to keep the mime from collapsing to the floor. "But not until I'd already left the grocery store—I'd barely gotten to the dairy aisle when I realized I didn't have my keys. Then I came back here and checked with Harry and Larry downstairs at Klassy Kitchens. They didn't know where their keys to my apartment were. They came with me to double-check that my street door was locked. It was. We all tried it. They let me out the back door of their store so I could cut through the alley." She spoke quietly to the mime. "Try to relax and breathe. I know it hurts. We're trying to help you." Nina looked up at me. "I was almost at your place when I remembered that I'd forgotten to turn on my ringtone after the carnival. My phone was in my pocket. I was going to call you, but I found your message that you were on the way here. I turned around and walked back. My street door looked like someone had broken in. I was about to call the police when I heard you up here shouting my name." Her dark eyes showed the empathy that I was also feeling for the mime and her la-bored breathing. Nina was also breathing heavily, more from emotion, I thought, than from the exertion of trying to prevent the mime from lying down and giving up. I stood and stretched.

Behind the fallen ladder, a chip of white plastic lay on the floor near the base of the painting. I eased around spilled sugar for a closer look. The chip could have broken off the bucket, which supported my theory that the bucket had fallen from high on the ladder.

Something gold gleamed near one of the splotches of sugar near where the ladder's feet must have been. I stooped for a better look.

It was an ornate gold locket.

Nina was concentrating on the mime. Neither of them was facing me.

A little voice in my brain told me to leave the investigating to the police.

Had the mime dropped the locket when she fell? Would it yield a clue to the mime's identity? Maybe it contained important medical information that could help EMTs save her life.

With the toe of one sneaker, I slid the locket away from the sugar. I didn't see a chain, and I wasn't about to dig around in the sugar for one.

Out on the street, a siren ended abruptly.

I worked a thumbnail between the two sections of the locket.

Chapter 6

❣

The locket opened easily.

On the left side was a sepia-toned photo of a stern-looking older gentleman dressed in what appeared to be a suit from the 1890s. The photo was blurry as if the man hadn't sat still.

A newer piece of paper was crammed into the locket's other side. Maybe I'd been right that the locket held information that could help the EMTs save the mime. I popped the scrap of paper out and unfolded it. I had to hold it under Nina's brilliant floodlights to read the tiny, light gray pencil marks. They were no help. The number 971 was followed by the capital letters W I S T S and an upward-pointing arrow.

Feet thudded on the stairs. I shoved the disappointing scrap of paper and the locket into my shorts pocket for safekeeping.

Samantha and an EMT I didn't know ran into Nina's loft carrying a wheeled stretcher with its wheels folded underneath it and blankets and cases of equipment on top. I was used to seeing Samantha in her uniform, but lately I'd been picturing her in the wedding dress that another friend, Misty, and I had helped her choose. Now, in contrast, Samantha's black uniform and heavy boots looked almost shocking. Her dark brown eyes concerned, she threw me an assessing glance, and then she and her partner eased the stretcher down beside the mime.

I picked up my phone, blew sugar off it, told the 911 dispatcher that help had arrived, and disconnected.

Nina stood up. She was pale and trembling. Afraid she might faint, I guided her to one of the two chairs in her kitchenette. "Put your head down between your knees."

"I'm okay."

To distract her, I opened the locket and handed it to her. "I think she might have dropped this."

Nina studied it in silence. "It's mine. Where'd you find it?"

"Near the ladder." I put the scrap of paper on the table in front of her. "This was inside, instead of another photo, I guess."

She stared at the locket and the paper. "She must have stolen my locket."

"Who's the man?"

"One of my great-great, I forget how many greats, grandfathers. His wife's picture was in the other half." She had regained some of her color.

"Where was the locket?"

Nina swallowed and let her gaze travel around the high-ceilinged loft. Finally, she pointed a shaking finger toward her screened-off sleeping cubby. "My jewelry box." Her words were soft, as if she hoped to wake up and discover she was only in the middle of a nightmare. She rubbed a thumb against the front of the locket. Fine white sugar remained lodged in its indentations. She stretched one leg out, leaned back in her chair, and shoved the locket and the piece of paper into the front pocket of her shorts.

I said sympathetically, "And then she vandalized your painting."

Still looking lost and bewildered, Nina shook her head. "I don't understand. Why would she do all this?"

Someone ran up the stairs.

Nina and I both stood. Eyeing the door, she covered her mouth. I braced myself for attackers carrying barrels of powder.

Brent strode into the apartment. He was still dressed casually in his jeans, T-shirt, and jacket. He looked so comforting that I took a couple of steps toward him and might have thrown myself into his arms if the situation hadn't been dire and sad. He met my gaze with a grim look of his own. "You called this in, Emily?"

"Yes. I guess we found our missing bucket of confectioners' sugar. When I arrived to deliver Nina's tote bag, her locks had been forced open. I heard noises up here and found the mime who was at the carnival. She was lying on the floor about ten feet from the ladder she must have fallen from, and her head was inside the bucket of sugar. With two broken wrists and one broken ankle, she didn't seem able to escape."

Brent obviously caught on that someone must have moved the mime and thrust the bucket of sugar over her head. "I'll need to talk to you both."

More people ran up the stairs. Nina drew in a halting breath.

Tall and composed in her police uniform, Misty preceded her patrol partner and Samantha's fiancé, Hooligan, into the loft. Hooligan glanced toward Samantha, then quickly turned his attention to Brent. As the responding detective, Brent was in charge of the investigation.

"Hooligan, go back down to the street door," Brent said. "Keep unauthorized people out." Hooligan started down the stairs.

I told Brent, "There's a balcony in the back of the apartment. We think the attacker climbed down Nina's chain fire escape ladder when he heard me coming. He or she, that is."

Brent looked at Nina. "Where would that take them?"

"It goes down to a ledge, and then you have to crawl along

the ledge to the slanting roof of an addition to the building next door, make your way down that slope, and then climb down that building's fire escape. You'd end up in the alley behind Klassy Kitchens."

Brent asked Misty, "Can you secure the rear of the building? Radio other officers to take over. After they do, come back and help take statements."

"Okay." Talking into her radio, Misty headed downstairs.

Brent asked Nina, "Have you ever used your escape ladder?"

"It's for emergencies." She shuddered. "I'd be scared to use it unless I had to."

Whoever attacked the mime, I thought, *was probably desperate.* Nina had told me she'd pulled the ladder up and put it away to keep anyone from climbing it. Judging by her description, making one's way up to the bottom of it would be difficult and dangerous. However, Nina's concern was legitimate, especially considering how violated she must have been feeling.

Brent, Nina, and I moved aside while Samantha and her partner wheeled the mime, wearing an oxygen mask and proper splints, toward the door. Samantha's lips thinned. If she could save the mime merely through the strength of her will, she would. I was again struck by how wonderful my friends were.

Nina and I showed Brent the bucket and the sugar-dusted floor where I'd found the mime. I admitted, "We both stepped in the sugar and knelt in it, and it looks like the EMTs walked through it, too. Nina tracked some of it out to the balcony and back."

Brent examined the footprints and the screen door.

Nina explained with a noticeable shiver, "I locked that door this morning before I left for work, and the screen was fine. But when I came back just now, the door was open, and the screen had that hole. The door can be unlocked without a key from inside."

He pointed downward. "What about these spoons and things on the floor?"

"First aid," I explained. "I made impromptu splints. Should we pick them up?"

Brent wrote in his notebook. "Leave them where they are."

I showed him the black scuff near the bottom of one of the ladder's legs.

He asked Nina, "Was the ladder lying down like this when you left this morning?"

"It was standing up, with its feet about here and its top above the painting."

I prompted her, "You said that someone threw powdered sugar at your painting."

Brent asked, "Where?"

"See those white blobs up there near the top of the painting, and dribbling here and there, all the way down?" Nina's voice quivered. "They appeared after I left this morning."

Brent looked at the base of the painting. "Sugar is spattering the floor."

I pointed at the small pile of sugar near the fallen ladder. "I think this is where the bucket landed. And there's a chip near the wall that must have broken off it."

Without touching it, Brent took a look at the chip. He left it where it was and walked around spilled sugar, kitchen utensils, and wadded scarves to the bucket. "I'm almost positive that the chip came from the rim at the bottom of the bucket." He looked up toward the top of the painting. "And I suspect you're right that the bucket was either dropped or thrown from high on the ladder. It landed over there but must have been carried, upright, here."

Nina's eyes widened as if she were trying to blink back tears. She covered her mouth with her hand.

Misty ran into Nina's loft. Brent had Misty write down my statement while he took Nina's. When we were done, he told us we could go.

Nina's forehead wrinkled. "Go?"

Brent apologized. "You'll have to stay out of your apartment until we finish our investigation."

"You can stay with me, Nina," I offered. "As long as necessary."

Tears welling over, she thanked me. "I . . . my painting. I need to clean the sugar off it and finish it so it can be shipped to the gallery in time for the opening."

Brent said gently, "We'll get you back in here as soon as we can."

Misty offered, "I'll help you pack. Gather everything you might need for a week or so."

"Do you mean I should take my outfit for the wedding on Wednesday?"

"Definitely." Misty followed Nina into her sleeping cubby.

I told Brent that I'd brought my backpack and Nina's tote bag into the scene after the mime was attacked.

"Okay," Brent said. "Take them. I'll make a note of it."

Wearing a black nylon jacket over her white shirt and black shorts and carrying a large black duffel bag with red piping at the seams in one hand and a grass-green silk dress on a hanger in the other, Nina stumbled out of her sleeping cubby.

She and I made our way down the lit stairway. I told her, "I couldn't find the light switch when I came in. Did you turn the lights on?"

"Yes. The switch is behind the door when the door's open. Not a great design, but the building's old."

We told Hooligan good night and went up the street.

The donut car, which usually made me smile whenever I caught sight of it, looked innocently sweet but terribly vulnerable outside in the dark.

Chapter 7

Driving home, I asked Nina, "Do you have any idea why that mime was in your apartment vandalizing your painting?"

She drew a shaky breath. "No."

"Will you be able to fix the painting before your show?"

"That depends. I might be able to brush some of the sugar off it, but the paint was still drying, and some of the sugar will have stuck to it, and I might need to scrape and repaint. That will take a couple of days, then I'll need another couple of days for the new paint to dry. The painting needs to be shipped in two weeks at the latest to make it to the show in time. That mime set me back a few days, and now, if the investigators take a long time, my show will have to go on without that painting."

"Could you tell if the painting was damaged by anything else, like the fall of the ladder or the bucket or the mime herself?"

"I didn't see anything like that, so if there's damage, it can't be too bad. Maybe there won't be any." Her voice held little hope. This new, almost despairing Nina contrasted with the bright and enthusiastic Nina of that morning when she and I had been heading down the sunlit grass-covered hill toward the carnival grounds.

I wanted to turn on the donut's colorful sprinkle lights and let them dance over Fallingbrook's shops and restaurants. I could even broadcast music over the siren-shaped loud-speaker mounted in front of the huge donut. I restrained myself and suggested, "Don't give up."

I heard her nylon jacket rustle, saw her hands clench each other on her lap. "It might be beyond my control."

"You can take time off. Jocelyn will be working with us at Deputy Donut until she goes back to school, and by then, many of the summer tourists will have left."

"No, I can't."

I knew what she meant. Art supplies were expensive. She lived very frugally except for probably splurging on renting that high-ceilinged loft with its oversized doors and wide stairway.

She fiddled with the handle that cranked down the old car's window. "I'll be okay if I sell some of the smaller paintings. That big one doesn't have to be in the show, and I'm not going to put it there if it isn't ready."

I knew how excited she'd been to display that painting and possibly sell it. "The gallery owner really wants it to be in the show, doesn't he?"

"Mr. Arthurs said to take my time, and if it doesn't make it to this show, he'll display it in his gallery later. After, he said, this show makes me so famous that my work will command higher prices."

I turned onto my street. "That's quite a vote of confidence. I mean, in addition to inviting you to have a one-woman show in his gallery."

"He might have been joking."

"He didn't seem like the joking sort the one time I talked to him."

"He doesn't to me, either." She sounded a little happier. I slowed in front of my sweet little yellow brick Victorian cottage. The porch and living room lights were on. Sitting straight up with her ears at their highest, my cat was on the windowsill looking out toward the street. "There's Dep!" The smile was back in Nina's voice. "Aww, she's been watching for you." I pulled into my driveway beside my own car, a sports car with my kayak fastened on top. Nina teased, "You must be notorious for cars with large and sometimes peculiar objects on their roofs. At least in the darkness, no one can see how the red of your kayak clashes with the red of your car." Her shoulders drooped. "Sorry for forgetting my tote bag in your car. You wouldn't have gotten mixed up in that mess at my place and you would have been here with Dep long ago."

"But then you might have walked in at the wrong time. You could have been hurt."

Nina opened her car door. "Or I could have kept it from happening."

I reminded her, "Someone broke in."

"Maybe I could have stopped them."

"Maybe. Despite everything that mime did, I hope we saved her."

We got out of the donut car. Nina reached into the rear seat and pulled out her duffel bag and her dress on its hanger. Carrying them, she climbed the porch steps ahead of me. "Samantha and the other EMT looked serious, but I suppose that's normal for them. I couldn't do their job."

I admitted, "I couldn't either, though we both did pretty well with our first aid this evening." Working at 911 had to be easier than coping with the sorts of injuries and illnesses that Samantha and her partners faced, but I hadn't been able to stand working at 911 after Alec was shot. I'd taken that night off to go to dinner with out-of-town friends, and a new employee had filled in for me. Brent had been with Alec and had been only grazed. He had assured me that he had radioed for an ambulance even before a civilian phoned 911, but I would always wonder if I could have sent help to Alec faster than the new 911 employee had. Brent also tortured himself with questions about whether he could have done more to save Alec.

I looped the straps of my backpack and Nina's tote bag over one arm and opened the front door. The lamp in the living room spread a warm glow through the pine and white room with its jewel-toned furnishings and stained-glass windows. Nina and I both kicked off our shoes. Purring loudly, Dep wound around Nina's legs. Dep was a tortoiseshell tabby, also known as a torbie. She was ginger, cream, and dark gray with tabby stripes and adorable circles that resembled donuts on her sides.

Nina put her duffel bag down and picked up the cat. "Hello, darling kitty. You're nice to come home to." Nina's wistful tone barely hid the anxiety she had to be feeling. Dep must have recognized it, too. She snuggled into Nina.

I scratched the striped ginger patch on Dep's forehead. "Sorry we're late. I brought a friend." Dep arched her neck and purred even more loudly.

She helped me take Nina and her things up to the guest room, open the sofa bed, and spread out sheets and my grandmother's gorgeous blue and white quilt. Making the bed without Dep's help would have been quicker, but less amusing.

I brought Nina towels. "Are you hungry or thirsty?" Since breakfast, neither of us had eaten much besides fritters and other delicious, but maybe not terribly nutritious, fair foods. "Tea? A snack?"

"No, thanks."

"I'll get you a glass and some water in case you get thirsty in the night."

Usually, Dep trotted downstairs ahead of me. This time she stayed upstairs. She apparently thought Nina needed her more than I did.

My house was small, with no hallway on the first floor. I

crossed the living room and turned on lights in the dining room. With its pine plank floors, white walls, white furniture, and stained-glass windows high on the walls beside the fireplace, the dining room was nearly as welcoming as the living room.

I went on into the kitchen. Alec had been at least as fond of cooking as I was, and we hadn't held back when we designed and renovated our kitchen. We'd installed pine cabinets to go with the woodwork in the rest of the house, but everything else was meant to contribute to the fun of cooking—oversized stainless fridge and range, granite countertops, and handmade terra-cotta tiles in warm autumn shades on the floor.

I ran cold water into a cute pitcher with a matching tumbler that served as a lid. The set was brown ceramic. Alec's mother, Cindy, taught art at Fallingbrook High. She had made the set and many of my other dishes. She'd made Dep's dishes, too.

Brent phoned. "I need to ask you and Nina more questions. May I come over?"

"Sure."

I took the pitcher of water upstairs. Nina was standing near my desk and looking out the window over the top of my dark computer monitor toward the maple tree and the street beyond it.

I set the pitcher on the bedside table. "Brent's coming over to ask us more questions."

She yawned. "Okay."

Dep led both of us downstairs.

Brent showed up almost immediately. Dep sat down in front of him and looked up—way up—into his face. "Meow."

He picked her up. Based on the defeated expression in his eyes, I expected to hear that the mime had worsened. Brent sat in my cobalt blue wing chair and cuddled Dep.

Nina and I faced him on the deep red, mahogany-trimmed

velvet couch, another of the furnishings I'd inherited from my grandmother. Dep didn't seem to make Brent feel better. I braced myself for bad news.

Brent took out his notebook. Dep jumped off his lap and headed toward the kitchen.

Unable to stand the silence any longer, I croaked, "How's the mime?"

Brent stared at my face for several long seconds. "She survived until a couple of minutes after she arrived at the hospital. But that was it."

Although I wasn't surprised, I felt shocked and horrified. "If only I'd arrived sooner," I whispered, "she might still be alive. I shouldn't have toured every aisle of the grocery store."

Nina twisted her hands together in her lap. "You couldn't have known. And you did your best when you got there."

"My best wasn't good enough." I asked Brent, "Do you know who she was?"

"We have a name for the pink car's owner, but we can't release it until we get a definite identification and notify her family."

Nina's knuckles were big, even for long fingers like hers. They were also starkly white compared to the rest of her skin. "It's sad, but I can't help being angry at her for breaking into my loft and trying to ruin my painting."

Brent didn't look up from his notebook. "How do you know that she was the one who threw sugar at your painting?"

Nina stared at him. Pasted together with tears, her long eyelashes looked even longer and thicker than usual. "Her wrists and one ankle were broken. She must have been the one who fell off the ladder, from near the top, so she must have been the one who threw the sugar."

Brent suggested, "Someone else was there, too, right? Someone who made a hole in your screen and hung your fire escape ladder over the railing."

Dep returned and jumped onto Nina's lap. For a few seconds, all I heard was Dep purring. She was comforting even when she wasn't on my lap. Nina drew a long, quavering breath. "Maybe two people worked together to break in and vandalize my place, and the other one attacked her." She stared at the pillar candles I'd arranged inside my fireplace for the warmer months. "None of it makes sense."

Brent leaned toward her. "A screwdriver was on the landing outside the door to your loft. Was it your screwdriver?"

"No. I don't have one like that. I saw it there and figured that someone had used it to pry my doors open." She seemed to be trying to suppress a yawn. The whites of her eyes were bloodshot.

Brent quickly said, "You're worn out. That's all I needed to have you fill in for me. You can go to bed, Nina. Emily and I will go over the statement she gave Misty."

Nina set Dep on the floor and asked if I minded if she took a shower.

"Of course not."

Dep scurried up the stairs ahead of her.

I turned to Brent and tried to inject some lightness into the situation. "I seem to have lost my cat to my house guest."

Brent remained serious. "Is your guest room still the one in the front of the house?"

"Yes." The cottage had only two bedrooms. Mine was the one that looked out at the walled garden in back.

"Let's go to the sunroom where we'll be less likely to disturb Nina."

I translated that as, "Let's go to the sunroom where Nina won't hear what we say," which was almost, but not quite, the same thing.

Could Brent actually believe that Nina was involved in the mime's death?

Chapter 8

I led Brent through the dining room and kitchen to the sun-room. It was in the back of the house, separated from the kitchen by a half-height wall. Two other sides were windows above radiators and shelves, while on the third side, windows and shelves flanked the back door.

I closed the wide-slatted wooden venetian blinds and turned on lamps at both ends of the two-seater couch. Under the circumstances, I tried not to think of it as a love seat. We sat facing the rear windows, but angled toward each other. I tucked a foot underneath my other leg and waited.

Brent paged through his notebook. "You told Misty that the woman said something. Do you remember what that was?"

"I couldn't make sense of it, and I'm sure I didn't catch everything she said, but it sounded like 'a die a seized her.'"

"'A seized her?'" he repeated, "not 'I seized her'?"

"It could have been 'I.' She wasn't speaking clearly." I tried I's instead of a's. "'I die. I seized her.' Maybe she was trying to say, 'I'm dying. I seized her.'" The thought that she knew she was dying was so sad that I stopped talking. I heard water running upstairs and Dep thumping down the uncarpeted stairs from the second floor. I spoke quietly. "Maybe the mime's attacker was a she, not a he. I've been picturing the magician."

"Why?"

Dep jumped onto my leg. I inched my fingers into her silky fur. "The mime failed to distract us enough to prevent Nina from noticing he was robbing us. I'm guessing he had to leave the carnival right afterward for fear of being caught. That could mean his day's work didn't bring in as much as he'd hoped, and he could have blamed the mime. Also, except for his white shirt and bow tie, he was wearing black, and if his shoes had been any color besides black, we probably would have noticed. If his shoes were black and his soles were, too, they could have made the mark I showed you on the ladder." Brent wrote in his notebook and then looked up at me, and I added more theories. "The magician wasn't the only one wearing black shoes that might also have had black soles. Marsha Fitchelder's sandals were black, and she quarrelled with the mime. Marsha looks muscular, besides, so she might have been able to restrain the mime and hold her down."

"Marsha Fitchelder also quarreled with you and Nina, didn't she?"

I couldn't help making a face like I'd bitten into an onion. "It was more of a discussion. She told us we couldn't drive to our tent to unload the donut car. We asked to unload close to the entry gates. She said we could, but we'd have to move our car later."

"Who moved the car?"

"Nina."

"Did she have any arguments with anyone while she was doing that?"

"Not that I know of."

"Did you see or hear of Nina arguing with anyone else during the carnival?"

"She didn't argue with anyone, including the magician and the mime, but they did make her angry. She was embarrassed about yelling at the mime." Gazing back into Brent's unwavering stare, I stopped petting Dep. "You can't suspect Nina of attacking the mime. She would never hurt anyone. Besides, she was wearing turquoise shoes with white soles all day, and she still had them on when she returned to her apartment. She wasn't the one who kicked the ladder out from underneath the mime."

Brent only looked at me without saying anything.

I admitted, "Okay, we're not sure anyone did kick that ladder."

"It's a good guess, but it's only a guess."

"True. Anyone could have caused that ladder to fall."

"Including the person near the top of it. The ladder will be dusted for fingerprints, and the scuff mark will be analyzed. Do you have any idea why the mime went into Nina's apartment without Nina?"

"No, and I'm sure that Nina doesn't either. And I'm also sure she didn't let them in. The latch plates of her street door and her apartment door were damaged as if someone had pried at the locks using the screwdriver you asked her about."

"We'll check the latches and that screwdriver, too, for fingerprints." He reminded me, "Nina didn't have her key. Maybe she broke into her own apartment."

"That doesn't make sense. She knew she'd left her purse in the donut car, so she set out to find me, and then she got the message saying I was bringing it to her. Besides, she looked really shocked when she came home and saw me trying to rescue the mime."

Dep stretched, leaving her back feet on my leg and placing her front paws on Brent's. The rest of her body followed. She curled up on Brent's lap.

I put both of my bare feet on the love seat and hugged my knees. "Also, someone stole that locket from Nina's jewelry box. If the mime took it, she did it before she fell and broke her wrists and ankle."

Brent didn't blink. "Tell me about the locket."

The house's old pipes clunked. Dep seemed to recognize that as a sign that Nina had turned off the shower. She jumped off Brent and bounded away. I wasn't sure if Brent had known about the locket before I mentioned it, but I described what I remembered. "It was on the floor near the fallen ladder. It's gold, probably an antique, and ornate. I didn't notice a chain. Was the chain in the mime's pocket?"

"I don't know those details yet. Did you open the locket?"

I gave him a sheepish smile. "You know me too well."

His lips twitched, but he didn't quite grin. He merely waited, so of course I went on. "I didn't know yet that it was Nina's locket. I thought it might have been the mime's, and I wanted to know if it held the mime's identity or any medical information that could help the EMTs. They were on their way, and I didn't want to lose a second in case there was crucial information in the locket that could save the mime, so I opened it."

"That's understandable, considering that your biggest concern was the mime. Did you find identifying or medical information?"

"No. In one side, there was an old photo of an eighteen-nineties gentleman, but in the other compartment, there was only a scrap of paper with something printed in pencil. The printing was teensy. Nina said that the gentleman was one of her ancestors but she didn't understand what was on the paper."

"What was it?"

I tried to picture the tiny pencil marks. "There was a number, nine hundred something, I think, and a word, all in capital letters, like 'wrist,' but I don't think that was it. Both of the mime's wrists seemed to be broken, so 'wrist' would probably have stuck in my memory. After the wrist-like word, there was an upward-pointing arrow." I couldn't control a shudder. "What if the word was 'wrist,' and it was a warning? Could someone be going around breaking over nine hundred wrists?"

"Not that I've heard. Where are the locket and the photo and the piece of paper now?"

"Last I knew, Nina had them. She said the locket was hers and the mime had taken it from her jewelry box. Didn't she tell you about it?"

Brent didn't answer.

I easily found an excuse for Nina. "She was distracted. And she must not have thought the locket had anything to do with the attack on the mime."

He tilted his head slightly in apparent acknowledgment.

I again spoke to fill the silence. "Would you like me to go ask if you can see them?"

He removed a paper evidence envelope from his pocket. "Yes, if you can. Do you know why Nina seems to believe that the mime stole that locket? Her attacker could have been the one who took it."

"If the attacker had wanted the locket, he probably would have taken it with him."

"From what you told me, he or she left in a hurry."

"True." I took the envelope and stood up. "I'll try not to handle the locket and the piece of paper much, but I suspect that Nina and I replaced any fingerprints on that locket with our own."

Upstairs, Nina's door was ajar, and her room was dark. She must have heard me, though.

She stage-whispered, "I'm not asleep."

I put my face near the crack in the door. "Brent would like that locket and the piece of paper from it."

I heard springs creak, and then the bedside lamp went on. "Just a second. I have the locket, but the paper didn't belong in it, so without thinking, I tossed it." After a few seconds of rustling, she handed them both to me.

I thanked her, slipped them into the envelope, took the envelope downstairs, and handed it to Brent. "It's not exactly an unbroken chain of custody, especially considering that I didn't find a chain." I knew the joke was lame.

He got it, anyway, and smiled. "At this point, I want to consider everything."

I apologized again for removing the locket and its contents from what I'd already suspected was a crime scene. "I don't know what else the mime or her attacker might have stolen from Nina's apartment. Maybe the mime vandalized the painting in anger because the only valuable thing she found was the locket. But that doesn't explain why the mime, or whoever, stole our bucket of confectioners' sugar early this morning, ripped most of the label off it, scrawled the word 'paint' on the bucket, and took it to Nina's apartment."

"Since we can't ask the mime, I don't know if we'll ever find an explanation."

"I hope you do."

He tossed me a half grin. "Good. You understand that we're doing the investigating, not you."

"I never interfere."

"Not on purpose, exactly." His smile warmed. "I should go." He closed his notebook and stood up.

At the front door, he told me, "As for all serious crimes, an agent from the Wisconsin Division of Criminal Investigation will manage the case, and I'll report to him or her."

Him, I hoped. I'd met two female DCI agents. One had been incompetent, and the other had been competent but too interested in Brent, I thought, to focus on her investigation. I would be happy if Brent found someone to love for the rest of his life, but Detective Kimberly Gartborg seemed too cold and hard for him. The male DCI detective I'd met was quick and intelligent and didn't worry me on Brent's behalf. And I was fairly sure that the male DCI agent now understood that I was not a murderer.

Telling me to give Dep a hug, Brent wrapped an arm around

my shoulders for a second and then let himself out. I closed the dead bolt. He trotted down the porch steps.

Earlier, when I'd held his hand and we'd toured the carnival like two people on a date, seemed like a long time ago. My face heated. I murmured, "Pretending wasn't hard." It wasn't the first time we'd held hands. We sometimes grasped each other's hands to keep our kayaks from drifting apart on calm lakes so we could stay together without paddling and without colliding with each other. I didn't consider those incidents as romantic, and I doubted that he did.

I made certain that my doors and windows were locked, and then I turned out the lights and went upstairs.

This time, Nina didn't call out to me. Figuring she might be sleeping or almost sleeping, I tried to be quiet while showering and padding back down the hall to my own room. I climbed into bed. Dep pushed my unlatched door open, jumped onto the bed, landed behind my knees, and purred.

It was late. I had to get up early, but I couldn't sleep.

Maybe Nina was tossing and turning, also. Dep left my bed several times and returned a few minutes later, landing more heavily on me each time as if she could press me into a deep sleep.

I kept seeing that mime, first alive at the carnival, and then barely alive in Nina's apartment.

I die. I seized her.

What had the mime been trying to say? What else did she say that I hadn't caught? Nina had said that the cryptic note didn't belong in the locket. Had the mime put it there? Or had her attacker? Maybe the note held a clue about who had killed the mime and why.

I turned over and wrestled with my pillow. I hadn't reread that scrap of paper before I put it into Brent's evidence envelope. What had been written on it? A number, nine hundred something, and a word like "wrist" or the card game whist, but I didn't think it was either of those. W I S T? Had there been an *s* at the end? W I S T S? And after that meaningless word, there had been an upward-pointing arrow. Except for the arrow, the numbers and letters could have been copied from a license plate.

I had almost drifted off when a possible meaning came to me and I sat up, wide awake. Muttering, Dep jumped off the bed. WI was the abbreviation for Wisconsin. ST was an abbreviation for street. S was an abbreviation for south. An upward arrow could mean upstairs.

Had someone written a shortened form of Nina's address on that slip of paper? I'd picked her up and dropped her off many times without paying attention to the number near that oversized door. I didn't remember her address from our records at Deputy Donut, and I seldom programmed addresses into my phone, but I was sure that her apartment was in or near the nine hundred block of Wisconsin Street South. I wanted to wake her up, ask what her exact address was, and find out if she agreed with my deciphering of the code, but that was silly. In a few hours, we both had to go to work.

I flopped down but fretted about who had printed that coded address. I knew what Nina's printing looked like from shopping lists she'd made at Deputy Donut. The printing in the locket hadn't resembled Nina's. Had someone been carrying Nina's address around?

It could have been the mime or the magician or maybe Marsha Fitchelder. Any one of them could have targeted Nina's apartment and folded the coded address into the locket after pilfering the locket from Nina's jewelry box.

Any one of them could have targeted Nina.

The mime was about Nina's height and weight, and they both had prominent cheekbones and short brown hair. The mime had covered her red-and-white-striped shirt and her chartreuse suspenders with a plain white shirt like the ones we wore at Deputy Donut. When she'd been in Nina's apartment, she'd been wearing the black shorts she'd had on ear-

lier in the day. Although baggier, those shorts were similar to
the ones that Nina and I—and Jocelyn, too—had worn at the
carnival. Someone, probably the mime, had torn most of the
label off the bucket of sugar and scrawled the word PAINT
across it.

The mime could have disguised herself as Nina carrying a
pail of paint so that no one would think anything was wrong
if they saw her going into Nina's apartment.

And then, someone who was looking for Nina could have
mistaken the mime for Nina.

The murderer could have believed he was attacking Nina,
not the mime.

Chapter 9

Unable to lie still, I sat up again. If the attacker had been try-ing to kill Nina, she would be in danger the moment the at-tacker discovered she was alive, which could be as soon as the actual victim's name was released.

I grabbed my pillow and hugged it on my lap. I had told Brent I wouldn't interfere in the investigation, and I wouldn't, unless I thought I could learn something that would put a killer behind bars before he could attack Nina. Or anyone else.

I would keep my eyes out for that magician, and for Mar-sha Fitchelder, and I would . . . I wasn't sure what. I threw the pillow back where it belonged, plunked my head down, and turned onto my side.

Ideas, each more bizarre than the previous one, floated in front of my eyes, and the next thing I knew, my alarm was going off and Dep was leaping off my bed.

I went down to the kitchen, fed Dep, and started Wiscon-sin aged cheddar and spinach omelettes. Dep nibbled at her kibble.

Her makeup failing to conceal the dark shadows around her eyes, Nina joined us. Gold glinted at her throat under-neath the collar of her Deputy Donut shirt.

Folding her omelette, I asked, "Is that the chain for your locket?"

"Yeah. It was in my jewelry box. She didn't steal other pieces of jewelry, as far as I could tell. I hope I get my locket back soon."

Hiding my doubt about how quickly belongings might be returned after a serious crime, I put her omelette onto a plate and set it on the granite counter. "Have a seat." I poured us each a glass of cranberry juice. "I'm sorry, but you know I had to tell Brent about the locket and the coded message inside it."

"I'd have told him if I'd thought about it, but with everything going on, I just wasn't thinking. And even if I had thought about it at the time, I don't see how her stealing my locket can possibly tell anyone anything about who attacked her. I was just glad to get my locket back, for all the good that did. I hope Brent decides my locket has nothing to do with the murder and gives it back to me soon." She perched on a stool. "Thank you again for letting me stay here. You're a real lifesaver."

I hoped it wouldn't come to that.

We ate breakfast, and I made a marinade with rice vinegar, maple syrup, and grated fresh ginger. I put a pork tenderloin into the marinade and refrigerated it.

Despite Dep's high-volume protests, Nina and I eased her into her soft-sided carrier. Dep was even less happy about being put into the donut car. I couldn't blame her. She'd gone to all the trouble to learn to walk in a harness with a leash attached to it. She knew she shouldn't have to suffer the indignity of riding in a carrier in a car, even a charming antique car with a large plastic donut lying on top.

Pulling out of the driveway, I pitched my voice above Dep's complaints. "Nina, it occurred to me that the mime's murderer could have been after you."

"How could that be?"

I pointed out that the mime had dressed like her, had probably carried a bucket labeled PAINT, which was something that Nina might do, and was in Nina's apartment. "Someone could have mistaken her for you."

"That makes no sense."

"Can you think of anyone who might see you as an enemy?" While Nina had been working at Deputy Donut, she'd never come near making enemies.

"No." She drew the word out.

I teased, "Did you have to think about it that long?"

"Going back to when I was three takes a while." Her sense of humor was returning.

"What's your address on Wisconsin Street?"

"Nine seventy-one."

"Wasn't that what was on the slip of paper in the locket? Nine seventy-one W-I-S-T-S, which could stand for Wisconsin Street South, and there was an arrow pointing up, like for the upper floor of a building."

"I didn't pay much attention, but you could be right, if that was what was on the paper."

I tried to help her understand the danger she could be in. "Someone—either the mime or her attacker—was carrying around an abbreviated version of your address. And then someone stole your locket. Whoever it was didn't want to leave a copy of your address behind, so they hid it in your locket, probably meaning to take it with them and discard the coded address later. But the locket was left behind."

Nina leaned forward and brushed a speck of dust off the dashboard. "Here's what I think happened: The mime was mad at me for chasing her away from the carnival and telling her to stay away from us. Remember when we found Marsha Fitchelder yelling at that mime to move her car?"

"Yes."

"That mime looked at Marsha's clipboard, and then pretended she had her own clipboard and was reading the pages on it. She pointed at you and me. She must have been looking at Deputy Donut's registration form, which showed our photos and addresses. And she guessed we were from Deputy Donut because of our donut car and our hats."

"I think you're right. When Brent and I were talking to Marsha Fitchelder, our application was still on top of the papers on Marsha's clipboard."

"That's strange, but so is Marsha Fitchelder, so I'm not surprised. After I chased the mime away from our tent, she must have remembered one of the addresses she'd seen on that form, so she went to that address to get back at us. Stealing valuables and vandalizing the painting she found at the address were going to be her revenge, but she fell off the ladder."

I pointed out, "Your theory has a hole in it. The mime stole the sugar hours before you chased her, so are you saying that she was planning revenge for your yelling at her before you did it? We noticed that it was missing before our customers told us that Marsha had called the police to tow the mime's car away."

"Yeah, but it was after we witnessed Marsha scolding her and probably after that mime memorized my address."

I shuddered. "The way the mime gave us that visual warning that she was watching us was creepy. She must have taken the sugar right after that, when our arms were so full that I forgot to lock the car. Her desire for revenge was extreme considering that all we did was watch her miming her side of an argument with Marsha Fitchelder."

"That mime was stranger than Marsha. Maybe she stole the sugar just to cause some sort of mayhem, and she didn't care what kind. Maybe she was hoping to cause a dramatic confrontation at the carnival so she could mime another argument."

"Is that a little farfetched?"

Nina sat back and folded her arms. "Maybe not. You cause a little tension here, you cause a little chaos there, you put people on edge, and someone might create a scene that a mime can borrow for her performances. Or maybe she just wanted a lot of sugar, to start a bakery or something."

I warned, "Until her murderer is caught, don't be alone."

"I'll try."

I pulled into the lot behind Deputy Donut. It was early. Very few cars besides Tom's SUV were there. Nina offered, "I'll take Dep inside while you park." I stopped near our back door, the one that led into our office. Nina scrambled out of the car and carefully removed Dep's carrier from the rear seat.

I backed the donut car into its garage. When I arrived in the office, Nina had let Dep out of her carrier and had gone on to the kitchen. Dep had scurried up carpeted ramps and kitty-proportioned stairways to her highest catwalk near the ceiling. Eyes wide, she peered down at me. "Mew!"

I called up to her, "No more car rides today, Dep! You can relax."

Maybe batting that catnip-filled toy parrot down onto my head was her way of relaxing. I shoved my backpack into the lockable drawer where Nina had already stowed her tote bag. Inside our combination kitty playground and office, we also had a gas fireplace for the cooler seasons, a big desk and chair, a filing cabinet, a coffee table, and a couch that Dep would sleep on later, probably.

The office was thoroughly enclosed so Dep couldn't go out and mingle with our customers, or more importantly, according to the health department, mingle with our donuts. The office had windows on all four sides, allowing Dep to gaze at whatever she wanted—the driveway, the parking lot, the dining area, or the kitchen.

The kitchen was in the rear of the building, between the office and our storeroom. I peered through the window into it. Tom was the only one facing me. Standing at one of the stainless-steel fryers, he frowned at me. Behind him, Nina was rolling out dough on the marble counter in the middle of the kitchen. Jocelyn was pouring coffee beans into a grinder near the kitchen's far wall.

I smiled and waved at Tom. He only nodded. His frown reminded me of Alec's whenever a case was bothering him, and I again felt sad that Alec would never reach the age his father was now. He would probably have looked like Tom by then, square-jawed and often serious, fit and above average height, with dark eyes that easily showed compassion. I could tell by Tom's expression that he'd already heard about the death, probably from his network of retired police friends and other officers who were still in the Fallingbrook Police Department.

I shut Dep into the office and went into our dining room. As always, it looked inviting. The sun had risen, and the front windows and door let in early morning light that showed off the rock maple floor, the peach-tinted white walls with interesting artwork hanging on them, and our round tables. With Cindy's help and encouragement, Tom and I had painted the tabletops to resemble donuts. We had protected our paintings with glass. Chairs with their backs and seats upholstered in dark brown leather were pulled up to the tables.

I walked between the serving and eating counter and the half-height wall that separated the kitchen from the dining room, and then turned and walked around the end of the half wall. Tom and I had designed the space so that when we were standing in the kitchen, we could see our customers, but they wouldn't be able to see the potentially cluttered parts of the kitchen, like the deep fryers. Customers might see beyond the serving counter to the marble-topped work surface and the row of coffeemakers.

I waved a greeting at Jocelyn, now grinding coffee beans. Nina started cutting donuts out of dough, fragrant with yeast, that had risen overnight in the perfect temperature and humidity of our proofing cabinet. A pan of chocolate frosting sat in a bowl of warm water to soften it for spreading. As always, the fragrances added up to a mouthwatering kitchen.

I went through a doorway at the end of the kitchen farthest from the dining room. In our well-stocked and neatly arranged storeroom, I put on a clean apron. Now, except for my shoes, my outfit matched the others'—white shirts, black shorts, logo-trimmed aprons, and Deputy Donut hats. I passed our other back door, the one that opened to the loading dock, and returned to the kitchen. Jocelyn shut off the grinder.

In the sudden silence, Tom lowered a basket of donuts into hot oil. "Emily, I heard that you and Nina ran into a little excitement last night." His voice was gruff. He always treated me like a beloved daughter, and he was very fond of Nina and Jocelyn, too. Like Brent, Tom did not approve of my snooping around in what should be police-only business, but I'd always had good reasons.

And now I had a crucial one. Whether she believed it or not, Nina could be in danger.

"Yes," I said.

"It was horrible," Nina added.

Her dark eyes bigger than ever, Jocelyn stared at Nina and me.

I started measuring ingredients for the donuts that used baking soda and baking powder as leavening. I felt like all of us—including Nina, even if a murderer was after her—were safe with Tom nearby. Although he had retired from being Fallingbrook's police chief and a detective before that, he was a very young and fit sixty-four. I suspected that he would probably never lose that careful attentiveness to his surroundings and the ability to cope with nearly any danger.

Nina and I told Tom and Jocelyn about our evening and

that Nina was staying at my place until the investigators finished at hers. I added, "I've told her not to be alone until the
guy who attacked the mime is caught."

"That's silly," Nina said.

Jocelyn retorted, "No, it's not."

Tom reminded us that our customers would want to ask
questions about the murder. "Deflect their questions. We
don't know anything, okay?" He looked straight at Nina and
me. We agreed.

Jocelyn and I went around putting creamers and sugars on
our donut-like tables.

Our first customers of the day arrived. Jocelyn and I served
them warm donuts and fresh coffee. There were no questions
about the death the night before. While our customers enjoyed their donuts and coffee, we returned to the kitchen to
prepare more donuts.

The front door opened. A man and a woman I'd never
seen before were hesitating near it. They both carried cases
that could contain small laptop computers or tablets.

Tom beckoned me to the deep fryer. "Can you manage the
donuts? I'll look after those two characters."

The fryer's timer went off. I lifted a basket of golden
donuts from the bubbling oil and hung it on the side of the
fryer to drain. After a few seconds of watching and listening
to Tom, who could be quite intimidating, the man and woman
left.

Tom returned to the kitchen.

"That was quick," I teased him.

A twinkle lit his eyes. "I told them where the police station
was, that I was no longer police chief or a police department
spokesperson, and that my former colleagues would be better
able to answer their questions."

Jocelyn gazed toward the front door. "Where were they
from? I've seen lots of reporters covering gymnastic events,
but I didn't recognize those two."

Tom picked up a carafe of coffee. "They didn't know that the murder had anything to do with us. They came in here because it's the first place they found that was open this early. They drove all the way from Wausau. I'm afraid we might expect people from even farther away. This pair was particularly interested because the deceased was a mime, and they seemed to think she'd been traveling the carnival and festival circuit this summer and might have been in other towns and cities, and their audience in Wausau might have encountered her or her murderer, or the murderer might show up in someone else's hometown."

He insisted on taking over serving customers. Since it was a Saturday, we didn't have our weekday regulars to question why Tom was working the dining room while those of us who usually waited tables stayed in the kitchen.

I was lowering donuts into bubbling oil when Nina looked toward the front door. A perplexed frown wrinkled her forehead. "Is that . . . ?"

I followed her gaze. "Detective Gartborg. She must be the detective the DCI sent to direct the investigation into the mime's murder." I wondered why Brent hadn't come with Detective Gartborg. He seldom took his breaks at Deputy Donut, though. I beckoned to Tom to return to the kitchen and watch the frying donuts. "Let's go say hello."

Nina's grin was a little crooked. "I guess Tom doesn't have to protect us from her."

Tom took over at the deep fryers, and Nina and I headed for Detective Gartborg's table. The DCI agent was every bit as glamorous as she'd been almost a year before, tall and thin with prematurely silver hair that she wore in a smooth, short bob. This time, it was cut with one side angled longer in front than the other. She wore a tailored navy linen dress and a white linen jacket with navy trim. Her shoes were navy and spotless.

I welcomed her to Deputy Donut, and Nina repeated it. I

added, "Nice to see you again." That sounded silly considering that the last time we'd seen her she'd been investigating a murder. I quickly added, "I'm sorry for the reason you had to come."

Nina rescued me from my babbling. "What can I get you? Our special coffee today is a medium-roast Nicaraguan blend with hints of fruit and chocolate, and we have our usual mellow Colombian coffee, plus all sorts of teas and fried goodies, including the s'mores donuts we just invented."

"No donuts for me, but a small Colombian coffee would be great." She smiled. "The Fallingbrook Police Department could use a few lessons about making coffee."

Nina quipped, "We can't teach them or the fire department. They'd stop coming here."

Detective Gartborg's laugh was low and musical. "Yes, I guess you can't. Do EMTs take their breaks here, too?"

I made a fake sad face. "Not often. They buy roasted beans from us and grind their own coffee, and they seem to do it right, or at least if they cause any medical emergencies with their coffee-brewing, they handle them themselves. And their headquarters aren't easy walking distance from here."

Gartborg teased, "They could come in ambulances, lights flashing and sirens blaring."

A pair of people we'd never seen before came in. These two were holding their computers in plain sight.

"Reporters," Nina told Gartborg. "Tom will want us to skedaddle so he can look after them."

Gartborg nodded and took her phone out of her expensive-looking navy handbag. I'd seen the ploy often and had used it myself. When dining alone, fend off unwanted company by pretending to check for messages and calls, and then answer the messages and calls whether or not they existed.

Nina and I returned to the kitchen. I made more donuts, and Nina took Gartborg her coffee before hurrying back to the kitchen to avoid talking to anyone who might be from the press.

Gartborg didn't stay long.

About a half hour after she left, Nina received a call. She listened for a few seconds, said, "Okay," and disconnected. She smiled at me. "Brent wants me to go to the police station."

Chapter 10

✣

Nina's smile grew. "I hope the police are going to tell me I can go back to my apartment tonight so I can start repairing my painting."

Tom and I exchanged looks. *It was a homicide*, I thought. *They won't have cleared the scene.* I was sure Tom was thinking the same thing. Neither of us said it, and neither of us mentioned that if the police were only going to tell her she could go home, they probably would have said it over the phone.

Jocelyn was the first to speak. "You're not going alone, are you?"

Nina opened her eyes to their widest in pretend shock. "To the police station? It's all of two blocks, and it's the middle of the day, besides. No one could possibly be after me, and if they were, having someone with me wouldn't stop them, even if that person can knock someone out with her feet."

Tom and I laughed. Jocelyn's gymnastic skills allowed her to do amazing things.

Jocelyn protested, "I never knocked anyone out. And Emily came as close to it as I did. Dep, too."

I backed a step and put my hand over my heart. "In my case, it wasn't skill."

Jocelyn retorted, "In Dep's case, it was. Maybe you'd better take Dep with you, Nina."

Nina grinned at her. "That would impress the police."

Jocelyn had an answer for that, too. "Brent would understand why you brought a feline bodyguard, at least that one."

Nina untied her apron. "I'd better go before the police send out a search party." She went into the storeroom.

Jocelyn called after her, "They should have offered to pick you up!"

Nina returned to the kitchen without her apron and hat. "I'm glad they didn't." She waved her hand toward our dining room, almost completely full of customers. "That could be bad for business."

Tom asked her, "Do you have your phone?"

She patted her shorts pocket. "Yep. And I turned on the ringtone. Don't worry. I'll be fine." She danced away. "See you soon!"

Tom went back to frying donuts. Jocelyn decorated the ones he'd just made. I toured the dining area, refilled coffee mugs, and then went behind the serving counter for a fresh pot.

A woman who looked slightly familiar slipped into Deputy Donut. Her oversized navy cardigan looked too hot for the day outside, but it was unbuttoned, showing the lacy front of the flowing lime-green top she wore over greenish-gray cropped pants. Her tentative way of walking made the name of her white shoes, "sneakers," seem entirely appropriate. She twitched the end of her ponytail from her back to her front, and I recognized her hair's ombre shading of blond near the top and chestnut near the bottom. She was the woman I'd seen peering into the donut car while I was climbing the hill above the Faker's Dozen Carnival to look for the missing sugar.

The woman came to the serving counter and asked me in a voice barely above a whisper, "Could I fill out a job application?" She was younger than I'd originally thought. Her apparent shyness and her smooth, pale skin made me think she was in her early twenties.

We didn't need staff, but Jocelyn would be returning to college in a couple of weeks, and despite what I'd said to Nina the night before about taking time off, we could use extra help during the late summer and especially in the early autumn, when tourists visited Fallingbrook to admire waterfalls and hike in forests while leaves were turning their most glorious colors.

But even if we had no expectation of ever needing another employee, I wanted to learn more about this woman whom I'd first seen the day before, the day that someone had stolen our sugar, the day that maybe a different someone had broken into Nina's apartment, and also the day that someone had fatally injured the mime. I told the woman, "We don't have openings at the moment. Would you like to fill out an application in case we need someone later?"

"Yes, please."

I showed her to the table nearest the office. Dep was sleeping on top of the back of the couch. I opened the office door. Dep stood and stretched, arching her back. Cooing to her, I retrieved a blank application from the filing cabinet and a pen from the desk. I made certain that I closed the office door behind me, returned to the woman, and gave her the application and the pen. "Can I get you a coffee and a donut? Our treat, so you can taste some of the goodies we serve."

She hesitated. "That would be nice." Luckily, she didn't glance toward the office. Dep had puffed herself up into a scary monster and was staring straight at her.

I brought the woman a mug of our special Nicaraguan coffee and a strawberry donut with vanilla frosting topped by dark chocolate shavings. Barely looking up from the application, she thanked me. Dep's fur was still on end, and the tip of her tail twitched.

I went around offering more coffee and donuts and smiling and chatting with customers, but all the time, I was wondering if the woman sitting near the office and filling out an
application had killed a woman she thought was Nina in
order to create a job vacancy. It hardly seemed likely.

Dep must have decided something similar. Her fur smooth
again, she sat with her tail wrapped around her feet. She was
still facing the woman, but her eyes were mostly closed as if
she were about to go back to sleep.

I hoped Nina would return while the woman was still in
Deputy Donut. If the woman believed she had killed Nina
the night before, how would she react when she saw Nina?

The woman shoved the application across the small table
and laid the pen across it. I went back to her table and picked
them up. Her name was Kassandra Pyerson, and she had experience as a waitress at Suds for Buds. Although it sounded
like it could be a dog groomer, Suds for Buds was a pub south
of downtown Fallingbrook. Alarm bells in my head clanged
so loudly I was surprised that no one turned to stare at me.

Suds for Buds was across Wisconsin Street from Nina's loft,
a couple of buildings farther south, but, as far as I was concerned, suspiciously nearby.

I told Kassandra, "I'll keep this on file and let you know if
we need you to come in for an interview."

She'd eaten her donut. She pushed her empty coffee mug
toward the center of the yellow-frosted donut painted on her
table and gazed around the room at our art-covered walls. "I
see that you have lots of artwork for sale. Would you let me
display some of my paintings here?" Bracing her shoulders,
she sat a little straighter. "I'm an artist, and I'd like a place to
show off my work and get my name out there."

An artist. The alarm bells clanged even more loudly. *Had
Kassandra heard about Nina's show, and was she jealous
enough to break into Nina's loft, vandalize her painting, and
attack a stranger she mistook for Nina?*

I glanced around at some of the art on our walls. "We don't make the arrangements with the artists themselves." Hoping she wouldn't suggest that we needed to hire her as a liaison between us and the artists, I added rather lamely, "The system works well."

"I'll show you." The woman reached into a brown, tan, and white crocheted bag with a long braided strap that she wore over one shoulder and across her body. She spread about a dozen photos on the table. "I painted these." I heard pride in her voice, and also the hesitancy of someone fearing rejection.

I was afraid to look at her photos for fear I wouldn't like the paintings and wouldn't be able to hide my feelings. Reminding myself that art was subjective and my opinion couldn't be very important to her, I adjusted the photos to eliminate reflections from the pink glass fixtures hanging from the ceiling. The photos were blurred, and I couldn't be certain the colors were true, but I suspected that the paintings themselves were very good. I'd thought the same about Nina's work, and so had Arthur C. Arthurs when he'd come to Fallingbrook to see it. "These look wonderful, but the displays in here and the sales of the artwork are done through The Craft Croft."

Kassandra looked bewildered.

"It's an artisans' co-op a couple of blocks south on Wisconsin Street." I pointed. "You might like to join it. Many of the artists and crafters whose work we show in here also display their work at the co-op, and the co-op arranges for displays at other shops and businesses around Fallingbrook. What we have here is only a small representation of what artists and craftspeople around Fallingbrook can do."

She showed the closest thing to a smile yet. "Thanks. I'll go see them." She stood.

I offered, "I'll call if we need you."

She thanked me and walked cautiously, as if she were afraid that someone might actually look at her, outside.

I had been careful not to say that I would call her if we had an opening. Nina and Jocelyn and their enthusiasm and genuine fondness of other people had spoiled me. Folks came to Deputy Donut for our delicious beverages and treats, but they also came because Jocelyn and Nina—and probably Tom and I, too—were like friends and family. I wasn't sure that Kassandra was outgoing enough to make people want to return to talk to her.

I also wasn't certain that her main aim was to find a job. Maybe she only wanted a place to display her paintings.

Besides, I'd seen her peering into the donut car around the time our sugar was stolen and before the mime was killed. I put Kassandra's application with others in the filing cabinet.

Nina was gone longer than I expected. When she came back, her face was bright red. She stormed into the kitchen where Tom, Jocelyn, and I were making more donuts. She looped one finger underneath the gold chain around her neck and pulled the chain out from underneath her shirt. "They wouldn't give me back my locket!"

"Who?" Jocelyn asked. "Thieves?" I could almost see her mentally kickboxing the locket out of a thief's hand.

"No. The police." Nina turned to me. "It was that Detective Gartborg from the DCI who was in here this morning. She didn't like me the last time she was in Fallingbrook, and although she was friendly this morning when we were chatting with her, she still doesn't like me."

I asked, "Was Brent in on the interview?"

"Yes, and I don't think he was playing at being a good cop. He really is one. He seemed empathetic. I told them the locket was mine, and that the mime stole it and dropped it in my loft. It was mine all along and I got it back, so that crime—the theft—was solved. I don't see what it has to do with whoever attacked that mime. That woman!" I wasn't sure if Nina was talking about the mime or Detective Gartborg. Nina flung herself into the storeroom. She returned with her Deputy Donut hat on crooked. With jerky movements, she brought her apron strings around to the front and tied them. "It's that mime's fault that I lost that family heirloom. Now I might never get it back."

"You will," Tom said, "if I have to go get it myself. But it might be awhile. It depends on how soon they catch the person who killed the mime and how long the trial takes."

Nina knocked her hat into place with a fist. "That locket has nothing—probably has nothing—to do with the killer. It could be years before I see it again, if ever."

I pushed the rolling pin over the dough with more force than was absolutely necessary. "I'm glad to have the company, and you can stay at my place as long as you need to, but did they say anything about when you could return to your apartment?"

"Oh, maybe in a week or so. But what if it's so long that I won't be able to repair my painting and have it shipped in time for my opening?" She waved her hands in the air like she was describing a vast space. "There's going to be this big blank wall at the gallery and it's all that mime's fault." Nina seemed at least as angry as she'd been when she chased the magician and the mime away from our tent the day before.

Customers were coming in. Nina glanced toward them. "I'm okay, really. Don't worry, I won't bite anyone's head off. I'll go look after them. It'll take my mind off that Gartborg woman and help me calm down."

"Wow," Jocelyn muttered when Nina was in the front of the shop laughing and talking to the new arrivals. "She really has it in for that DCI detective, and for the dead woman, too. But I understand. That art show means a lot to her, and I really want her to become a famous artist."

I pushed a round cookie cutter into my rolled-out dough

and twisted to make certain the cutter went all the way through the dough. "So do I."

Tom put dough for the next day into our proofing cabinet. "Whatever works best for her and makes her happy." His wife, Alec's mother, Cindy, had been well-known as a ceramicist. The MoMA had at least one of her pieces in its collection, and so did other museums, but when Alec was a teen, Cindy had given up that world to teach high school art. As far as I knew, she had never regretted it. She believed that helping kids grow and learn was more important than making pretty things that ended up unused and barely touched in glass cases. Her work—and Tom—made her happy.

The last of our customers left. We tidied the shop for the Jolly Cops Cleaning Crew, a group of retired police officers who came in during the night to clean everything and haul away the used cooking oil. Tom drove home to Cindy, and Jocelyn pedaled away on her bicycle.

Nina and I went into the office. Dep had climbed to her highest catwalks and seemed uncertain about coming down, but when I rattled her harness, she trotted to me. She stayed far from the cupboard we'd built for her carrier, but after we put her into her harness and snapped her leash on, she pranced outside ahead of us.

It was a hot, hazy evening. We walked several blocks south on Wisconsin Street before we turned west onto my street. The sun was still high, but the haze made the light almost painfully bright. We both put on sunglasses. I could hardly see through mine. "Ugh, I should clean these once in a while."

Nina laughed. "Me, too. How do we manage to get so many smudges on them?"

Tail up, Dep marched ahead of us. Nina was next to the grass between the sidewalk and the road, and I was next to the front yards. I turned my head away from the sun and toward the houses lining the street. Close to Wisconsin, they were large and old, frame with gingerbread trim, wide porches, and charming paint choices showing off architectural details. In the next block, houses were a little smaller and closer together. Some were brick and some were frame, but they still boasted whimsical gingerbread trim. Most of them had gardens in front boasting the season's last roses and first mums, and nearly all of the gardens were lined with hedges or low fences next to the sidewalk.

Dep zigzagged back and forth in front of Nina and me. She meandered to the other side of Nina and walked on the grassy area close to the road.

I was about to hand Nina the leash when Dep puffed up and raced toward the hedge beside me, nearly tripping both Nina and me. I might have thought that Dep was playing one of her cat-and-mouse games, but she leaped onto the flat top of a privet hedge.

Dep never climbed trees and bushes.

Behind us, a car's engine raced. I glanced over my shoulder.

A gray car swerved over the curb and across the grass between the street and the sidewalk. Its right wheels were on the sidewalk.

The car was heading straight at Nina.

Chapter 11

❧

I yelped, threw one arm around Nina, and hurled both of us into the base of the hedge.

Twigs snapped and scratched my face and arms. Tiny leaves cascaded over us.

Rattling, the car thumped off the curb and sped away as if the driver hadn't noticed the near collision.

Nina struggled to a sitting position with her feet below her on the ground sloping toward the sidewalk and her head still among twigs and branches. "What was that?"

Dep let out an indignant howl.

I brushed leaves off my face. "Dep! Are you all right?"

Something tugged at my ankle. Dep's leash was tangled around it, but Dep wasn't anywhere near my ankle. Behind me, her leash led upward.

"Meow!"

I looked up and over my shoulder. Dep was still near the top of the hedge. With her toes spread and her claws extended, she was clinging to branches that didn't look strong enough to support her.

Her fur was fluffed. Her pupils huge, she stared down at me. "Mew." She wriggled and let go. Using my head and one shoulder as a stairway, she landed on my lap.

I stroked her soft fur. "Hello, baby."

"Mew."

I felt her all over. She hadn't damaged anything besides her dignity. I picked bits of brush off her and set her on the grass beside me.

Nina helped me untangle the leash and crawl out of the hedge.

Dep licked one of her shoulders as if trying to smooth down hairs that were still standing on end. She had leaped into the top of the hedge and had made a reasonably soft landing up there. I had flung myself and Nina into the hedge's trunks. Our landings, at least mine, had not been soft. Belatedly, I asked Nina, "Are you okay?"

"I'm fine. What happened?"

"Someone nearly hit us. Did you get a look at the driver?"

"I heard a car and the next thing I knew you were throwing me into a bush. Did you see the driver?"

I resettled my even-more-smudged sunglasses on my nose. "I caught a glimpse of the top of a baseball cap behind the steering wheel. The driver must have been looking down instead of where he was going."

"Was it a he?"

"I couldn't tell. I think the car had Wisconsin plates, and there were two fives on it, beside each other."

"I thought I saw Wisconsin plates, too, and a four and a five." She grinned down at me. "You're strong for someone so small."

I flexed my arm. "You're light for someone so tall." My voice was shaking almost as much as I was.

"Thanks for saving me."

"That's two possible attempts on your life in two days."

"Or zero. If that was an attempt on my life, it was a brazen one. In full daylight, with a witness."

"Exactly." My voice was as dry as the dust I was brushing off the back of my shorts.

"It could have been an accident. Besides, who knows?

Maybe it was an attempt on your life, and I just happened to be in the way."

It was a good argument, but mine was better. "You were closer to the street."

"Collateral damage. But really, I doubt that anyone tried to hit us. I think it was a distracted driver. Probably texting, and even when they looked up and drove off the sidewalk, they might not have noticed that they'd scattered pedestrians and pets into bushes. It's so hazy out here that they might not have seen us at all, especially if the windshield was as dirty as our sunglasses."

I teased, "You don't own a car and we keep the donut car pristine. How do you know about dirty windshields?"

"I've driven other cars, but even someone who doesn't drive knows what it's like to try to see through a dirty windshield." She pushed her glasses up her nose. "Or smudged glasses."

"Especially if she's an artist."

"Yep. Artists might make more smudges than other people, but we're also super-observant."

I thought, *Except when cars are aimed at you.* "Just be careful, okay?"

"I am. See? You told me not to be alone, and I walked with you and you saved me from a reckless driver."

I wanted us to run home and lock ourselves inside, but a quavering voice called out, "Hello?"

I picked Dep up and cuddled her whether she wanted me to or not. I backed a few steps to see around the hedge.

A tall and wiry white-haired woman in a ruffled lavender tunic and black yoga pants stood beside the house. She was carrying some very businesslike pruning shears.

"Hi," I said. "I'm afraid we might have damaged your hedge by falling into it."

Nina muttered, "Or being thrown."

The woman slid the shears onto her porch and then faced

us again, barehanded. Had she come outside planning to wield pruning shears as a weapon against people and animals barging into the hedge in front of her house?

I apologized for the snapped-off twigs and leaves.

The woman joined us on the sidewalk side of her hedge. "It's nothing, I was just coming out to prune it, anyway. Don't worry about it. You probably saved me some work." She looked from one of us to the other. Nina had debris in her hair, and I probably did, too, while Dep had acquired a few more leaves on her back and head. "How did you manage to fall into the hedge? All three of you?"

"All three of us," Nina concurred. "The cat jumped, and Emily threw me and landed there, too."

The woman raised her eyebrows about as far as they would go. "You *threw* her? It was an accident, surely."

Nina smirked at me.

Clutching the squirmy cat to me, I stood as tall as I could. The woman was closer to Nina's height than to mine. "I did it on purpose." I turned around and pointed at the street behind us. "A car was speeding. It drove up onto the sidewalk. It nearly hit us."

The woman placed one hand on her heart. "That's terrible. The street is perfectly straight and it's not raining or anything. Why would anyone jump the curb?"

Nina answered quickly, "We figure the driver was distracted, and the sun could have been in his or her eyes. If the windshield was dirty . . ."

The woman peered up the street as if watching for the distracted driver to turn around and come back. "Nothing like that's ever happened before in the sixty-however-many years I've lived here!" Either she was exaggerating, or she had lived in that house since she was in grade school.

I asked her, "Did you see or hear the car?"

"No, I'm sorry, I didn't. It must have happened when I was

out in the shed rummaging around for pruning shears. Are you three all right?"

I hugged Dep. "We are." Dep twitched her ears. A teensy leaf fell off her head.

The woman called across the street, "Did you see a car drive up on the sidewalk over here?"

I couldn't see anyone, but a man answered from behind a screen of morning glories climbing a lattice on the front porch. "No. I just came out."

The woman confided quietly, "He probably did. He sits on his swing every evening about this time and reads the paper while he sips a glass of wine. He probably wouldn't have noticed a bulldozer tearing up his front lawn." She frowned. "Or the old lady across the street pruning her hedge." She scratched Dep's forehead. "I had a kitty almost like you about fifty years ago. She was the best pet ever."

Dep turned her head away from the woman.

The woman laughed. "After you, of course."

Dep looked up at the woman's face. "Meow."

We laughed, but our laughter ended when the woman pointed out a strip of flattened grass between the street and the sidewalk. "The grass will straighten up," she assured us, "but you three could have been badly injured or worse." She clasped my wrist. Her hand was bony and her skin felt paper-thin, but her grip was strong. "I'm glad you weren't. But if you run into any more trouble around here, you just come pound on my door."

I thanked her and promised to ask for help if I ever needed it. I wanted to hug her, but my arms were full of a purring fur ball. Also, my eyes felt suddenly wet. Nina gave her a hug.

The woman peered more closely at me. "You live in that cute two-story yellow brick cottage up the street, don't you? With the walled garden and the red kayak on the red car?"

"Yes." Naturally, a woman who knew about the reading

and wine-drinking habits of the man behind tangled vines across the street would know more about me than I knew about her. She probably also knew that I was a detective's widow. It wasn't a secret, but people seldom mentioned it to me. I was no longer as fragile as I'd once been and was probably less fragile than people thought I was.

She promised, "I'll ask around. Maybe another neighbor saw or heard something."

I thanked her again, and we headed home to the yellow brick cottage with its own share of whimsical gingerbread trim, painted a lovely, fresh cream.

After we were securely locked inside and Dep was freed from her harness and leash, I told Nina, "I'm calling Brent in case that driver has anything to do with the mime's death."

"I don't see how that could be, but who am I to stop you from calling your handsome detective?"

Grumbling that he wasn't mine and was probably dining with DCI Agent Kimberly Gartborg that very minute, I speed-dialed Brent's personal line. It went to message. "Nina and I have something to tell you," I said into the phone.

"Right," Nina muttered, "*we.*"

I put my phone into my pocket. "No answer. He probably really is on a date with her." Seeing pity in Nina's eyes, I added quickly, "She's welcome to him."

"Sure, sure."

Nina cooked rice and made a salad in the kitchen and I grilled the marinated pork tenderloin outside with Dep playing nearby. As the woman with the pruning shears had mentioned, my rear yard was completely walled in. The wall had been constructed with smooth yellow bricks. When Dep was a kitten, she got stuck high on a tree trunk, didn't know how to back down, ended up in a humiliating position, and stopped climbing trees. Until this evening, she'd avoided bushes, too. I turned away from the fragrant meat. "Dep, after you jumped onto that hedge today, are you still safe from climbing into bushes and jumping to the top of the wall?"

She stared down at a worm or a bug. Swishing her tail back and forth in the grass, she ignored me.

"Good thing I keep everything pruned far from the wall," I muttered.

We ate outside. The evening was warm. The earlier haze became a pinkish softness in the sky, with breezes caressing our faces. I took our dishes inside and put a kettle on for tea. Nina stayed outside with Dep.

I checked my phone in case I'd missed Brent's return call. I hadn't, but there was a headline: Deceased Mime Identified. I opened the article. The mime's name was Zipporah Melwyn, also known as Zippy. She was thirty-one, and she was from Lapeer, Michigan.

I went outside. "Hey Nina, guess what?"

Nina dragged a string with a bright red pompom attached to it through the grass. "What?"

I showed her my phone. Dep subdued the pompom.

Nina studied the screen and then tugged at the string again. "I guess they notified the mime's next of kin. Get it, Dep!"

"Zipporah Melwyn. With a name like that, she should be, I mean she should have been, a movie star."

"Or Zippy, the vandalizing thief. She sure was zippy when she was running away from me at the carnival. Sorry, Emily, but I'm finding it hard to forgive her for causing so much trouble."

Maybe I shouldn't have brought it up. Nina didn't need to be reminded of the horror of the previous evening. Still, I couldn't help reminding her, "She could have been an innocent victim of someone else."

Nina ran with the string. Dep chased the pompom. "She got into my apartment somehow. Someone could have carried her in against her will, but . . ."

"It doesn't seem likely. Maybe someone broke in, pretended they lived there, and invited her in."

"That's creepy."

"Sorry," I said. "Maybe the police will let you go back soon, and you can finish that painting."

"I hope so, even though you're trying to scare me away from it." She was obviously exaggerating to punish me for my creepy theories.

Dep raised her cute little bottom high and wiggled it. She pounced on the pompom again. "There's a funny coincidence," I told Nina. "Zipporah Melwyn was from Lapeer, Michigan. Lapeer, spelled the same as your last name."

"That is a funny-strange coincidence, but the name isn't unusual."

"Could your ancestors have founded Lapeer?" I was picturing the man whose photo was in her locket.

"No. As far as I know, none of them ever visited the place. I've never been there."

"Do you know any other Lapeers besides your family?" I wasn't trying to interrogate her. I was merely interested. She never talked about her family. I didn't think she had siblings. Jocelyn and I didn't. Alec had been an only child, too.

Nina lifted her head as if listening. "What do I hear?"

"Oops! The teakettle."

"Something else, too. Your doorbell?"

She was right. I ran toward the house. "Maybe it's Brent."

"I'll stay here with Dep to give you two some alone time."

I stuck out my tongue. In the kitchen, I turned off the gas underneath the teakettle.

I was halfway through the dining room when the doorbell rang again. Still fearful for Nina's—and my—life after that car had nearly rammed us, I set my feet down quietly to keep whoever was on my porch from detecting that someone inside was approaching the door. Tentatively, I peeked out the peephole.

Misty and Hooligan, both in their Fallingbrook police uniforms, were on the front porch. I loved them both, but I couldn't help feeling disappointed that Brent had sent them to hear my story instead of coming himself or returning my call.

I flung the door open. "I'm glad you're—" And then I noticed the sad and apologetic look on Misty's face, and I couldn't finish my sentence.

"We'd like to talk to Nina Lapeer." Misty's voice was quiet, but full of steely determination.

Chapter 12

✼

"Nina's outside with Dep," I told Misty and Hooligan, stern and businesslike in their police uniforms. "Would you like me to get her?"

"Yes, please." Misty was as formal as I had suddenly become. She looked miserable.

Hooligan shot me an empathetic glance. Both he and Misty knew Nina from their breaks in Deputy Donut, and they liked her. Everyone did, except for the person, if there was one, who was trying to kill her. And maybe Wisconsin DCI Agent Kimberly Gartborg.

I invited Misty and Hooligan in and went back to my walled-in garden. Shade cast by the western side of the wall had crept over more of the grass, and Dep must have lost interest in chasing a pompom. Nina was sitting in one of my patio chairs with Dep purring on her lap.

"Nina?" I said.

She looked up.

"Misty and Hooligan would like to talk to you."

She studied my face for a moment and looked away. She took a deep breath. Shoulders tense, she walked to me. She didn't meet my gaze as she lowered Dep into my hands. She turned and headed toward the living room.

Whatever was going on, I didn't want her to face it without a friend. Two friends, counting Dep. With the warm cat nestled in my arms, I followed Nina.

Misty and Hooligan had barely moved from the front door. Her back to me, Nina faced them. She stood stiffly with her hands at her sides and her fingers straight.

Misty acknowledged me with barely a flicker of her eyes and then said in a gentle but firm voice, "I'm sorry, Nina, but we'll have to place you under arrest for the murder of Zipporah Melwyn and ask you to come with us."

I croaked, "That's impossible. Someone tried to run Nina down today. Someone else killed the mime and is trying to kill Nina." I knew my guesses were wild. I added, "I called Brent and left him a message. I thought he sent you to take our statements. About . . . about nearly being hit by a car."

Misty's lovely face became even grimmer. "Brent's been occupied tying up loose ends."

I felt my mouth twist in shock and pain. Loose ends? I forced out an offer that seemed outlandish to me, knowing Nina as well as I did. "I'll talk to Tom about finding you a lawyer, Nina."

She raised her head and stated firmly, "I can't afford one."

I promised, "Tom will know what to do. Where's your purse, Nina?"

"On your guest room bed."

I asked Misty, "Is it okay if I get it?"

"Sure. No rush."

I ran up the stairs, picked up the tote bag, and trotted back down.

Nina's hands were behind her back, and Hooligan was apologizing as he fastened handcuffs around her wrists. Nina didn't show signs of resisting, but I wanted to scream at my friends not to cuff her. I knew it was procedure, however, and no amount of arguing could change that. My mouth in a grim line, I handed Nina's purse to Misty.

Nina seemed as wooden as the door she was staring at. "Bye, Emily, and thanks for everything. Bye, Dep."

I'd carried Dep upstairs and down again without noticing. Certain that the police would realize their mistake and release Nina quickly, I told her, "If you come back after I go to bed, keep ringing the doorbell until I wake up and let you in."

Nina only nodded. It seemed like she had given up and expected to be convicted.

Not if I could help it.

Deep sadness shone from Misty's Scandinavian-blue eyes. "Emily, Brent said he'll come talk to you later."

Hooligan opened the door. I watched until he and Misty helped Nina into the back of a cruiser.

I closed the door. If Dep hadn't been in my arms, I might have been tempted to pound my fists on walls and furniture. Dep wasn't purring. Maybe she hadn't heard the part about Brent coming over. Or maybe she blamed Brent for depriving her of Nina's attention and was no more eager to see him than I was at the moment. I'd left my phone outside. I got it, brought it into the kitchen, called Tom, and poured out the details of Nina's arrest.

"I know just the guy to handle this," he told me. "He's an excellent lawyer. Nina's my employee as much as yours. Let me take care of it, okay?"

"Okay, but we'll split the cost. And there's one more thing, Tom. You know how I guessed that Nina was supposed to be last night's victim? This afternoon on our way home from work, a speeding car came up onto the sidewalk and almost hit her. The driver kept going, but I wonder if, now that the deceased's name has been released, the murderer realized he'd failed to kill Nina yesterday, so he tried again today."

There was silence on Tom's end of the line. "Were you almost hit, too?"

"I was farther from the car. Dep noticed it first and leaped out of the way. None of us were hurt."

Tom sighed. "I'm glad." He was quiet again for a second, and then he stated, "So she wasn't necessarily safer with you."

"Or with anyone, not if this guy is as determined as he seems."

"Guy? Did you see him?"

"No, only the top of a pale-colored baseball cap. Guy or whoever. The car was gray, and we both thought it had Wisconsin plates." I told him the numbers we thought we'd seen.

He suggested, "Nina might be safer in police custody."

My mouth went dry. "Maybe, but only if they catch the real murderer, and Nina doesn't end up spending most of the rest of her life in prison." Fortunately, Wisconsin didn't have the death penalty.

Tom promised, "I'll do whatever I can. See you at work tomorrow?"

"Definitely. We'll manage without her if we have to. I talked to a job applicant today, but I didn't think she had the right personality. She seemed too shy and introverted."

"People like you and Nina and Jocelyn aren't easy to find."

"And you!"

"Ha." He disconnected.

I wandered into the living room and sat on the couch. I didn't try to read. I knew I wouldn't pay attention to the words. Outside, the sun set. Dusk arrived, and then twilight. Despite the purring cat on my lap, I sat wrapped in misery for my friend, her talent, her enthusiasm, and the joy that had just been dashed from her life. It became fully dark outside. I didn't move. I didn't turn on lights.

On the street, a car door closed. Dep jumped down and padded to the door. Someone climbed my porch steps, slowly and quietly.

Nina, back already, and it had all been a terrible mistake?

I checked the peephole. I'd neglected to turn on the porch

light, but I recognized Brent's silhouette against the dimly lit street. I opened the door.

As if afraid of disturbing someone, he walked in softly. "I wasn't sure you were still up." He didn't make a move toward one of our usual hugs.

I didn't, either. I led him inside. "Sorry, I didn't turn on lights." I switched on the lamp near the wing chair where he often sat. "Have a seat. Can I get you something?"

He sat down, leaned forward, and rubbed his forehead with both hands. "No, thanks."

"A glass of water?"

"I'm good." He was also being unnaturally formal.

Hiding a sigh, I plunked onto my spot on the couch and sat far enough forward to place my feet flat on the floor. I held my palms together in my lap. Every muscle in my body felt tightly coiled.

Brent straightened. Those usually lively gray eyes had become dark with fatigue. Dep jumped into his lap. He eased his fingers into her fur. After a few seconds, he said softly, "I'm sorry, Em."

I might as well say it. "Nina didn't kill anyone."

"Why are you sure?"

I didn't have a good answer. I wished I could say I was with her from the time we left the carnival, and that we'd gone up to Nina's apartment together and found Zipporah Melwyn. Even if I wanted to lie, which I didn't, Brent would see through me. "She just wouldn't, that's all. She's worked for us for almost a year. I know her pretty well."

"We often think we know people well when we don't."

The backs of my eyes heated. I bit my lip. I would not cry. "Someone tried to kill her yesterday but killed the mime instead. Someone tried to kill her today. That's why I called you."

"Misty mentioned that." He had me describe the car and where we'd been. Dep was sitting squarely on Brent's lap, making it difficult for him to write in his notebook, but he managed by balancing the notebook on the wide arm of the wing chair. He finished writing and told me, "I'm glad no one was hurt, and I understand how you can believe that someone is trying to kill Nina. But there are facts. Someone attempted to kill Zipporah—apparently, everyone knew her as Zippy—Melwyn. You entered the apartment and tried to save her. Nina came in."

"But someone broke into Nina's loft and then broke out through the screen."

"Probably." He paged back in his notebook. With the only light in the room shining down on him, he looked like he was the one being interrogated. "Nina's footprints were in the sugar and her shoes made partial prints out to her balcony and back."

"I saw her step in the sugar and then go out to her balcony and return. And I'd seen the floor before she went out. There were no footprints there until I saw her make them."

His eyes seemed to pierce my brain and my heart. "You're sure?"

"Yes. You believe me, don't you?" I didn't know what I would do if this good friend believed I would lie to him.

He said gently, "Of course I do."

"You might as well suspect me. I was first on the scene. As you said, Nina found me there, alone with the victim."

"You called me a few minutes before that, concerned that the victim might be injured and inside her car."

"That could have been a ploy."

He stared at me as if asking why I was trying to make myself into a possible suspect. Maybe he thought I was testing his friendship and the belief that I hoped he held, the belief that I couldn't be a murderer. But as he'd said, we sometimes think we know people well when we don't.

I mumbled, "It could have been a ploy, but it wasn't."

"Other evidence points to Nina."

I shook my head, and whispered, "No."

Running his index finger down notebook pages, he summarized what he'd learned. "Zippy Melwyn was seen around the corner from Nina's apartment. Melwyn was dressed like Nina and carrying a white bucket labeled PAINT. The direction she was heading could have led to Nina's apartment. It appears that Melwyn broke in through the street door and then the loft door, climbed Nina's new ladder, and threw sugar onto Nina's painting. We believe that Nina came home, found Melwyn trying to ruin the painting that was to be the centerpiece of Nina's show, and lost her temper. She toppled Melwyn off the ladder, injuring both of Melwyn's wrists and one of her ankles. Nina was so angry that she dragged Melwyn out of sight of the apartment door, put the bucket of sugar over Melwyn's head and held it there, and Melwyn couldn't fight back. Then Nina heard you on the stairs and broke her way out through her screen."

I held up a hand to stop him. "Nina wouldn't have dragged Zippy Melwyn out of sight of her door. She wouldn't have been expecting anyone to come in."

I knew as soon as it was out of my mouth that it was wrong, and Brent said it for me. "Nina was expecting you, wasn't she?"

"Yes, but since she was expecting me, she wouldn't have attacked an intruder. She probably would have run downstairs to her landlords' shop and called the police, and then she would have waited for them and for me."

"If the attacker was someone besides Nina, and he believed he was attacking Nina, he might not have expected anyone and would not have dragged his victim out of sight, either. But someone did, and we believe it was Nina. People in that situation don't always think things out perfectly. Nina must have panicked."

I shook my head. "Nina said her screen door was wonky and had to be jiggled for it to slide open. She knew how to do that. Whoever ran out of her apartment must have had trouble with it, and in his hurry, he punched his way out."

"Maybe Nina was in too much of a hurry to jiggle it. Or she knew she needed to make it appear that the person who attacked Melwyn didn't know how to open the screen door."

I leaned back and folded my arms. "If I came up with a theory like that, you'd say it was a stretch."

The slightest twitch of a grin tugged at one corner of his mouth. "Probably. But Nina kept her fire escape ladder stored underneath an Adirondack chair, out of sight. Someone apparently hooked it over the railing and climbed down. Quickly. Who else would have known about that ladder, and how to get off the ledge below her balcony to the slanted roof below the ledge? She told us she is probably the only one who knew about the fire ladder."

"Wouldn't a desperate person look everywhere for a way to escape? They'd find the ladder and use it, and they'd figure out getting off the ledge and the slanted roof, too."

"We considered that. But there are other sides to Nina that you don't know. Dark sides. Kim Gartborg noticed it last October when she was here."

"Detective Gartborg took a dislike to Nina." She'd taken a dislike to me, too, but I didn't mention that. I slid my hands, palms against the velvet upholstery, underneath my thighs.

Brent looked up from his notebook. "Did you know that Nina officially changed her last name about five years ago?"

"To Lapeer?"

"Yes."

"I didn't know that." I inched forward on the couch. "Why did she change it?"

"She said she just wanted to, which doesn't seem likely. Why go to the bother for a whim?"

"I don't know why she did that, but I suspect it's a total coincidence that her new name is the same as the name of the city where the mime was from."

Brent didn't say anything.

I pointed out, "The woman was attacked five years after Nina changed her name. What was Nina's last name before?"

"I can't tell you that."

"Can't or won't?"

"Can't. She won't tell us without a lawyer present."

"I'm glad she's willing to accept one. Tom's going to arrange it."

"He did. The lawyer will be there tomorrow."

I guessed, "Maybe, for the past five years, Nina's been hiding from someone who's a danger to her. And that person has tracked her down. I'm glad you have her in custody, and I hope she'll be safe there until you find the right person."

"I'm sorry, Em, but I'm afraid we have the right person. We discovered evidence besides Nina having the motive, the opportunity, and the means. Zippy Melwyn had a diary in her car. In it, she wrote that her distant cousin, Nina, was trying to harm her and might even kill her."

I pulled my hands out from underneath my thighs and waved them dismissively. "That's impossible. It can't be the same Nina."

"There's more in Zippy's diary. Zippy was an artist."

"Not another one!"

He leaned forward slightly. "What?"

"Go on. I'll tell you later."

He eased back underneath the light from the lamp. "Zippy had approached the Arthur C. Arthurs Gallery and had gotten some nibbles about displaying her art there. She claimed in her diary that Nina sabotaged her and was offered the art show that Zippy thought she should have been offered."

"That's not true. Do you remember Rich Royalson?"

"Yes." Of course he did. He and Detective Gartborg had investigated the man's death.

"Royalson came into Deputy Donut and admired one of

Nina's paintings. At my suggestion, he went to The Craft Croft to see her other work. He told Mr. Arthurs about Nina. Mr. Arthurs came to Fallingbrook and assessed Nina's paintings before he ever spoke to Nina."

Brent smiled. "I was on the phone with you when Arthurs made the offer. You were very excited."

"Zippy wasn't telling the truth in her diary. Nina did nothing underhanded to be offered that art show."

"But it sounds like it has to be the same Nina. Zippy said that although she, Zippy, that is, did not attend art school and Nina did, Zippy was a better artist, and Zippy deserved the art show."

"None of that makes Nina a murderer. But it does make Zippy look like the nasty and jealous kind of person who would break into someone's apartment and vandalize a painting in an attempt to destroy that other person's artwork."

He agreed. "It also makes Zippy look like a person that a distant cousin might want to remove from her life."

"I think that the printing on that tiny piece of paper in the locket was an abbreviation of Nina's address." I reminded him that Zippy had taken a good look at Marsha Fitchelder's clipboard and could have seen Nina's address.

"I'll double-check, but I suspect you're right about the abbreviation." He wrote in his notebook and then looked up at me again. "I also believe that the locket was originally Nina's, and that Zippy stole it, but she stole it a long time ago, not last night."

"What? How?"

Brent searched through his notebook, read silently, marked his place with a finger, and told me, "We looked into Zippy's connections and her past. Going way back, we discovered that Zippy was at a Melwyn family reunion in Pennsylvania the summer she was thirteen. A distant cousin named Nina, who was eight at the time, was also there. When Nina was packing to leave, she couldn't find her locket. The same man owns the resort today. He remembers this determined eight-year-old marching into his office and describing the locket she'd lost. She drew pictures of it, too, and of the man and woman whose photos were in the locket. The resort owner kept those pictures. He's been sorry ever since that the locket didn't turn up. Even afterward, he held on to the pictures in case someone found the locket and because they were cute and he thought the spunky eight-year-old had a surprising amount of artistic talent." Brent's words put me somewhere between denial and disbelief. Ignoring my head shaking, he went on. "The resort owner scanned the drawings and sent them to us. He was right about the eight-year-old Nina. She was quite an artist, and observant, too. She caught the old gentleman's stern expression and replicated the design on the outside of the locket. It has to be the same one."

"The resort owner must have known Nina's last name. Was it Melwyn?"

"He didn't think so, but he apologized for not remembering it. Many of the people at the reunion had last names that weren't Melwyn. He said he's afraid he's forgetting a lot of things lately, and he's glad his grown children have taken over the running of the resort." Brent stroked Dep with his free hand. "He lost track of Nina's name and address. He'll contact us if the name comes to him. We don't like to put ideas into people's heads, but we did give him a list of possible names, most of them towns and cities in Michigan, and Lapeer was one of them. He didn't recognize any of the names we suggested." Brent tilted his head and gazed at me. "And maybe this is a coincidence, and I don't see it as conclusive evidence of anything, but Nina and Zippy resembled each other. It's easy to believe they could have been related."

Chapter 13

I took a deep breath. "You're right about the resemblance. I already guessed that Zippy tried to look like Nina when she broke into Nina's apartment, probably because she didn't want anyone to question her. And your description of the eight-year-old girl does sound a lot like the Nina we know. Nina didn't say when Zippy stole the locket, but she didn't dispute it when I implied that Zippy had stolen it yesterday."

Brent reminded me gently, "It doesn't matter when it was stolen. Nina could have seen it in Zippy's possession after Nina knocked the ladder down. That could have been enough to make Nina want to do more harm than she'd already done to Zippy. Could Nina have recognized Zippy from having met her before, even a long time ago?"

"I'm not sure about when Zippy was made up as a mime. When Nina came in and saw me trying to revive Zippy, Nina seemed to go into shock, which was understandable considering that a nearly lifeless person was in her apartment. But maybe it was because she'd recognized her distant cousin after her makeup had been replaced by powdered sugar."

"Or before that, when Nina saw her without the makeup. And near the top of Nina's ladder."

I shook my head. "Stealing a locket, writing what I suspect were lies about a cousin, working with a thief at a carnival, breaking into and vandalizing someone's apartment—Zippy was not a nice person. She must have had other enemies. Like that magician. Even if Zippy wasn't working with him to rob people, she probably saw what he was doing. Maybe he thought she knew too much about him and might report him to the police." I thought for a second and asked, "Whose fingerprints were on the screwdriver and the bucket of sugar? Mine would be on the bucket from when I removed it from Zippy's head, plus the fingerprints from any of us at Deputy Donut could be on it. Yesterday morning, Nina carried the bucket from the shop to the car, and then someone stole it from the car—Zippy, I guess, from what you said about someone seeing her carry it last night."

Still sitting underneath the only lit lamp in the dark room, Brent nodded. "The prints on the screwdriver were Zippy's, underneath prints from someone wearing gloves, so the screwdriver might have belonged to Zippy. The prints on the bucket were yours, consistent with your pulling it off Zippy's head. The bucket had been wiped clean before you touched it."

"Nina didn't need to wipe prints from that bucket, since everyone would expect her prints to be on it. Could you tell what kind of gloves the person who handled the screwdriver was wearing?"

Apparently, he decided that the information didn't need to be kept secret. "Woven, with traces of white cotton fibers. I expect we'll discover that they were Zippy's gloves, and she touched it both before and after she put on the gloves."

"Did you see any evidence that someone in that apartment was wearing leather gloves, like black ones?"

He gave his head a definitive shake. "No leather gloves at all."

"That doesn't rule out the magician handling things and wiping off his glove prints."

"It doesn't." Did he have to be so agreeable about everything except freeing Nina?

Although I wasn't sure how it would help her, I tried another question. "I'm sure that most if not all of the white powder in that bucket was sugar, but has it been tested for additions like poisons or drugs that might have been added after the brand-new pail was opened?"

"Nothing has been found so far besides sugar, but the investigation continues. Nina's hair and clothing were spattered by white powder when I arrived." Dep stretched and curled up again on his lap.

"So were mine. And when Nina first got there, she didn't have a speck of sugar on her. I would have noticed. It wasn't like I hadn't been thinking about white powder."

"You could have been distracted."

"That's an understatement, but I'm sure I would have seen at least some white powder on Nina if it had been there."

He looked down and wrote in his notebook. "I believe you, Em, I always believe you, but—"

I finished for him. "Detective Gartborg is sticking to her own theories."

He looked up at me then, and I thought I saw pain in his eyes.

I conceded, "They're good theories, but they don't fit with what I experienced and what I know about Nina. Someone else had sugar on himself or herself that night. It's a pity we didn't find them then."

"It is."

"They'll have removed it by now."

"They will." Hugging Dep close, he stood, turned on the lamp nearest me, and sat down. Dep looked boneless and completely contented and relaxed on his lap. He flipped to a new page in his notebook. "You told us that you did an abdominal thrust to help clear Zippy's airways, and then Nina took over holding Zippy upright to help her breathe. Did you ask Nina to take over, or did she offer?"

"I asked her if she would prefer holding Zippy up or

splinting her wrists and ankle. She chose holding Zippy up, so I put the splints on." I winced. Could Nina's choice put her in prison for life? And destroy her dream at the moment when the dream was about to come true?

"When Nina took over, was Zippy breathing?"

"Yes, with difficulty."

"Samantha said that Zippy was barely breathing when she got there. They put her on a respirator, but the powdered sugar had done its work."

"Nina was trying to help Zippy. I'm sure of it. And there are other people you should probably investigate besides that magician. Marsha Fitchelder, the carnival organizer, quarreled with Zippy yesterday morning. Marsha was angry and shouting, while Zippy only mimed her side of the argument, which seemed to infuriate Marsha. I understand that, a little later, Marsha called the police to tow Zippy's car, but the police refused because the car was on public property."

"I've read that report."

"Zippy was proud of herself." I described Zippy's chalk-one-up-to-me miming reaction when one of our customers told us about the police refusing to tow the Mime Mobile. I admitted, "Maybe it's a stretch that Marsha was mad enough to attack Zippy, but I never like to leave a theory un-theorized."

"I've noticed. If you had joined the police force immediately after college like Misty did, you could be a detective by now."

"Not ahead of Misty."

"She doesn't want to be a detective."

"Fallingbrook doesn't need another detective. You'd have to join the DCI."

"You're not the first one to say that today. Kim also mentioned it."

Detective Gartborg. She would. Hiding my own feelings about the possibility of a friend moving away, I tried to think of what might be best for him. "Would you like working for the DCI? You'd be in charge of serious cases."

His face gave nothing away, and he answered the question with a question of his own. "Who doesn't like being in charge?"

"Probably someone. Nina is not a killer. I can't tell you how I know that. I just do."

He stroked Dep. "I'll keep an open mind, Em. Earlier this evening, you started to say something about another artist. What was it?"

"One came into the shop today, supposedly looking for a job, but I think she was actually looking for a place to display and sell her art. The name she wrote on her job application was Kassandra Pyerson." I spelled it for him. "The photos she showed me of her paintings were good, so I suggested she should join The Craft Croft. I don't really think she killed someone she thought was Nina in order to open a job vacancy, but there's something off about her. The first time I saw her was yesterday morning at the carnival. I was climbing the hill to look for the confectioners' sugar, and she was peering into our donut car. I called out and asked if she wanted to see inside the car. I was sure she heard me, but she turned away and started toward a gray car. I know there are zillions of gray cars, so I'm not saying that she tried to run Nina down on our way here from work this afternoon, but I can't help wondering if there's a connection between the bucket of sugar, Zippy, Kassandra Pyerson, and the gray car. Oh, and as I told you, that black windowless van was parked nearby when Kassandra was hanging around the donut car, also."

Brent finished writing what I told him, stood, and handed Dep to me. She jumped off my lap, landed silently on the wide planks of the pine floor, and rubbed against Brent's ankles, the little traitor. Brent scooped her into his arms. "Thank you for your help, Emily. I'll go over all of it with Kim. As I said, she thinks we've got the right person."

I stood and put my fists on my hips. "Do you think Nina could have killed someone? Her cousin?"

It took him a second to answer. "I don't know her as well as you do, but the evidence against her is strong. Remember, she let you believe that the locket had been stolen yesterday, when it appears to have been stolen a long time before that. Nina keeps secrets, even from you. I'm sorry to have to disillusion you, Em. Good night, you two." He gave Dep a knuckle rub, handed her to me, and left.

Knowing he'd stay on my porch until he heard me lock the door, I set Dep down and pushed the dead bolt into place with as much force and as loudly as I could.

I picked Dep up, turned out both lamps, sank into the couch cushions, and let bleakness descend with the darkness. I hadn't told Brent about the way that Zippy had leaned away from Nina. I'd thought that Zippy was too weak to stay upright, even with help, but had she actually been afraid of Nina? She must have been certain that Nina was the same Nina as her distant cousin, and jealousy and long-held grudges must have made her break into Nina's apartment. She could have been dodging Nina because she was afraid of what Nina might do to her, not because she believed that Nina had already attacked her. Zippy could have seen her attacker. If Nina and I had managed to keep Zippy alive, Zippy could have told the police that Nina had not attacked her. What had Zippy tried to tell me? *A die. A seized her.*

I muttered to Dep, "I can't possibly be wrong about Nina, can I?" Dep only purred. I asked her, "Should I have told Brent about Zippy maybe cringing away when Nina approached her?"

Purr, purr.

"That means no, right, Dep?"

Purr.

"What if Nina is jailed for murder, and Brent joins the DCI and moves away? You'd be losing two of your favorite people—Nina and Brent."

Dep stopped purring.

Finally, I went to bed. I'd been up late the night before, also.

Falling asleep quickly was hardly likely though, considering that I couldn't help listening for Nina to run up onto the porch and ring the doorbell, either completely free or free on bail.

"And maybe," I muttered to Dep, "it would be a good thing for you-know-who to join the DCI and move away. Then you might learn to stop sitting by the front door waiting for him to show up." When Brent wasn't around, I didn't dare say his name aloud in Dep's presence. She would go downstairs and sit by the front door. I needed the comfort of her warm little body.

I did sleep, eventually, and woke up forlorn because that morning, Nina was not going to join Dep and me for breakfast. "Nina will be out soon," I said. Dep grabbed the end of her tail and smoothed the fur on it.

It was Sunday, the day that Deputy Donut opened late. Dep walked nicely on her leash to work. No one tried to run us down. No one went speeding past along our route. Dep didn't attempt to fly to the top of anyone's hedge.

Jocelyn arrived shortly after I settled Dep into our office. Tom and I told Jocelyn about Nina's arrest. Red flooded Jocelyn's face, and then she went pale and tears filled her eyes. "That's all wrong. No one could think that Nina would hurt anything."

Tom and I agreed.

Jocelyn promised, "I'll work extra hours and extra hard until she comes back."

Tom reminded her, "You already work just about all day every day." It was true. Thanks to Jocelyn and Nina, Tom and I each took two much-needed days off most weeks. A teasing glint lit Tom's dark eyes. "You mean you haven't been working at top capacity already?"

I caught a glimpse of the dimple beside one corner of Jocelyn's mouth. "Almost."

Again, the first customers of the day were reporters. A cameraman waited on the patio while a woman in a heathery gray sleeveless dress came in.

"I'll talk to her," Tom said. Their discussion was brief, and then the woman joined the cameraman. They both stood on our patio while Tom returned to the kitchen.

I asked him, "Did they know that Nina works here?"

He shook his head. "If they did, they didn't admit it. They wanted to chat—just off the record, they said—but I was not exactly welcoming." Outside, the reporter and her cameraman had made it as far as the sidewalk. Pedestrians waved them away or shook their heads and kept walking. Tom folded his arms. "No one seems to want their fifteen minutes of fame." He grinned. "Aha. Maybe I know why."

In their patrol cop uniforms, Misty and Hooligan came up the walkway between our twin patios and headed for our front door. The reporter and her cameraman got into a car parked beside the patio.

"Misty and Hooligan are the ones who came to my place last night and arrested Nina," I told Tom and Jocelyn. "I'll serve them, okay, Tom?"

"Sure, but leave the paparazzi to me if you can."

I watched the latest pair of reporters drive away. "Gladly."

Jocelyn asked me, "Are you going to scold Misty and Hooligan for arresting Nina, Emily?"

"What? And get arrested, too?" Teasing was one way to keep myself from collapsing on the floor and refusing to move until the world started turning in the correct direction again.

I'd barely gotten to Misty and Hooligan's table when Misty

stood, gave me a quick hug, and said, "I'm sorry for what we had to do last night."

Hooligan apologized, too.

I admitted, "It was your duty. But I'm certain you have the wrong person. How's Nina doing?"

Misty raised her clear blue eyes to mine. "She didn't have a good night. Her lawyer was there first thing this morning. Nina's adamant that she's innocent."

I resisted stomping a foot on our gorgeous maple floor. "Won't they let her out on bail at least?"

Misty straightened her spoon. "The earliest time for a bail hearing is tomorrow. And she might not get bail. The crime is serious, and besides . . ."

Hooligan spread his hands wide on the glass tabletop. "There's something she's not telling us. I mean there's something she's not telling the detectives."

I chewed on a lip. "I suggested to Nina that whoever killed Zippy might have actually been after Nina. Maybe she's realized that being in a cell in the basement of the police department is safer than living with me and working here."

Wearing the casual navy blue pants and shirt that he wore when on duty at the fire station, Scott came in with Samantha. She was in her EMT uniform.

I tried not to think about the fact that get-togethers with these four good friends often included Brent. "You all came to cheer me up, didn't you?" I asked.

Scott laughed. "Don't most of us come here most days?"

I couldn't help grinning back at him. "All of you except Samantha. Besides, you cheer me even when I don't need cheering."

Hooligan and Samantha gazed into each other's eyes.

I asked, "What can I get you? Our featured coffee today is from Kenya. Although it's a light roast, it has a good, strong flavor. We also have fresh blueberry fritters. They're coated in granulated sugar, not confectioners' sugar."

Misty shuddered. "I don't ever want to see powdered sugar again."

"Did you have to remind us?" I smiled to show I was joking.

"Yes, I had to. I need comfort food. Just bring me an un-raised chocolate donut with fudge frosting. And a mug of the Kenyan coffee."

Hooligan opted for a blueberry fritter and Colombian coffee.

Samantha asked for green tea, but no donuts, fritters, or anything else delicious and high in calories.

Scott never seemed to fill out his tall frame. He wanted the Kenyan coffee plus a cinnamon twist and a long John.

I brought them their beverages and then returned to the kitchen to plate everyone's donuts and fritters. The shop wasn't busy, so I sat at the table with my friends for awhile. All of us except Samantha teased Hooligan that at his wedding, we would find out his real first name.

Scott asked him, "Have you told Samantha what it is?"

With his auburn hair and freckles, Hooligan's lopsided grin made him look even more boyish. "Nope. I didn't want to take a chance that she wouldn't marry me."

Samantha slapped at his arm. "As if. And although he didn't tell me what it was, I saw it when I signed the mar-riage license." She giggled. "It's not that bad, but I'm sworn to secrecy."

The rest of us groaned, but Hooligan gave Samantha a ten-der smile. "It's not bad, just embarrassing."

Samantha leaned forward. "Misty and Scott will see it when they sign our marriage certificate as witnesses. They'll be sworn to secrecy on pain of—"

I squawked, "I'm a bridesmaid, too! Won't I get to see and sign the marriage certificate?"

Hooligan gave Misty a teasing look. "We chose Misty be-cause she and I might be in life-or-death situations together.

She has to be able to trust me, and who knows what I would do if she divulged my deepest secret?"

I sat back and made a pretend sulky face.

Hooligan told me, "You can continue calling me Hooligan. Or simply call me the luckiest man in the world."

Samantha rolled her eyes. "You hope."

Misty stared at Samantha. "Your hair is its natural color." Samantha often streaked her dark brown hair with bright colors to give her patients something to smile about. When she and Hooligan first got engaged, she said she might have a winter wedding and powder her hair to look like snow, but she was getting married in August.

"What color is your hair going to be when you walk up the aisle?" I demanded.

"You mean down the grassy slope toward the beach? You'll see."

Misty and I looked at Hooligan.

He continued gazing at Samantha. "Don't ask me. I don't know. She'll be beautiful no matter what."

After my friends left, I helped make donuts until we had more than enough for the rest of the day, and then I went outside and parked the donut car next to the loading dock so I could vacuum and tidy it before we needed to make deliveries.

I cleaned the trunk first, and then the passenger compartment. Pushing the vacuum brush underneath the seat behind the passenger seat, I heard a strange, fluttery-paper noise. I yanked the brush toward me.

The vacuum cleaner was trying to suck up a manila envelope.

Chapter 14

Shutting off the vacuum, I muttered, "How long has that been there?" I'd swept the donut car shortly before Friday's Faker's Dozen Carnival. If the envelope had been underneath the seat then, I had missed it.

Nothing was written on either side of the envelope, and it felt almost empty. I untucked the flap and pulled out part of a letter written in choppy blue script with a pen that must have gone past its best-before date. Both the top and the bottom of the pale gray stationery had been torn off, and the letter was missing a salutation and a signature. Only a few lines remained.

was going to catch up on the rent I owed, and it wasn't that much, so you had no right to change the locks on our apartment. Give me a key or let me in so I can have my belongings and paintings. OR ELSE.

Who had written the letter? I peeked inside the envelope and almost missed the tiny piece of thick paper stuck in the bottom fold. I turned the envelope upside down and tapped it.

A photograph fell out, faceup, on the seat.

I couldn't help a gasp of recognition. The photo had been cut in the shape of Nina's locket. The woman in the picture appeared to be a perfect match for the man that Nina had said was an ancestor. The woman wore a black dress with puffs at the tops of the sleeves and a high collar. Her hair was pinned in horizontal rolls. Stiff black feathers stuck up from one side of her black hat. She'd been better at holding still than the man had been. Her face wasn't as blurred, but her expression was every bit as severe. They both might have been Nina's ancestors, but tall Nina with her big, waiflike eyes didn't resemble either one of them. Maybe she would if she ate lots more donuts, which wasn't likely to happen if she stayed in jail.

I left the car and the vacuum cleaner, hurried into the office, phoned Brent, and told him, "I'm at Deputy Donut. I found something in our delivery car that might have a bearing on the Zippy Melwyn case."

He said he'd be right over.

"I'll be in the office. Coffee and a donut?"

"Just coffee, thanks."

When Brent arrived, looking groomed and calm but also a little distracted, in his light gray suit and deep blue tie, I'd already photographed the torn letter and the locket-shaped photo so that I'd have copies. I placed a mug of fresh, hot coffee on our office coffee table for him.

Dep pelted down her stairways and ramps and meowed at Brent until he picked her up. We sat on our office couch. Dep curled between us, but she snuggled up to Brent's leg, not mine. I handed him the envelope. He pulled out the partial letter, studied it, set it on the table, and looked at me questioningly.

"There's more," I told him, "inside the envelope."

A grin twitched at the corner of his mouth. "You mean I failed to detect something?"

"I'd never say that."

Dep flopped over to her side with her back against Brent's leg and stretched her own legs toward me. "Mew."

Brent removed the tiny photo and held it by the edges between his thumb and forefinger. "I . . . see," he said. "This looks a lot like the eight-year-old Nina's drawing. It must have come from Nina's locket. Could Nina have left this envelope in your donut car?"

"Possibly. She could have dropped it, or it could have fallen out when she tossed her tote bag into the rear seat. But if it's true that Zippy stole Nina's locket a long time ago, Zippy was the one who had the photo from the locket, and Zippy must have left that envelope in the donut car. It was close to where we'd put the sugar. Maybe Zippy accidentally dropped the envelope when she stole the sugar. Maybe she intended to keep that written threat with the diary you told me about."

Brent conceded, "They do seem to belong together."

I pointed at the envelope. "I don't have a clue why the eighteen-nineties woman's portrait was also in the envelope, unless it was a convenient place to keep the portrait when Zippy hid Nina's coded address." I reminded Brent that Zippy had gotten a good look at the top page on Marsha Fitchelder's clipboard and had apparently connected Nina and me to Deputy Donut. "I thought it was probably because of our hats, but if Zippy was in Fallingbrook looking for Nina, which if you're right about their relationship seems likely, Zippy might have recognized Nina, either by remembering Nina's appearance when she was eight, or by noticing the family resemblance."

"It's possible that Nina gave Zippy her address. They could have stayed in touch over the years. We have no reason to believe that they didn't, and this letter makes me think that they might have."

I argued, "Then Zippy would have known Nina's address and wouldn't have needed a coded version of it."

"Maybe she wrote it as a memory crutch."

"It's also possible that they didn't stay in touch and Nina changed her name because she was afraid of Zippy, but Zippy tracked her down."

"Choosing someone else's city as a last name isn't the greatest idea if one is hiding from that particular person. I know you'd like to help Nina, but none of this does."

"Not if Nina wrote the threat. But I don't think she did." Seeing the look of pity on his face, I asked, "What?"

"It's the wording. Two different witnesses heard Nina yell at Zippy to stay away from the Deputy Donut tent 'or else.'"

I remembered Nina confessing that she'd yelled at Zippy to stay away from the Deputy Donut tent. I didn't remember her saying anything about a nonspecific threat. "Lots of people say 'or else' when they can't come up with better wording on the spur of the moment. Or maybe the witnesses merely imagined it because people often add those words. Zippy probably tore off the signature because it was hers, and it would have contradicted her diary entries about Nina threatening her, and she tore off the salutation because she wrote the letter to someone else, not Nina. Or maybe there never was a salutation or a signature. Zippy could have torn off the top and bottom of the sheet of stationery. She could have written those threats herself in the hope that anyone who read them would mistakenly believe that Nina wrote the threatening letter to Zippy. It wouldn't be easy to tear a letter the way this one's torn. Wouldn't we usually lose part of the writing above and below this snippet? This looks staged to me."

"It would to me, too, except that the lines in the snippet are widely spaced, so the rest of the letter could have been also." Brent pointed at the fragment of paper. "Do you know if Nina has ever had a roommate?"

"I don't know about ever. Maybe in art school? I think she's lived alone in that loft above Klassy Kitchens ever since she started renting it. She'd been there a couple of years already when we hired her. It's possible that she had a roommate before I met her." I picked up a shopping list from our desk. "Nina printed this. I don't have a sample of her handwriting, but it's hard to imagine Nina, who prints shopping lists with such elegant printing, writing in such a choppy way." I gave him the list.

He studied it and set it down.

I handed him Kassandra's job application. "Here's yesterday's job applicant's printing. It's more like the writing on that piece of a letter."

"I'm not sure we need to add Kassandra Pyerson to this mix."

I reminded him that she'd been hanging around the donut car on Friday morning. "She could have put the envelope in the car and locked it before I saw her. And she came here looking for a job, she said, but she also claimed she is an artist and asked to display her paintings here, so I'm not sure she's quite what she pretends to be. It's possible that she followed Zippy into Nina's apartment and attacked her there."

"I can take the envelope and its contents. They might point to clues that would help us solve the case, but it's like with the locket. You, and not the police, found them, so we don't have a proper chain of custody, and they wouldn't help much in court. Which might be a good thing if Nina wrote the letter."

"I don't think she did." I changed the subject. "Did you find Zippy Melwyn's name on Marsha Fitchelder's list of exhibitors?"

"More or less. Zippy registered under the name of Zippy the Mime and was honest about her car's license number."

"What about the magician?"

"There were several magicians. None of them gave the license number you found on that black van, but one of them, who called himself Marv the Marvelous, applied with a Wis-

consin license number that does not exist. He claimed it belonged to a dark brown van."

"Was it the license number the pickpocketing magician
used when he applied to other carnivals and fairs?"

"No. One of the reasons we're having trouble catching him
is he never gives the same name, vehicle, and license number
when he applies to perform at events. And some of the other
magicians at the Faker's Dozen Carnival worked at other fairs
where your thieving magician was picking pockets."

"Don't call him mine! Is Marv the Marvelous your prime
suspect in the pickpocketing case? Because of the faked license number?"

"Yes."

"And he might not have anything to do with the windowless black van?"

"I'm not ruling that out. Thank you again for getting those
photos of it. Before I go, would you like me to search your
donut car in case there's anything else?"

I jumped up. "Good idea. The car's beside the loading
dock. It's not locked."

He gave me a look but said nothing about my failure to
lock the car. He thanked me for the coffee and asked, "Would
you like to be present while I search your car?"

"I would, but I should probably go back to work. And I
trust you."

He looked up toward Dep's catwalks as if answers to questions and solutions to crimes might be up there, but he only
said, "I'll let you know what I find." He picked Dep up, gave
her a quick hug, handed her to me, and carried the envelope
out to the back porch. I made a show of locking the door behind him. He didn't turn around.

I shut Dep inside the office and washed my face, hands,
and arms before I put on my apron and hat and returned to
making donuts.

About ten minutes later, Brent came in through the front. I joined him near the door. "Did you find anything else?"

"No. You can finish vacuuming and lock your car."

I made a face at the reminder to lock up. "And put it into its garage. Which we always lock."

He smiled. "Good. Call us if you think of anything else." He held up the envelope. "Thanks."

"You're welcome."

I watched him until he turned toward the police station and went out of sight.

I took off my apron and hat and finished vacuuming the car. I didn't find anything else that didn't belong in it. I backed the car into its garage, put the vacuum cleaner away in the storeroom closet, washed up, and served customers. Some of them asked about Nina. I told everyone, "I'm sure she's innocent."

None of us usually took much time off for lunch. When we were really busy, we grabbed snacks. Sometimes we took turns joining Dep in the office for a few minutes to eat. All of us liked exercise. Whenever we could, we went for walks. Jocelyn might have done more than walk, though. I could easily imagine her cartwheeling through town.

We weren't terribly busy. I told Jocelyn and Tom I had an errand to run.

Naturally Tom saw through me. "The police will sort it out, Emily."

"It's not about Nina, it's about Kassandra, the woman who applied for a job yesterday. I don't want to hire her even if Nina can't . . ." My voice broke. "Even if she doesn't come back, but I told Kassandra she should join The Craft Croft. It's a nice day, so I'll go down there and find out if she did. And I like to see the new artwork they're displaying."

He narrowed his eyes at me. "Stay out of trouble."

"I will. And I have my phone. If it gets busy in here, call me. I'll be right back."

Jocelyn grinned. "Okay."

In the office, I started to file Kassandra's application. I glanced at the back and then read it more carefully.

Kassandra's home address was in Lapeer, Michigan, the city that Zippy was from, the city with the name that Nina had adopted as a last name.

I was certain that Brent had not looked at the back of the form. I gave Dep a short cuddle. "I'll tell him later, but I need to take this opportunity to visit The Craft Croft before Deputy Donut becomes busy again." Dep wanted to come with me. I squeezed out the back door without her.

At the Wisconsin Street end of the driveway, I turned south. Thinking about Nina, I barely noticed the displays in the shop windows I passed. As far as I knew, Lapeer wasn't a big city. Had Zippy and Kassandra known each other? Could they have conspired with each other? Possibly, both of them had worked with the magician to distract people from noticing what the magician was really doing. I still believed that the magician had killed Zippy, but now that I knew that Zippy and Kassandra were both from the same small city in Michigan, I moved Kassandra higher on my list of murder suspects, right below the magician and above Marsha Fitchelder.

I went into The Craft Croft and almost ran into Kassandra Pyerson.

She was wearing a white boyfriend shirt over another gauzy skirt, this one a batik print in shades of red, orange, and yellow. Instead of tying her hair back in a ponytail, she wore a stretchy blue headband with purple flowers printed on it, allowing her long hair to flow down her back. She edged behind the reception desk and sat down. "May I help you?" Apparently when I wasn't wearing my Deputy Donut hat and apron, I wasn't recognizable.

"Is Summer here?"

Kassandra looked confused. "It's August." She blushed. "Oh, you mean Ms. Peabody-Smith."

I smiled. "Yes."

A strident voice called from Summer's office, "I'll be right out, Emily!"

Kassandra suggested politely, "Have a look around."

"I see you found a job." Seeing no recognition on Kassandra's face, I added, "You talked to me at Deputy Donut yesterday."

Kassandra blushed again. "Oh, sorry. I thought you looked familiar."

Summer strode out of her office. Being six feet tall did not deter her from piling her red curls on top of her head and wearing high heels. These shoes were scarlet and contrasted beautifully with her white knee-length, sleeveless dress, a classic style that skimmed her curves. "Kassandra's going to bring some of her paintings for me to see," Summer told me, including Kassandra in the conversation. "From what I saw of her photos, she should join the co-op and display her work here."

I smiled at Kassandra. "Your photos look good."

"Thank you for sending her here, Emily. We've been short-handed for a while." Summer asked Kassandra, "When will we see the actual paintings?"

Blushing more furiously, Kassandra seemed to shrink away from her glamorous boss. "As soon as I can get them out of storage and shipped here."

Summer tilted her head. "Where are they?"

"In Michigan. I'll get them." Kassandra tucked her lips into her mouth and seemed to bite down on them.

Michigan.

Summer turned toward me. I was sure that her polite smile was an attempt to conceal concern. About Kassandra? "Emily, you're just the person I wanted to see. Do you have a moment?"

"Sure."

She led me to her sleek white and brushed nickel office and closed the door. "I was just on the phone with Arthur C. Arthurs." I'd had a small part in connecting Nina with the gallery owner, but Summer had done more. "It was distressing," she said. "The news about Nina's arrest has reached Madison. Mr. Arthurs is considering canceling her show."

Chapter 15

✀

I stared in horror at Summer. "How can Arthur C. Arthurs cancel Nina's show? Didn't they sign a contract?"

"Mr. Arthurs told me that the contract will be null and void if the artist's behavior might cause harm or embarrassment to the gallery. They added that clause to their basic contract after one of their artists went on a damaging social media rampage."

I leaned toward Summer. "Nina has done nothing wrong. She wouldn't hurt anyone." I sounded confident, which I was, and also calm, which I wasn't.

Summer twisted her lips and looked at me from underneath half-lowered eyelids. "That's what I told Mr. Arthurs."

"Do you have his number? I'll call him."

She scrolled through her phone's screen and read his number aloud. I added it to my phone and then asked, "Why did you hire someone who lives in Michigan?"

Summer's forehead wrinkled. "Who?"

I cocked my head toward the showroom behind me. "Kassandra."

"Michigan? She gave me an address here in Fallingbrook. At least I think she did." Summer walked her fingers through a file drawer. "Aha." She pulled out a piece of paper. "Here it is. Second floor, nine seventy-six Wisconsin Street South, Fallingbrook."

"But that would be . . ."

"What?"

I couldn't tell Summer that Kassandra's apartment had to be almost across the street from Nina's. I didn't want to frighten Summer about having hired a possible murderer, and I also didn't want to make accusations about someone who might be innocent. "I mean, Kassandra could have moved recently and automatically listed her old address when she filled out the application at Deputy Donut."

Summer placed the application in the file drawer. "She did say she was new in town, and her paintings are in Michigan, so that could explain why she forgot and gave you her old address."

I didn't mention another possible explanation. Maybe Kassandra and Zippy had been roommates, and after Kassandra filled out the application at Deputy Donut, she realized she needed to conceal her connection with Zippy, so when she'd applied at The Craft Croft, she'd given a local address.

Had one of them written that threatening letter to the other? If so, which one had fallen behind on her rent and which one had prevented the other from retrieving her paintings and other belongings? Maybe Zippy had changed the locks on an apartment she shared with Kassandra for a very good reason, like being deathly afraid of Kassandra.

I asked Summer, "Do you mind if I take pictures of the photos Kassandra gave you of her paintings?"

"Of course not."

With my phone, I took pictures of each of the photos of paintings that Kassandra had said were in storage. As far as I could tell, these were the photos that Kassandra had shown me.

Women were streaming in from the sidewalk. Summer

sighed. "That tour group is early. I guess I should go out there."

I blurted, "Be careful around Kassandra."

"Why?"

"Just a feeling that she's not quite what she says she is."

Summer confided, "I have the same feeling. She looked away from us when she said her paintings were in storage, like she was making it up. But maybe my first guess was right. I thought she was desperate for money and had to pawn her art. I hoped that by hiring her, I could help her get on her feet and redeem her paintings."

That theory sounded likely but also very sad. I asked Summer, "How much money could someone get from pawning paintings by an unknown artist?"

Sighing, Summer tossed a sympathetic glance toward Kassandra. "Not much."

We left Summer's office. Summer greeted the women browsing through The Craft Croft.

I'd walked about a half block in the afternoon sunshine when I heard footsteps behind me, running and coming closer. "Emily!"

Despite the large number of potential customers in The Craft Croft, Kassandra had followed me.

I stopped walking and let her catch up. She twisted her hands in her long skirt. "Did Nina Lapeer, that woman who was arrested for murdering Zippy Melwyn, work in your donut shop? I . . . I thought I recognized her. Like, wasn't she at the carnival with you?"

When had Kassandra seen Nina and me together at the carnival? The only time I'd seen Kassandra there was when I'd climbed the hill to search the donut car for the missing confectioners' sugar. Nina hadn't been with me. Maybe Kassandra had passed the Deputy Donut tent when we were both working, and I'd been paying more attention to the fritters than to people in the crowd. Or maybe Kassandra had seen both of us at the carnival in our Deputy Donut hats and figured out that we worked together.

Kassandra and I were about the same height. I stood as tall as I could. "Yes. And I'm sure the police will come to their senses and let her go." I hoped Kassandra wasn't about to ask for Nina's job. Or about to thrust my head into a bucket of powder or anything else. What could she do to me on a glorious Sunday afternoon in downtown Fallingbrook among all the other people out on the street?

She leaned toward me and spoke quietly. "Did Nina know Zippy?"

"I don't know." It was true. I didn't know for sure.

"Like, with the last name of Lapeer, I thought maybe Nina had been to Lapeer and had met Zippy." There was something about Kassandra's tone that made me almost certain that she'd known Zippy.

I tried to sound innocent. "Was Zippy from Lapeer?"

Kassandra turned her face away from a couple of pedestrians brushing past us. "That's what they said on the news. I thought maybe Nina and Zippy were related."

"Why did you think that?"

"Oh, the Lapeer connection, I guess."

"You're from Lapeer. Did you know Zippy?"

Kassandra shivered as if standing in the hot sunshine in a long-sleeved shirt and long skirt was making her cold. "I . . . I moved away. I might have met her."

"What was she like?"

"I don't know. Isn't Nina Lapeer the artist who's about to have a show at the Arthur C. Arthurs Gallery?"

I figured it would be okay to answer that question. "Yes. We're all very excited about it."

Kassandra glanced toward my face and then away. "How did she luck out with that?"

"One of the gallery's clients saw some of her paintings in Fallingbrook and alerted Mr. Arthurs."

Kassandra licked her lips. They looked chapped. "So, displaying my work in Fallingbrook might be a really good idea."

"Could be, especially in The Craft Croft. We get lots of tourists in Fallingbrook."

Kassandra watched a man go into the bookstore. "Was that client who saw Nina Lapeer's paintings a tourist?"

"He's no longer in Fallingbrook."

Kassandra's shoulders drooped. "It must be nice, you know, to have a dream come true."

"Yes, but Nina might not have that happen, after all."

"It has to. You need to get her out of jail." Kassandra's voice had become surprisingly tough and earnest. She glanced at my face for a second and then looked away again and shifted back to her usual soft voice and tentative manner. "You've solved crimes before, haven't you?"

"Not by myself. The police are very good at it." I hoped that was still true.

Kassandra looked into my face again and gave her head a quick shake. "Don't you want to help her? If she's innocent, she shouldn't be in jail. She should get to attend her opening, and . . . everything."

"She's innocent, and I'd like to know who killed Zippy."

Kassandra eased toward the street and away from a laughing family carrying bags of books out of the bookstore. "I might know." Kassandra's fists were now almost completely tangled in her skirt.

I hoped I kept a neutral expression. "Did Zippy have enemies?"

Blushing, Kassandra let go of the front of her skirt. "I don't know about enemies, but I was working at Suds for Buds the day Zippy was killed. That's almost directly across the street from where she was killed. A man was in the pub half the afternoon and all evening. He ordered only one beer that entire time. It must have gotten pretty warm by the time he finished it, only I'm not sure he did finish it." She took several shallow breaths and then went on. "He was sitting by one of the windows, and he was looking out, like he was watching for someone or something. I mean, if you're going to sit in a pub for hours by yourself and you don't bring anything to do, you'd look out the window, right? Except this guy must have brought something to do. He had a briefcase."

I immediately pictured the magician and the briefcase he was carrying while he went around pulling four-leaf clovers out of ears and cash out of pockets and drawers. "What did he look like?"

"Oh, you know, a kind of roundish or squarish face. About average height and weight."

"How old?"

"Old."

The magician could have been in his fifties or even his sixties. I asked, "Clean-shaven?"

"I guess. Like, he didn't have a full-on beard, but he didn't get up and shave while he was there, and he was there a long time." Kassandra's tight little smile was apologetic as if she didn't think it was appropriate to say something even slightly funny under the circumstances.

"What was he wearing?"

"A suit. We didn't get that many suits in Suds for Buds." She blushed. "He was sort of interesting, even if his nose was big and reddish like a drinker's. Only he didn't drink much, so maybe he'd just been out in the sun."

She was almost perfectly describing the magician. But she could have been making up a story to throw suspicion on someone besides herself. Maybe no man had been watching out the window at Suds for Buds half the afternoon and all evening on Friday. Kassandra could have noticed the magician at the carnival and described him. Establishing that Zippy's killer was a man could help Nina, but it could also help Kassandra if she was the killer. Maybe that explained why she'd followed me out of The Craft Croft even though it had become crowded.

I asked, "Did the man's jacket have tails?"

Her face wrinkled in confusion. "Tails?"

"Like a tuxedo."

"I don't think so. But I didn't see him when he walked in or when he walked out." She glanced uncertainly at a couple of nearby women and lowered her voice. "When I was about to go on my break, I saw him start to get up, and I thought he was leaving, but he stared out the window for a few seconds, and then he took off his jacket as if that was why he'd stood up. I don't remember any tails on his jacket. He sat down again. He hadn't finished his beer. He took another sip and stared out the window. And then he seemed more interested in the window than in me, so I went and waited on other people." If she was making the story up, she was throwing in a lot of believable details.

Hoping that none of the people passing us were catching much of our conversation, I leaned closer to her. "Did he tell you his name?"

"No, and I wasn't about to ask. That would have been too much like flirting with a customer." She gave me a sideways glance as if checking to see if I noticed what a good employee she was.

"Do you know when he left Suds for Buds?"

"No. I went out for a break like I always did around ten if it wasn't too busy." She paused as if our discussion had tired her. I suspected she wasn't used to talking so much. She continued in an even softer voice. "When I came back, he was gone. Not long after that, there were all these sirens and an ambulance and police cars. I decided I didn't want to work in that part of town anymore."

"It's usually pretty safe. It's not far from here."

"Yeah, I guess. Driving in a new place, you don't get a feel for how far apart things are."

Driving. After she'd been peering into the donut car at the carnival, she had headed toward a gray car, but I hadn't actually seen her in a gray car. I wanted to ask her what color her car was, but if Kassandra had been the driver who had almost hit us, she might suspect correctly why I was asking, which could mean trouble for me.

Either the magician or Kassandra—or both—could have stayed in Suds for Buds until Zippy entered Nina's building. Had the killer known that the woman was Zippy, or did he or she think Zippy was Nina? Had he seen Nina try her door, and was that why he'd stood up as if about to leave? But Nina hadn't gone inside. That could be why the man sat down again and watched. And then Zippy could have come along with a screwdriver and a white plastic bucket labeled PAINT. And the man could have left the pub and followed her.

I wanted to ask Kassandra where she'd gone and what she'd done on her break and whom she'd seen, but I didn't want her to notice that I'd realized she'd placed herself close to the scene of the crime at about the time it was committed.

And I still wondered if the man Kassandra said she'd seen really existed. I asked her, "That man who sat in Suds for Buds all afternoon and evening—what color was his suit, and what color was his briefcase?"

"Both dark. Maybe black or dark brown or even dark blue. He was beside the window, but it's tinted, and there are colored lights from a sign in the window. Mostly, the pub is dark inside, even during the day."

Kassandra seemed so nervous and hesitant that I suspected she'd spent most of her life being told what to do, so I didn't want to tell her outright what I thought she should do. Hinting was probably no better, but I suggested, "Maybe you should call the Fallingbrook police and tell them what you told me."

Apparently, she wasn't about to take the hint. "I'm not . . . it's not really . . . well, you know, I don't know if it means anything."

I tried to sound encouraging without frightening her into silence. "The police are nice people, and they'll figure out if it means anything."

She looked away. "But if it didn't, they might just get mad at me. I don't like being involved, but I thought maybe I could help you get your assistant out of jail. You seem nice, and so did she, from what I saw of her."

"Thank you. What you've told me could help."

She rewarded me with the briefest of half-frightened smiles. "I need to get back to work." She turned around and ran in a girlish way, her hands out as if for balance, toward The Craft Croft.

Wondering if she'd been trying to help Nina or rehearsing a story about a man in a suit in case she needed to explain herself to the police, I watched her go. Below the hem of her gauzy skirt, her black boots thumped on the pavement.

She'd worn sneakers when she came into Deputy Donut to apply for a job the day before, but had she worn those boots to work at Suds for Buds Friday afternoon and evening? Their heavy black soles could have made the scuff mark on Nina's new ladder.

Chapter 16

With all of the other people around, many of whom knew me, I couldn't stand on Wisconsin Street gaping at Kassandra running back toward The Craft Croft, and it wasn't a great place to call Brent, either. I hurried up the street and around to the back door of Deputy Donut. In the office, Dep leaped to the desk and rubbed, purring, against my arm. Brent's phone went straight to message. With Dep attempting to chew on my phone, I said, "Kassandra Pyerson, the artist who applied to work at Deputy Donut, wrote on our application that she lives in Lapeer, Michigan. She's now working at The Craft Croft. On her application there, she said she lived in Fallingbrook. Also, she told me that on Friday, a man sat in Suds for Buds most of the afternoon and evening and stared out the window. He left Suds for Buds around ten Friday night. You probably know that Suds for Buds is across Wisconsin Street from Nina's apartment, but a couple of doors south."

I tried to leave the office. Dep pounced on my shoes. I managed to let myself out of the office without her, and with my shoelaces tied. I washed up and put on my hat and a clean apron. I made certain that my phone went into the apron's front pocket, along with my pen and notepad.

Brent didn't return my call during Tom's break. Maybe I'd

given Brent enough information for him to go talk to Kassandra at The Craft Croft. Tom returned, and Jocelyn left for her lunch break.

A couple came in. It took me a second to recognize them. They were Alf, the tourist I'd met briefly at the Faker's Dozen Carnival, and Connie, the woman who'd been telling him about sights to see in and around Fallingbrook. Instead of a hot pink shorts outfit, Connie wore a purple sundress decorated with giant poppies the same crimson as her lipstick. Her lips were pursed as if she were about to bestow a kiss on someone. She was hanging on to Alf's arm. He looked relaxed in khakis, loafers with no socks, and a light blue dress shirt worn unbuttoned over a T-shirt. Neither of them was wearing a hat.

With a determined look on his face as if he expected to fend off more reporters, Tom started out of the kitchen. I waggled a hand at him. Tom tilted his head as if to ask if I was sure he didn't need to intervene. I nodded and then turned to the couple. "Welcome to Deputy Donut!"

Alf smiled back at me. "I told you I'd come see you. Sorry we didn't make it sooner. We've been sightseeing."

Despite the puckered-up lips, Connie managed a coy smile. "Not all of the time."

Afraid she was about to offer too much information, I quickly showed them to one of our cute tables for two and asked what they would like.

Alf wanted to try our Nicaraguan single-origin coffee. "I've probably been to that particular coffee plantation," he told me. "All of the ranches from that area grow fantastic coffees." He studied our blackboard listing the day's special donuts. "And how about a pistachio saffron cream donut?" He had chosen the most expensive items on our menu that day.

Connie told me, "I want iced tea, but it should be brewed, and not out of a can or bottle or made from syrup."

I assured her, "We always brew our tea."

She didn't want either sugar or lemon. Judging by the simper, she'd already been into the lemons. "No donuts, either," she told me. "Too much sugar and fat."

I wanted to explain that plain donuts didn't contain much sugar, and ours were fried at a temperature that prevented them from absorbing much oil, but I only smiled, returned to the kitchen, and explained to Tom, "He's visiting Fallingbrook, and she's showing him around. I accomplished some matchmaking at the carnival!"

Tom sighed. "You and your matchmaking."

"I'm good at it. Samantha and Hooligan. Misty and Scott."

He gave me a side-eye.

"Okay, Samantha and Hooligan didn't need my help, but maybe Misty and Scott did. Not that they're engaged. Yet."

After Alf and Connie ate, Alf signaled for the bill and paid me. "We'll be back."

Connie had barely touched her tea. "If we have time."

Walking out, Connie clung to Alf's arm again, maybe because her high heels had an unfortunate tendency to wobble.

I cleaned their table and then joined Tom in the kitchen. He glanced toward the opening front door. "That's an odd getup for a journalist."

Near the door, a man in a fringed suede vest, blue jeans, a red plaid shirt with pearl snaps, and black, pearl-trimmed cowboy boots removed his white felt cowboy hat and held it at his side. "I don't think he is one," I told Tom. "He was at the carnival on Friday. He told us he's Rodeo Rod. He's performing at the rodeo out at the fairgrounds this coming Saturday. I'll take his order."

I showed Rod to the table that Connie and Alf had vacated. Instead of sitting down, he peered toward the kitchen. "Where's that gal who was working with you at the carnival? Please don't tell me she's the one who was arrested for murder. I thought I recognized her picture in the news from when

I saw her racing around the carnival threatening people and from later, when I saw her with you."

I had to defend Nina. "They've got the wrong person. She would never hurt anyone."

"I can believe that. She has the look of an angel. But that mime she was threatening ended up dead, didn't she?"

"I didn't see Nina threaten anyone."

His handsome face was sad. "She was yelling at the mime to stay away from your tent, or else. That was the threat. Or else."

"Did you tell the police?"

"They talked to me, but no. It wasn't that big a threat, you know?" He smiled down at me in a way that was almost flirtatious. He still didn't sit down.

"I agree. Are you from around here, Rod?"

"Just passin' through, always looking for greener pastures and more rodeos."

"What made you come to Fallingbrook a week before the rodeo here?"

He set his hat carefully, its crown down, on a chair. "Oh, you know. I had some extra time after my last rodeo in Iowa, and I mostly travel around, and it just happened that I got here early." *Just happened*, I thought. *He just happened to arrive over a week early and stumble into the carnival where Zippy Melwyn was doing her mime performances.* He didn't seem to notice that I might suspect him of ulterior motives, including planning a murder. He gestured at his hat. "And good luck, like at your carnival, always helps. Know why I set my hat upside down?"

"So you won't distort the brim?"

"That, and they say that if you put it right side up, good luck will fall out of it."

"Like upside-down horseshoes."

"You got it!" He beamed at me. "This Fallingbrook seems like a pretty nice place. Lived here all your life?"

"Yes, except for college."

"Figured. You look pretty happy here."

"It's home. Northern Wisconsin is beautiful, and the people are friendly. What can I get you?"

"Just plain coffee, nothin' fancy, and a plain, old-fashioned donut. Don't you be sprinkling nonsense like powdered sugar on it."

I nodded and headed to the kitchen. What had made Rod think of powdered sugar? I didn't think the police had revealed the details of Zippy's death.

I brought Rod his coffee and donut. He leaped up from his chair and thanked me. His manners were sweetly old-fashioned, like taking off his hat inside and standing in the presence of a woman even when he towered over her. He didn't spend long with his coffee and donut. He waved at me and clomped out in his flashy boots. His outfit lacked only a lasso, a couple of pearl-handled six-shooters, and spurs. And a horse.

Jocelyn returned from her break and apologized for being away so long. It had been less than an hour, but she seldom took more than twenty minutes.

She helped me clean Rod's table. "Nice tip!"

"I think he was hoping to see Nina. Did you see him?" I described Rod.

"He was dawdling in front of the library, then he got into a van and drove away."

"What kind of van?"

"Bigger than a minivan, but not much, like one of those small delivery vans. It was black with a galloping horse on the back where the window would be if it had windows."

I asked, "How big was the galloping horse?"

"Small, about the size of my hand. It was the silhouette of a horse. White."

I didn't remember seeing a decal like that on the back of the van that had been parked beside the donut car for a while on Friday morning, but it could have been there and I hadn't noticed. Or the galloping horse could have been a magnetic sign that Rod had stuck on his van later. Brent and I had not seen any windowless black vans when we'd toured the parking lot, but Rod had come to the Deputy Donut tent and talked to Nina and me after Brent left. Where had Rod's van been between when he saw Nina chase and yell at Zippy and when he talked to us at our tent? I was certain that the magician and Rod were two different men. Rod was taller than the magician, and it wasn't only due to the cowboy boots. I supposed it was possible that Rod and the magician shared a van.

Jocelyn's dark brown eyes were bright with excitement. "And do you know who else I saw, Emily?" She didn't wait for me to answer. "That deflated-looking woman who was in here yesterday applying for a job. I think she's working at The Craft Croft."

"She is. I talked to her there."

Jocelyn looked totally innocent. Surely she hadn't taken a longer break to search for clues to prove Nina innocent. I was going to have to keep an eye on Jocelyn. I wasn't about to tell her about the possible connection between a black windowless van and the magician who might have killed Zippy. Jocelyn was clever and spunky. What if she became overconfident and got herself into trouble? I wasn't certain that she thought about every angle before she leaped, sometimes literally, into something.

Tom probably thought the same of me, except unlike Jocelyn, I never added somersaults and backflips to my ventures into righting wrongs.

Knowing that Jocelyn could look after everyone in the dining room and wasn't likely to leap into any danger there, I joined Dep in the office. I would keep an eye on the shop. If it became busy or if the magician slunk inside, I would run into the dining area and kitchen to help.

Dep made it clear that I was to sit in the desk chair. I did, and she curled up on my lap and purred. I called Brent and left another message. "This is not connected to my call earlier about Kassandra Pyerson. Have the police publicly revealed the cause of Zippy Melwyn's death? I'm asking because Rodeo Rod, a rodeo performer who was at the carnival, was just here at Deputy Donut. He made a point of not wanting powdered sugar on his donut. I can't help wondering if he's squeamish about powdered sugar because he killed Zippy. Also, and maybe I shouldn't tell you this, but he said that at the carnival, he heard Nina tell Zippy to stay away from our tent 'or else.' I don't know if he heard the 'or else' or added it to deflect suspicion from himself."

Dep was asleep on my lap. Rather than disturb her by getting up, I phoned Mr. Arthurs and introduced myself. He remembered me from the short time we'd talked together in Deputy Donut. I told him, "I know Nina very well, and she would never have done anything like what she's accused of."

"I hope you're right. If you're not, and if we did open the show, I'd feel like I was exploiting the death of an innocent woman, and I don't want to make money on something that is really a tragedy for both women. You see, I knew Zipporah Melwyn."

If Dep hadn't been anchoring me in my chair, I might have tumbled off it. "You knew Zipporah Melwyn?" I'd dismissed Zippy's diary entries about communicating with Mr. Arthurs as the meanderings of a woman who was jealous of a distant cousin named Nina, but maybe Zippy had been writing the truth. Not that I believed that Nina could have hurt her or anyone else.

Mr. Arthur's voice was almost apologetic. "If it's the same Zipporah Melwyn, that is. But how many Zipporah Melwyns could there have been in Lapeer, Michigan?"

"Probably not many, unless the Melwyn family kept naming their daughters Zipporah. Apparently, she usually short-ened her name to Zippy."

"She communicated with me as Zipporah. The news said that the Zipporah Melwyn who was just murdered was thirty-one. That'd be approximately the same age as the Zip-porah Melwyn who contacted me about her paintings. Plus, I find it interesting that Nina's last name is Lapeer. Was Nina's family some of Lapeer's first settlers? Could Nina and Zippo-rah have known each other in Lapeer?"

"Nina told me that her family was not from Lapeer."

"Where is Nina from? I don't think she ever told me."

"I'm not sure, but right before she was arrested, she said she'd never been to Lapeer." I felt terrible about not knowing much about her. Was that because I'd never asked, had never wanted to pry, or did she have secrets she was afraid of shar-ing? She had never talked about siblings, which wouldn't be surprising if she didn't have any, but I didn't remember her ever mentioning parents, either, even when I talked about mine.

Mr. Arthurs went on. "I shouldn't have said I knew Zip-porah Melwyn. I never met her, but we talked. She was also an artist. She sent me photos, but I haven't seen the actual paintings. From what I could tell, she's not as original as Nina, and her work didn't warrant a separate trip to Michi-gan. However, I'm heading to Detroit next month, so I want to go on up to Lapeer and look into having someone show me Zipporah Melwyn's paintings. I guess I'll call your police department up there in Fallingbrook for guidance about next of kin and possibly getting access to her paintings. It seems to me that Nina mentioned that you folks at Deputy Donut have connections with the police department."

"My partner is Fallingbrook's retired police chief, and be-tween the two of us, we have lots of friends in the depart-ment. You could talk to Detective Brent Fyne. Tell him Emily Westhill sent you." I gave him Brent's work number.

He thanked me.

"Meanwhile," I said, "have you ever heard of an artist named Kassandra Pyerson?"

"The name doesn't ring a bell."

I couldn't tell him about Kassandra's possible connection to Lapeer, Michigan, and perhaps to Zippy Melwyn. For one thing, he didn't need to know, and for another, I wasn't about to tell anyone except police officers about my suspicions of Kassandra. "Summer Peabody-Smith and I both think, only from photos, that Kassandra's work is good, and as you might recall, Summer and I noticed Nina's talent before you heard of her. I think you might be interested in Kassandra's paintings, too. Do you mind if I send you a few pictures? She doesn't know I was thinking of doing this, so you don't have to say or do anything about them." My matchmaking had now extended to matching artists with art galleries.

"Send them along." Mr. Arthurs gave me his e-mail address. He was easier to talk to than he'd been on his first, nearly silent, visit to Deputy Donut. He'd come a second time, also, but I was inside when he waylaid Nina out on the patio and told her he wanted to feature her in a one-person show at his gallery. Remembering how thrilled she'd been that sunny Halloween afternoon, I felt even sadder about her being locked in the basement of the police department, and possibly about to have her show canceled. I hoped she had no inkling that Mr. Arthurs was considering it, but knowing Nina, she was already worrying about it.

A tall, thin man and a short, thin woman came into Deputy Donut. My parents.

Chapter 17

❧

Except for grocery shopping, my parents seldom ventured out of the campground at Fallingbrook Falls, where they lived in their RV during the warmest month or two of every summer. I ran out of the office and hugged first my mother and then my father.

Tom was right behind me. "Annie! Walt! Welcome. What can I get you?"

My mom said, "Nothing, thank you. I'm fine." She was in tight jeans and a peasant blouse she'd made and embroidered when I was a kid. As always, she wore strings of colorful beads over the blouse. Her hair was curly like mine, but hers had turned silver.

My dad said, "Coffee." He also fit into jeans that he might have had since 1968. He wore his loose blue chambray shirt untucked. Except for his hair, now white, and a few wrinkles, he had barely changed since I was a kid. My parents were in their early forties when they had me, and I'd always thought of them as old, but because of their youthful and idealistic outlook on life, and the way they'd always treated me as a beloved but surprising equal, they now seemed ageless.

Tom told me, "Sit down with them, Emily. I'll get the coffee."

I sat down.

My mother placed her hand over mine and squeezed.

"How's Nina?" Her eyes, the same brilliant blue as mine, were concerned.

"She didn't do it."

My mother patted my hand. "We know. She couldn't have."

Jocelyn brought them each a coffee and a lemon meringue donut, filled with lemon and topped by points of meringue. "How are you, Mr. and Mrs. Young?" Jocelyn's parents also spent their summers in an RV in the Fallingbrook Falls campground. My parents would be returning to Florida right after Samantha and Hooligan's wedding. Jocelyn's parents were much younger and commuted to their jobs near Fallingbrook during the summer. The rest of the time, they lived in a Victorian house in my neighborhood. When Jocelyn wasn't away at college, she stayed in their home and biked to and from work.

"We're fine," my mother said, "or we would be if you called us by our names, Walt and Annie."

My father added, "And when Nina is released from jail."

Without complaining, my folks ate the donuts they hadn't ordered and drank the coffee that my mother had pretended she didn't want. Although they were obviously concerned about Nina, they didn't make suggestions about how I could help her. They had always trusted me to do what was right, and except for a few little rebellions when I was a teen, I had attempted to live up to their expectations. Similarly, I seldom interfered in their lives, although I worried about them, and I loved visiting them out at the falls and listening to them play their guitars and banjos around a campfire. I might have inherited my mother's lack of height, blue eyes, and curly hair. I hadn't inherited either of my parents' musical abilities.

Although Tom and I told them the coffees and donuts were on the house, they insisted on paying for them, and on leaving a large tip for Jocelyn. My father explained, "She has college expenses."

Telling me to call them if I needed anything or if they could help with Nina, they got up to go.

My mother said softly, "See you at Samantha's wedding." She turned to go, but not before I saw the tears about to spill over. My mother was a prime wedding-crier. Also, she'd known Samantha since we were in junior high. Samantha's, Misty's, and my parents had always treated all three of us as daughters. Maybe my mom was also remembering Alec's and my wedding, and how young, in love, and full of hope for a long, happy life with Alec I had been.

I tried to put that self out of my mind. During the rest of the afternoon, I pondered how I could prove that Nina was innocent. I reminded myself that if someone was making attempts on her life, she was probably safest where she was.

After we closed, the evening was still warm. On the way home through our pretty Victorian neighborhood, Dep had fun creeping under hedges and leaping out at my feet. I laughed and scooped her up for snuggles. As soon as I set her down, she did it again. People on porches waved at me and called to her. The woman whose hedge we'd landed in came down the walkway from her house and pointed at the front of her hedge. "You barely damaged it, and after I pruned it, no one would ever be able to tell that anyone had fallen into it."

I picked Dep up and hugged her. "Thank you. I don't see any bare spots."

"I asked around. No one heard or saw the car that almost hit you and your friend. Where is she?" She scratched underneath Dep's chin. Dep purred.

The woman might eventually hear about Nina's arrest. I explained.

The woman folded her arms. "That's terrible. She seemed very sweet the other day. They have the wrong person, don't you think?"

"I'm sure they do."

She glowered at a car passing us and going sedately below

the already-low speed limit. "At least she's safe from reckless drivers."

The car was gray. An older man was driving it. He was not texting. Both of his hands were on the wheel. "Yes," I agreed. "She is."

The woman nodded. "Protective custody, I think they call it."

My answering smile was a little wan. I wished that Nina was only in protective custody.

Several blocks away, a windowless black van drove slowly south on Wisconsin Street. I couldn't see much of the driver, but I caught a glimpse of something white, possibly the size of a cowboy hat, just inside the passenger window.

I said goodbye to the woman and quickly carried Dep home. Running up my porch steps, I reminded myself that there were probably lots of windowless black vans in northern Wisconsin. I hadn't been able to see the back of this one, so I didn't know if there was a galloping horse where a rear window would have been. I also hadn't noticed lettering on the van's side. I took Dep inside and locked the door.

After dinner Dep ran up the stairs to the second floor ahead of me. Mentally apologizing to Nina for invading her room, which was also my home office, I turned on my computer.

I found references to Nina Lapeer in only two places on the internet. Her website showed photos of her paintings displayed dramatically on expanses of white, her name, and nothing else. No artist's bio, no cute stories about wanting to be an artist ever since she was a little girl or having suddenly decided to become one as an adult. No reference to her previous last name or why she'd changed it. Not even a middle name. The other place where she was mentioned was the Arthur C. Arthurs Gallery website. It announced her show. At least that hadn't changed. Yet.

It also mentioned that she was from Fallingbrook, Wisconsin. A headshot portrayed her high cheekbones, huge brown

eyes, and enviably long and thick eyelashes. Instead of smiling, she looked so serious that she was almost glaring at the
camera. I shivered at the thought that the Fallingbrook Police
might now have a mugshot of her wearing almost that same
expression.

Zippy must have visited the Arthur C. Arthurs website.
She would have seen Nina's new last name and her grown-up
face.

Zippy could have become enraged with jealousy.

And the website had told her that Nina lived in Fallingbrook. Zippy must have hoped that by paying Nina a visit
and destroying her artwork, she could stall Nina's career and
advance her own. Maybe she'd even hoped to find and damage all of the paintings slated for Nina's show. Luckily, all but
the largest one had been shipped.

Nina didn't seem to use social media, and I couldn't find
her named as one of the survivors in any online obituaries,
which was a morbid but occasionally useful method of learn-
ing the names of people's relatives. I might have found a
mention of her if I'd known her original last name.

Telling myself I could discover something that would help
her, I pushed my chair back and got up to snoop in the duffel
bag that she'd brought from her apartment and left on the
open sofa bed beside a nightgown and bathrobe. Dep had
beaten me to the bag. Its top was unzipped, and Dep was nestled inside. Her pupils wide, she watched me approach. I
baby-talked to her. "You know you're not supposed to be
there, don't you?"

She waggled her head in a playful way and then hid her
face behind one of the unzipped sides.

I scratched at the heavy nylon with a fingernail.

Dep flung a paw out and nearly caught my hand.

"Um, Dep, honey, I need to look underneath you."

Her head popped up again. I reached in, snugged my

hands around her warm little chest, lifted her out, and set her on the blue and white rug. She scooted beneath overhanging blankets and batted at Nina's slippers.

I found toiletries, a novel with a bookmark in it near the middle, lingerie, a pair of Deputy Donut shorts, and one of the white polo shirts that went with them. I opened the closet. Two pairs of comfy shoes and a pair of sparkly silver sandals were lined up on the floor. She'd hung up two blouses, a skirt, a pair of the black jeans we wore at Deputy Donut on cooler days, her black nylon jacket, and the green silk dress. Nothing was in the jacket pockets. I smoothed the dress on its hanger. Would she ever be able to wear it and the sparkly sandals she'd bought for Samantha and Hooligan's wedding? I eased the closet door shut and brushed a tear off my cheek.

I almost missed Nina's phone, plugged into its charger behind my computer. It was practically in factory condition and was not password-protected. She had only a few contacts— Arthur C. Arthurs, The Craft Croft, our landline at Deputy Donut, Tom's, Jocelyn's, and my cell phone numbers, and a number for Harry and Larry, her landlords at Klassy Kitchens. There was no one else, no doctor or dentist, and no one who could be a relative or friend that I didn't already know about. I hadn't realized how alone she was. I should have included her in more of my social life. Snooping among Nina's things hadn't given me any new leads that I could use to prove her innocence. It also didn't make me feel less unhappy about her and her plight. I could stay home and stew, making myself sadder and sadder, or I could try something else.

I looked down at Dep. "Sorry, Dep. I'm going out without you."

"Mew," Dep said.

Still in her playful mood, she ran down the stairs ahead of me and arrived at the front door first. I picked her up, opened the door, stepped out onto the porch, and set her inside on the living room floor. Tail up, she frolicked toward the back of the house.

"Good girl," I said approvingly, not that praise and compliments ever swayed her from doing whatever she pleased. I closed the door, locked it, and trotted down the steps to the sidewalk.

The evening was still sunny and warm. I cut through my neighborhood to Wisconsin Street and strolled south. Saddened by the sight of yellow police tape draped across the street door to the stairs leading to Nina's loft, I passed Klassy Kitchens. It appeared to be closed for the evening. The bakery selling gourmet pet foods next to it wasn't open, either. Beyond a barbershop, I stopped across the street from the address that Kassandra had written on her job application at The Craft Croft. I wasn't surprised to discover that the address was for Suds for Buds, the pub where Kassandra had said she'd worked.

Kassandra had written that she lived on the second floor.

That did not seem possible.

Chapter 18

Suds for Buds was on the first floor. Above it, the building had one of those false fronts designed to make it look taller. Maybe there was a second floor at the rear of the building, too far back from the street to be visible from where I was standing, but it appeared that Kassandra had lied about living on the second floor at 976 Wisconsin Street South.

I took a deep breath and crossed the street.

Inside, Suds for Buds was a welcoming pub, paneled in dark mahogany with green leather upholstery on seats in the booths and on stools at the brass-trimmed marble-topped bar. The room was about half full of people, most of them holding foamy glasses and talking quietly to one another. I stood between two of the bar stools and placed my hands flat on the smooth, gray-veined white marble.

An aproned man behind the bar looked up from drying a glass. He was probably in his fifties with kind hazel eyes, a wide smile, and brown hair thinning on top. He asked, "What can I get you?"

"Could I speak to the manager, if he or she can spare a few minutes? It's about a reference for a former employee."

"You're looking at him. Well, I'm Buddy. I own this place."

"I'm Emily."

He nodded, set the glass down, and picked up another glass. "Who's the former employee?"

Had Kassandra given Buddy the same name she'd given me? "Kassandra Pyerson."

Buddy nodded. "Kassandra. She was a good enough employee. Hard-working, that's for sure, no complaints there, and honest, but she wasn't as outgoing as I'd like in a waitress. Not that we expect them to become best friends with the customers, nothing like that, but she seemed almost too shy to smile or mumble more than a few syllables. But it turned out that she could carry on a conversation, at least I thought she could. Her last day here, Friday the thirteenth, we weren't very busy, and she talked to one patron a lot."

My pulse sped, and it was all I could do to prevent myself from nearly jumping over the bar in my excitement to hear more. "A man or a woman?" I almost sounded calm.

"A man." Buddy nodded toward a front window. "See that booth over there, the first one in from the front door? A man sat in that bench, the one with its back to the bar, from about five o'clock until about ten at night. He drank only one beer, as far as I know, that entire time, and he had a burger and fries, hold the onion. Mostly, he looked out the window, kind of ducking his head"—Buddy demonstrated bending his neck a little without lowering his gaze—"to see underneath the lit sign hanging there." It was a sign advertising a local craft brew. "Kassandra talked to that man more than she talked to most of our guests, but he was here for so long he must have begun to feel like family to her." Buddy winked to show he was joking. "She stood beside him, but where she could see me if I needed to signal her. She didn't talk to him all that time, but she definitely spent more time with him than she did with other patrons. He and Kassandra both left around ten."

"Together?"

"Kassandra left first. She said she was going for a short break, but she never came back. He didn't, either."

Kassandra had told me that she had returned to work after her break. "Are you sure that she didn't come back on Friday night?"

"Positive. It got busier in here, and I kept looking for her to help out. And then there were sirens and lights and police cars and an ambulance, and the next day I heard that a woman had been murdered almost across the street from us. Kassandra was probably afraid to venture anywhere near here after that. She was supposed to work on Saturday, but she hasn't shown up here since Friday night around ten."

Putting one foot on the brass footrail, I rested my forearms on the cool marble. "Do you think she could have been involved with the murder?"

"Nah. She wouldn't have had the gumption. If anything, I thought she might have gone off with the man, she was so friendly to him. Friendly for her, that is. She seemed kind of alone and lost. Or maybe they knew each other from somewhere else. She was new in town, she told me, and I don't know if he was local, but I don't remember seeing him in here before. That doesn't mean he wasn't. I just don't remember."

"She said she didn't think this neighborhood was very safe."

"It is."

"I told her that, too. She wanted to work at our shop, Deputy Donut, which is only about seven blocks away."

I could have sworn his ears perked up like Dep's sometimes did. "That's where she applied for a job? Deputy Donut?"

"Yes."

"Someone from there was the woman who came home and found a woman in her apartment and . . ." With an index finger, he made a cutting motion across his throat. "That doesn't sound like a safe place to work, except the murderer was caught. Were you scared, working with her?"

I shook my head so hard I risked becoming dizzy. "She was arrested, but I can't imagine her ever harming anyone. Ever. They got the wrong person. Can you describe the man that Kassandra was talking to? It could be important and might prevent an innocent person from going to prison." Although I expected Buddy to describe the magician, I tried to keep an open mind.

Buddy nodded, obviously wanting to be helpful. "Short hair, and he was wearing a suit and carrying a briefcase. I never saw him open the briefcase or take anything from it. He was looking out the window when he suddenly got up, took off the suit jacket, and stuffed it between the handles of his briefcase." Buddy moved his hands like someone tucking a jacket across the top of a briefcase and then pinching the top of the handles between a thumb and forefinger. "And then he sat down again. About ten minutes after that, he got up again and left. I never saw him again."

"How tall was he?"

"I don't know. Maybe about the same as me, five-ten, not particularly muscular, but not fat, either."

"Was there anything unusual about the suit?"

"Not that I noticed."

"Was it dressy, like a tuxedo?"

After a pause while his forehead became more and more creased, Buddy shook his head. "I don't think so."

"Did you see his shoes?"

"Nope, sorry."

"Did he have a beard?"

"I didn't notice, which means he probably didn't."

I guessed that the magician had taken off his fake beard and wig only moments after Nina had started chasing him. I asked, "A hat?"

"Don't think so. Not even a ball cap."

I hadn't really expected anyone to wear a top hat into a pub on a Friday afternoon. I tried another line of questioning. "Do you have surveillance cameras?"

Buddy winced. "The police asked that, too. I put some up. They worked for about a week, and then nothing. That was a couple of years ago, and I know I should replace them, for my own protection, you know? But I figure if they're not going to last more than a week, why go through all the expense and time of installing them?" He polished the counter with a towel, then looked up at me and asked, "When did Kassandra apply for a job with you?"

"Yesterday. The day after she left here, August fourteenth."

Buddy held a glass up to the light and studied it. "That's good to know." He set the glass down. "It did occur to me that something bad could have happened to her, too, and it hadn't been reported. The way she left was odd. We hadn't divvied up that day's tips. Plus, I owe her some back pay. Maybe she's too embarrassed to come back after leaving with no notice."

"Did you tell the police that she left here about the time of the murder and didn't come back?"

He turned around and lined up clean glasses in a row on the shelf behind where he'd been standing facing me. Catching my eye in the mirror behind the glasses, he said, "I didn't think of it, since I thought she was probably with that man, and then when they arrested a different woman, I was sure Kassandra had nothing to do with the murder. And you say you saw her the next day?"

"Yes, and I saw her this noon, too. She's working at The Craft Croft."

"That's a change from here. No chance for any tips there, let alone the good ones she could have earned here. I'll stop in and see her there. I never want anyone saying I don't pay what I promised. If you see her, tell her I have her wages and tips. The only address I have for her is in Michigan, but she said she wasn't going back there. She was moving here."

"I have her phone number, but not with me. It's at Deputy Donut, on the application she filled out."

"I have a phone number for her, too. She doesn't pick up. I've left her messages to come by." He gave the bar another swipe with the towel. "But she doesn't. Here." He inched a scrap of paper out from underneath an old-fashioned bronze cash register and slid it across the bar to me. "Does this look like the number you have for her?"

"I didn't pay attention to the one she wrote on our application. Do you mind if I take a picture of this one so when I go to work tomorrow morning I can see if it's the same one?"

"Be my guest."

I took out my phone and snapped the picture. "I'll let you know if I discover I have a different number."

"Much appreciated."

I put my phone away. "Do you know if any money went missing from your till or from any of your customers on Friday?"

"Not that I know of. And as I said, Kassandra seemed honest. I don't think she'd have stolen from anyone. She didn't seem interested in money." He shrugged. "Or she'd have stuck around long enough to get paid."

I'd been thinking of the magician, not Kassandra, but the thieving magician was probably too intent on watching for Nina to bother stealing from anyone in Suds for Buds that afternoon and evening. Nina must have infuriated him when she slammed the cash drawer on his hand. How had he found Nina's address? I wouldn't be surprised to learn that he, like Zippy, had sneaked a peek at Marsha Fitchelder's clipboard. Or maybe Zippy had told him where she was going, but not when. Whether Zippy or Nina was his actual target, he'd sat in Suds for Buds for hours looking out toward Nina's apartment.

I asked Buddy, "Did you notice if either of the man's hands was injured or if he had a bandage around a finger or two?"

"No, sorry."

That didn't prove anything. A drawer slamming on the magician's gloved fingers probably hadn't caused noticeable injuries. Knowing that Buddy was willing to help keep an innocent woman from going to prison, and also, like many people, he relished discussing dramatic events, especially when they'd happened nearby, I asked another question. "Do you remember how he paid for the beer and hamburger and fries?" If Buddy thought or knew that the man had paid by credit card, I should tell Brent about it so he could trace the man.

Buddy stated without hesitating, "Cash. I remember for sure, because he was a big tipper, and Kassandra could have used the money. He left the cash on the table, all crisp new fives. People tip us nicely, but not usually that nicely, even when they occupy a booth all afternoon and evening."

Crisp new fives. Now I was certain that the man who had sat watching Nina's apartment on the thirteenth was the magician, generously doling out some of his ill-gotten gains from the Faker's Dozen Carnival, probably the money he'd stolen from our Deputy Donut tent.

A man slipped onto the stool next to where I was standing. Buddy looked at him. "Your regular?"

Half afraid of seeing the magician, I took a better look at the man. He was shorter and older than the magician. He slapped his palm down on the bar. "You bet."

Buddy drew a pint of stout, slid it toward him, and returned his gaze to me.

"I'm sorry," I said. "You're getting busy in here."

"No problem, especially if you'd like to apply for a job."

I smiled back. He seemed nice. "I'd like it here, but I have to stay where I am. Oh, I have one more question. Is there a rental apartment in this building?"

"No." His forehead wrinkled in apparent concern. "Do you know someone who needs a place to live?"

"I thought that Kassandra told the manager at The Craft Croft that she lived on the second floor at this address."

"We don't have a second floor."

I apologized. "One of us must have gotten it wrong."

"Must have."

I thanked him again and headed toward the front door. If Kassandra hadn't noticed that Buddy's building had no second floor, she wasn't a very observant artist. Maybe, as I'd already guessed, Kassandra wasn't an artist at all, but had been trying to pass off Zippy's paintings as her own. Maybe she hadn't expected anyone to go looking for the address she'd given The Craft Croft.

Why had she lied about her Fallingbrook address? Was the Lapeer address also a fabrication?

I detoured past the booth the man had occupied Friday afternoon and evening. Hoping no one was watching, I bent a little to put my head at about the height of the magician's head if he was seated and peering underneath the craft beer sign. I shot a glance across the street.

The man would have had a clear view of Nina's street door and the sidewalk in front of it.

Chapter 19

᪥

As I'd noticed earlier, Klassy Kitchens wasn't open. Nina's landlords were in front of it. One was sweeping the sidewalk while his twin brother was cleaning one of the two large display windows flanking the front door.

I crossed the street. Harry and Larry were close to sixty, balding, rosy-cheeked, and cheerful. They'd helped Alec and me plan our kitchen renovations, and they always waved when they saw me pick Nina up or drop her off. As usual, they were dressed alike, this time in baby blue golf shirts and khaki slacks. I couldn't tell which one was Harry and which one was Larry.

They stopped what they were doing and came toward me, one holding his broom by his side and the other carrying a long-handled squeegee like a pole-vaulter about to vault. When they were close enough, I could read the names embroidered on their shirts.

Larry raised his squeegee higher. "Emily! We're so upset about Nina! We know she couldn't have done anything wrong."

We discussed how much we liked Nina and how kind she was, never wanting anyone to be hurt.

Harry slammed the bristles of his broom down on the sidewalk. "We'd do anything to help her. Anything legal, that is."

Larry teased, "Or mostly legal."

I grinned back. "We shouldn't have to go that far. Tom wouldn't approve."

Harry shoved at his little pile of dust. "Chief Westhill's a good man. We'll try to stay on his right side."

Larry winked at me. "Only for your sake, Emily."

"Good," I said, "thanks. Can you tell me about Friday evening?"

"We sure can." Harry sounded very sure of his memories. "Not long after ten, we were still in our shop, ordering a new line of elegant faucets. Nina knocked on the front door. She'd left her purse in your car and wondered if we had spare keys."

"We do," Larry added, "somewhere. We promised to look for them, but she said she'd head on foot to your place. We let her out into the back alley so she could take a shortcut. Oh! Sorry about dripping on you, Emily."

I brushed foam off my arm. "It's okay. Now I won't need a shower for another week."

After a second, they caught on and chuckled.

Harry took up the story. "Nina didn't seem involved in anything that could have upset her. She was her usual friendly self."

Larry agreed with his twin. "She wasn't acting like she'd just found an intruder in her apartment. How could she have? She couldn't get into her apartment."

I asked, "Did she try the door?"

Larry's arm moved in time with his nodding head. "She said she did, before she came to see us." Soapy water dribbled on all of us.

Harry dabbed soapsuds off his shoulder. "And before we let her out the back, we went to her street door with her, in case it was sticking or something, but it was thoroughly locked."

Larry waved that squeegee high in the air again. "Securely.

We both tried. So, as we said, we let her out the back way, and we haven't seen her since."

That corroborated my earlier guess about the man in Suds for Buds. Both Kassandra and Buddy had said that the man had stood up as if about to leave and then had sat down again. Now I was sure he'd seen Nina go to her front door and was about to follow her, but she left. He took off his jacket, stuffed it into the top of his briefcase, sat down, and watched for Nina to return.

Fortunately for Nina and for those of us who loved Nina, Zippy had come along looking like Nina and had broken in. That must have been when the man left Suds for Buds, crossed the street, and followed Zippy upstairs to Nina's apartment.

Leaving her tote bag with her keys inside it in the donut car could have saved Nina's life. I felt the blood rush from my face.

Harry bent forward and peered at me. "Are you okay?"

I assured him that I was, although I wasn't. How was I going to convince Brent and Detective Gartborg that Nina was innocent of killing the mime and that Zippy's killer posed a threat to Nina? I asked, "Did you see anyone else go to Nina's door?"

Larry aimed his long-handled squeegee toward Klassy Kitchens. "The police asked us that, too. Come over to our front door, Emily."

We trooped to the front door. Larry pointed northward. "See? We can't see Nina's door from here, or even the sidewalk in front of it, because of the way our door is recessed. We couldn't see it even if we went inside and climbed into the show windows. Want to try?"

Even though the squeegee must have lost most of its supply of foamy water, I backed away. "No, thanks. I can tell from here that you're right."

"We do look out a lot of the time," Harry admitted. "So many interesting people go up and down Wisconsin Street."

"And we got an eyeful that night." Larry nearly gave me an eyeful—of soapsuds. "With police cars and an ambulance, and then lots of police cars ever since."

I glanced upward. "Do you have surveillance cameras?"

Harry scowled. "We agree with the police that we probably should have them."

"Such an invasion of privacy," Larry contributed, "but—"

His brother finished the sentence. "If we had surveillance cameras, maybe that sweet Nina wouldn't be in jail and the person who deserves to be incarcerated would be there instead."

I told them about Kassandra's long skirts and hesitant way of moving and asked them if they'd seen her around the pub or on their side of the street or crossing toward Klassy Kitchens. They didn't think they had. I also described, as best I could, the man with the jacket stuffed between the handles of his briefcase.

Larry gazed across the street toward Suds for Buds. "We occasionally see men carrying briefcases, even on Friday nights."

Harry leaned his broom against the building. "You know, going straight from work to party with friends. I didn't see one on Friday night, though." He looked at his brother. "Did you?"

"Not a one."

They promised to call me if they thought of or learned of anything that might help Nina. "We have the number for Deputy Donut," Harry said. "Nina gave it to us when she first went to work for you."

"Do you still have my cell number?"

Larry hesitated. "It should be in our customer records somewhere." He darted inside, trotted back to us with a pen and paper, and had me dictate my number to him.

I walked home. The sun was nearing the horizon. The

western sky was tinged with orange, while the sky above was pale.

At the front door, Dep mumbled her grievances about my absence. I picked her up. She purred. I rubbed my face in her warm fur.

I called Brent's personal line and left a message that I had new and possibly important information. Waiting for him to call, I carried Dep up to the guest room. At my computer, I typed in the website address that had been on the black windowless van on the hill above the carnival.

The website featured a photo of empty wheelchairs lined up in a store window.

I looked more closely at the site and realized that although website visitors could click on a button to donate, the website didn't specify where the donations were going or what they'd be used for, except to "help veterans."

I found about a dozen recent complaints about the site. One outraged contributor mentioned that he had also fallen for a similar request at another site that was supposed to help veterans. After receiving none of the promised tax receipts, he had discovered that a man had been opening similar websites and then closing them after a few months—and probably after a few donations, besides. The researcher had found the man's name, Marvin Oarhill, and had posted a picture of him.

It was a portrait from the shoulders up. The man was wearing a black jacket, a white shirt, and a white bow tie. The jacket looked formal, as if it could have tails. There was no top hat, but the man had long white hair and a long white beard that looked like they were attached to each other but not to his face. He did not resemble Santa Claus, however. His eyes were cold and hard, and he wasn't smiling.

He was the magician who had registered for the Faker's Dozen Carnival as Marv the Marvelous and had robbed us there.

Dep was on the windowsill. I asked her, "Does Brent know this?"

She gave me a cross-eyed look before returning to her careful study of the tree outside and any creatures that might be bedding down in it for the night.

"You're right," I said. "I gave Brent the van's license number, so he knows who owns the van. But that doesn't mean that the van is registered to the magician, or that the magician's real name is Marvin Oarhill, or that the man uses that name when he's pretending to be a magician. It might be one more lead for Brent to follow."

Dep made a chirping noise. She wasn't answering me. She had spotted a bird in the tree. The end of her tail twitched in a warning the bird couldn't possibly see and wouldn't have cared about if he did.

I was about to shut down my computer when I noticed that Arthur C. Arthurs had replied to my e-mail. He'd looked at the photos of the paintings I'd sent him that Kassandra Pyerson had said she'd painted.

He wrote that Zipporah Melwyn had sent him photos of the same paintings back in December. Zippy had told him that she was the artist. The paintings in the pictures Zippy sent him were the paintings he was hoping to make a detour to see during his trip to the Detroit area. He attached a couple of the photos he'd received. They were less blurry than the photos that Kassandra had given Summer, but I had to agree with Arthur C. Arthurs. They were either photos of the same paintings or of some that were eerily similar.

Who was the artist, Zippy or Kassandra? One of them must have been lying, and the other one could have written the threatening letter that someone accidentally—or on purpose—tucked underneath the donut car's rear seat.

And very likely, Nina had not sent the letter, received it, or been in conflict with anyone over paintings left in an apartment.

It made sense that the letter's recipient had put it into the donut car.

Who was the recipient?

Perhaps it had never been sent, and as I'd guessed before, it might have been a decoy, a threatening message that Zippy had written and then torn from a larger piece of stationery to make it look like part of an entire letter.

I went downstairs. Dep beat me to the first floor, leaped onto the arm of the wing chair, and gave me imperious looks. I sat down. Dep stepped carefully onto my lap, turned around, curled herself into a ball, and purred.

My phone rang. Brent was finally returning my call.

"Hi, Brent, I have some things to tell you."

"About the Zipporah Melwyn case?"

"Yes. I was checking on a reference for that job applicant I told you about, the artist, and I learned some interesting things that you might or might not know. Can you come over?"

"Sorry, I have to go somewhere. Can you tell me over the phone?"

Explaining in person was usually easier. I tried to keep my disappointment out of my voice. "Okay."

"Just a second." He must have turned his head away from the phone because his next sentence was quieter. "I'll meet you at my car in a few minutes, Kim."

Chapter 20

✻

Even the backs of my eyes were blushing. Now that Detective Gartborg had someone in custody for the murder, I'd hoped she'd moved on to her next assignment and Brent would be free to come over and give Dep some of the attention she craved, even though she was contentedly purring on my lap.

And maybe, with the information I now had, Brent would have been able to overturn Detective Gartborg's decision.

Instead, it sounded like Brent and the glamorous detective were celebrating solving—or so they thought—the case by going somewhere together. And it didn't sound like the somewhere was my house.

Brent came back to the phone. "What did you learn?"

I repeated what I'd mentioned in my message about the man sitting in Suds for Buds until about ten Friday night. "Kassandra said he was looking out the window most of the time. The door to Nina's apartment would have been in his direct line of sight. Both Kassandra and Buddy told me that at one point, the man stood up as if about to leave, but he sat down again and stared out the window some more. That fits with what Nina and the twins who own Klassy Kitchens told me. Nina tried to get into her apartment, but when she didn't succeed, Harry and Larry also tested her lock, and then they let her go out through their back door to take a shortcut to my house. Zippy must have come along and broken in, and the man who'd been in the pub must have followed Zippy into Nina's apartment."

"That could have been coincidence, but we'll check into it all again. Anything else?"

I told him about the discrepancy in the addresses that Kassandra gave Summer Peabody-Smith and me and that the Fallingbrook address didn't exist.

He asked, "What was the address in Lapeer?"

I told him.

"Can you repeat that?" I thought I detected a tiny note of surprise in his voice.

I said it again, slowly.

He was silent for so long that I had to ask if the address I gave him was Zippy Melwyn's apartment.

I heard him sigh. "I might as well tell you, since you could get yourself into trouble trying to find out. It is the same address. But if Kassandra Pyerson said she now lives at an address that doesn't exist . . ." He stopped.

I finished the sentence for him. "She could be lying about all of it. Even if Kassandra didn't live there herself, it's interesting that she knew that address."

He conceded, "True. I can tell you one thing. The lock on Zippy's apartment appears to have been recently changed, and Zippy's apartment key is shiny and unscratched."

"Were there paintings in the apartment?"

"Yes. I've told Arthur C. Arthurs that I'll let him know when he can see them."

"Do you know if the paintings were signed?"

"Zipporah Melwyn signed all of them."

"Kassandra has been trying to pass those paintings off as her own. After she showed me the photos, I sent her to The Craft Croft. Summer Peabody-Smith hired her. Kassandra told Summer and me that the paintings were 'in storage.' I e-mailed the photos to Arthur C. Arthurs. He said they appeared to be blurrier versions of the photographs Zippy Melwyn sent him of her paintings."

Brent promised, "I'll look for Kassandra Pyerson at The Craft Croft. Would it be open now?"

"No. I think it's open from about ten to four on weekdays. If they were Zippy's paintings, Zippy could have written the threatening letter to someone else, but never sent it. So, it might not mean much except that the photo of the eighteen-nineties woman that had probably been removed from Nina's locket was with the fragment of the letter."

"Exactly."

"Nina has had her loft for a couple of years, at least. If Zippy ever locked Nina out of an apartment they shared or vice versa, it was a long time ago."

"People often wait many years to carry out their threats."

"Did investigators see any of Nina's paintings in Zippy's apartment?"

"No. If the letter was from Nina and was written many years ago, Nina could have retrieved her paintings and retained her grudge. We'll have the forensics guys verify that the signatures on the paintings in Zippy's apartment are Zippy's."

I pointed out, "Kassandra could have written the threatening note to Zippy."

"We'll talk to her and Buddy again. When we interviewed Buddy earlier, he didn't mention Kassandra or anyone looking out the pub's front window that afternoon and evening. Buddy must have thought we cared only about what happened across the street."

"Buddy also said that Kassandra and the man both left shortly after ten that night, and neither of them came back. Kassandra told me she went back to work that night after her ten o'clock break. Buddy said she definitely didn't return to work, that night or ever. She hasn't picked up her share of the tips or her pay, and he hasn't seen her. She also hadn't been answering his calls. I saw her early this afternoon when she followed me out of The Craft Croft to tell me about the man in the pub." I reiterated that Kassandra's and Buddy's descriptions of the man fit the thieving magician. My words tumbled out quickly as I stated a few obvious facts. "The magician was a thief. Maybe he decided to eliminate Zippy because she had conspired with him and could report his criminal activity."

Brent remained patient. "We asked witnesses at other fairs, and none of them reported seeing him collaborating with anyone."

"Maybe he tried it for the first time on Friday and didn't like it. And had a very extreme reaction."

"Very." Brent was quiet for a second, as if he were about to end the conversation and go somewhere with Detective Gartborg, but then he admitted, "We do have surveillance video from down the street from Suds for Buds and even farther from the entrance to Nina's loft. The street was dark except for streetlights and ambient light from shops and apartments. The video doesn't show the front of the Klassy Kitchens building or the door to Nina's stairway, but it does show the front of Suds for Buds. A man left the pub about ten after ten and walked across the street toward Klassy Kitchens. He was about average height and weight and dressed in dark pants and a pale shirt, and he was carrying something that could have been a briefcase with a garment slung across the top. There was no long beard, and his hair was not white or platinum blond."

"I think the magician's white hair and beard were fake. What were his shoes like?"

"Hard to tell, but probably dark. Thanks to your photos, we have the magician's actual license number, not the many versions he put on exhibitor applications, and we have the name the van is registered to. We have not yet located him, but we will."

"Good. The name I found for him is Marvin Oarhill."

Brent whistled. "I've told you before that you should have become a police officer. We're looking for Oarhill because of the thefts and his history as a suspected pickpocket, not because we suspect him of murder."

"Yet." I told Brent about the information I'd found about the magician's fundraising websites that were supposedly to help veterans. "If you dig around, you'll find his photo. He's definitely the man who robbed us."

"Can you send me the links you found?"

"Sure."

I heard a woman's voice in the background, and then Brent must have turned his head away from the phone again. He said from a little farther away, "I'm almost done. I'll be right with you." He asked me, "Was there anything else you wanted to tell me, Em?"

Yes. Detective Gartborg is not gentle and kind enough for you. I didn't say it. I merely asked, "Does Kassandra appear in that video?"

"Not at all."

"Nina?"

"No, and not Zippy, either, and not you or the Klassy Kitchens twins. Kassandra must have gone out the pub's back door, and Nina and Zippy and the twins must have been on the opposite side of the street from Suds for Buds."

"I was only on that side of the street, also. And I'd parked the donut car farther north."

"I saw it. Not in the surveillance video, but when I was driving to the alley you told me about to check out the little pink car."

I tried to put a smile into my voice. "Our donut car is hard to miss. Oh, and there's something else. I told you about

Rodeo Rod. This afternoon Jocelyn saw him driving a black van with a white galloping horse where a back window would be if the van had back windows. When I was walking home from work this afternoon, I saw a van that could have been his creeping down Wisconsin Street. I'd already turned the corner toward home and was several blocks away, so I don't think the driver saw me. The sun glared off something big and white on or near his passenger window that could have been the cowboy hat that Rodeo Rod brought into Deputy Donut earlier today. Rodeo Rod is flirtatious, so that could be why he might have been looking for me, if he was. Maybe he was driving slowly for some other reason. Anyway, because he was at the carnival on Friday, I wondered if you might be able to get more information about him from Marsha's list of exhibitors."

"Let's see." I heard computer keys clicking. "No Rodeo Rods, and no one listed as a rodeo performer."

"He did say he's here early for the rodeo this weekend. On Friday, his jeans were black, and his shirt was pale gray and white checked. And he was wearing black cowboy boots, but not a suit jacket. Both times I saw him, he had on a fringed suede vest."

"So you've added him to your list of suspects. I wouldn't mind being proved wrong about Nina, and now that you've told me about a man fitting the magician's description and sitting across from Nina's apartment, I'll pay more attention to the investigations into the pickpocketing magician."

I had to swallow hard to manage a thanks and a goodbye.

Dep must have recognized Brent's voice over the phone. As soon as I disconnected, she jumped off my lap and sat with her nose almost on the front door.

"He's not coming here tonight, Dep," I gently told her.
She didn't move.

I was almost as bad. I didn't stir from the wing chair where

I'd sat during the entire phone conversation with Brent. After I'd sat there numbly for ten minutes or more, the old teasing saying that Misty, Samantha, and I had chanted to each other as teens went through my brain like a fluttering banner. *When the going gets tough, the tough call their girlfriends.*

I was still clutching my phone in one hand when it rang.

Chapter 21

✻

It was Misty.

I told her, "I was just thinking about you and Samantha."

"What were you thinking?"

"When the going gets tough, the tough call their girlfriends."

She laughed. "That old motto still works for me. You talked to Brent a few minutes ago, didn't you?"

"How did you know?"

"He came storming out of his office."

I joked, "Do I always cause that reaction in him?"

"Not exactly. He's naturally upset about . . . everything."

"I gave him new information about the Zippy Melwyn case. And I made Detective Gartborg wait for him for several minutes, so he was probably upset about making her wait and rushing so he wouldn't be even later."

"Then he should have barricaded himself inside his office to stay away from her." I heard a smile in Misty's voice. "But that's not why I called." She turned serious. "Hooligan and I are outside with a search warrant for Nina's phone."

I set Dep gently on the floor, opened the door, waved to Misty and Hooligan to come up onto the porch, and sent them to my guest room. I waited downstairs. I wished I'd checked Nina's call history. I hoped it was as nonincriminating as her contact list had been.

They clattered back downstairs. "Got it," Misty said. "Is it okay if Samantha comes over? We've barely made plans for tomorrow night, Tuesday, and Wednesday about who's bringing what to the cabin at Lake Cares Away."

I'd been so concerned about Nina that I'd hardly given a thought to Samantha and Hooligan's big day. I wanted to do everything I could to help make it wonderful for both of them. One way to do that might be to show some excitement about their future and get into a celebratory mood with Samantha and Misty. "That would be great. Can you stay, Hooligan?"

He held up the evidence envelope that must have contained the phone. "I'm supposed to take this back, and then I'll be off duty like Misty is at the moment, but I'm not about to interfere with your bachelorette party plans."

Misty went outside with him and returned with a pair of jeans and a frilly top. While she was changing and calling Samantha, I went to the kitchen and put a round of brie, a package of sesame flatbreads, and a cut-glass dish of sweet yet savory caramelized onion jam onto the granite-topped island. I took a bottle of chardonnay out of the fridge and set small chocolate-brown plates that Cindy had made, wineglasses, and embroidered cocktail napkins at our places at the island.

I couldn't help worrying. I was afraid that Nina would not make it to the wedding. I would have to work on my own emotions and prevent tense undercurrents between my law-enforcement friends and me from marring what should be a carefree, jubilant occasion. And Nina had designed the flowers and had been excited about setting them up. I wondered how she was doing and what she was thinking and feeling.

Would Brent be able to attend the wedding? Neither of us had a date for it and the reception, and Samantha had invited us both, along with a plus one. Everyone assumed that neither of us would bring a date. Brent and I had been partying with Samantha, Hooligan, Misty, and Scott since before the other two couples had officially paired off. Brent and I wouldn't be together at the ceremony, but Samantha had placed us together at the reception's head table. Both of us had RSVP'd for only one person.

Dep batted a catnip-filled toy owl through the kitchen and into the sunroom. Leaving the owl behind, she dashed back to the living room. I called to her, "Tidying up for company, Dep?"

If she answered, I didn't hear her, but Misty laughed and joined me in the kitchen. "Samantha's on her way." She opened her official notebook. "Can you tell me about your new information? When Brent stormed out, he had that frustrated and distressed look he gets when investigations aren't going well. Maybe if you tell me what you told him, I can help him sort it out."

"I thought the investigation was over." I hadn't meant to sound bitter.

She glanced at me from underneath her eyelids. "You don't want it to be, do you?"

"No." We sat at the stools but decided to wait for Samantha before we started eating and drinking. I repeated my discoveries. Misty scribbled in her notebook. I added, "Do you think that Brent and Detective Gartborg are going to Suds for Buds to talk to Buddy now?"

"Could be. Last I knew, she was about to go on vacation."

"Where were she and Brent planning to go before I interrupted him with my phone call?"

Misty didn't answer, but I read sympathy in her eyes.

I caught on. "Brent was taking her out to a late dinner before she left."

Misty shook her head. "I don't know if that's what was happening, but even if it was, it would have been more like them going out together, not him taking her out."

"That's a fine line."

"Don't take it to heart. They're colleagues. They worked

together this time, and last October, also. Sometimes we just have to talk to other officers about things we can't talk to civilians about."

I knew that from Alec. And besides . . . "Brent is free to do whatever he wants. It's not like he and I are dating. We're just friends." I ignored Misty's smirk. "I hope he makes it to Samantha's wedding."

The smirk twitched. "His dinner with Detective Gartborg, if there is one, can't possibly last that long."

I pretended to brush her comments away. "Thanks." I pointed at her notebook. "Are you planning to apply to become a detective?"

"Someone will have to if Brent joins the DCI." She quickly added, "I hope he doesn't."

"Me, too. Then you'd join the DCI and move away, too."

"I like Fallingbrook and being near you and Samantha and our friends."

"Like Scott."

She agreed. "Yeah, him, too. I don't think he's about to leave his family and friends, either. Besides, being Fallingbrook's fire chief suits him."

I glanced at her left hand. No ring. Yet.

Unlike the rest of us, Brent and Hooligan hadn't lived in Fallingbrook most of their lives. I hoped both of them would stay and remain part of our close-knit group. Hooligan probably would, since he was marrying Samantha. But Brent? Could he resist a promotion plus a tall and gorgeous detective? Again, I thought, *She's too bossy and not kind enough for him.* I told Misty, "Brent claims that you don't want to be a detective."

"I've been known to say that." She stared at me intently. "I know that before Scott and I discovered each other, you thought Brent and I should be a couple. I like him, but he and I have never had a romantic interest in each other, even when Alec was alive. After Alec died, Brent dated for a while, but he seems to have stopped doing that. I don't think he's ever been seriously interested in anyone except you."

"He's not . . . that's impossible."

"Is it?"

"Definitely. And now that he's met Detective Gartborg, it's even more impossible. Besides, he just—" I shrugged. "He feels obligated to keep a protective eye on me, for Alec's sake."

"Did he ever say that?"

"No, but that's how everyone who loved Alec treats me—Brent, Tom, Cindy . . ."

The doorbell rang.

I ran to the living room, let Samantha in, and gave her a big hug. "Excited?" I asked her.

She pulled away from me. Those dark brown eyes twinkled. "Very!"

Misty came in from the kitchen and also hugged her. "Nervous? Scared?"

Samantha pushed her away. "Scared? Of course not. But I can't help being nervous that things won't go quite right."

In the kitchen, we poured glasses of wine and topped the flatbreads with brie and caramelized onion jam and discussed what to bring to the cabin the three of us were going to share.

"It's tiny," Samantha warned, "with three bedrooms that are more like cubicles, three of the world's smallest ensuite bathrooms, and a place to cook, eat, and sit. And a front porch with rocking chairs and side tables. Not much else."

I told them, "My parents offered to let Dep stay with them."

Samantha shook her head. "No way. Dep's coming with us. The cabin's big enough for her, and it's a pet-friendly resort."

Agreeing, Misty refilled our glasses. "How much cooking do we want to do?"

Samantha tapped her glass against Misty's. "Not much."

I clinked my glass against theirs. "How about eating leisurely breakfasts in the cabin and our other meals in the resort's restaurant?"

We all drank to that.

Samantha glanced toward the coffee station that Alec and I had set up. "You have to be in charge of coffee, Emily. I'll bring bacon and eggs."

Misty offered, "I'll bring Wisconsin cheddar and homemade bread."

I said I'd bring juice, butter, and jam. None of us thought we'd want tea, and we all drank our coffee black when the coffee was good. I promised it would be.

Misty threw me an impish smile. "We'll let you get there first, Emily. You're the best at organizing kitchens."

"It's fun." I asked Samantha, "What are you going to do about the flowers if Nina can't be there?"

"The florist will recruit her teenage daughters to help decorate. She has Nina's drawings of what goes where."

I studied Samantha's hair. It was still her natural deep brown. "What about your hair?"

"I can manage the color myself, and the three of us can help each other do our hair and makeup the way we practiced with Nina last week."

"Okay," I said, "but Nina is the artistic one. Maybe you can spring her loose, Misty, whisk her to Cares Away for the wedding and reception, and sneak her back into jail afterward."

Misty stared into her glass of wine. "And I'll get Hooligan and Brent to help me. Maybe Kim Gartborg, too, if she hasn't left town."

I snapped my fingers. "Maybe Brent's taking her to an airport right now!" I didn't really want that to be true. I hoped that Gartborg and Brent were together—talking to Buddy and Kassandra and deciding that the evidence against the magician was stronger than the evidence against Nina.

Misty had come to my place in a cruiser with Hooligan. She could have walked home, but since she needed to take her uniform, she accepted Samantha's offer of a ride. I opened the front door for them.

Samantha crowed, "See you tomorrow at Cares Away!" Her voice overflowed with excitement.

Misty teased, "Remember what we used to call that lake when we were teens, even though we never went there, except Emily had been there when she was little?"

Knowing what was coming, I again defended the lake. "I liked it."

Samantha punched at Misty's arm. "Nothing's going to scare me away from having my wedding there. 'Lake Scares Away,' indeed!"

Grinning, I closed the door.

Chapter 22

Thanks to Misty and Samantha, I'd started looking forward to our stay at Cares Away, to a relaxed Monday evening with only the three of us, to the rehearsal and rehearsal dinner on Tuesday, and to the wedding and reception on Wednesday. I woke up in the morning feeling like I'd had my first sound sleep in days.

But at Deputy Donut, I couldn't help worrying about Nina. Tom and Jocelyn didn't talk about her, but I knew they were also missing her cheery personality and good-natured willingness to do whatever needed to be done.

Her arrest had become old news, and media interest had died down. Our weekday morning regulars, however, were horrified. The Knitpickers came in at nine and sat at their table by a front window. Across the aisle from them and beside the other big front window, our usual group of retired men claimed their table.

Tom was in the kitchen. Jocelyn waited on the retired men while I served the Knitpickers.

Cheryl put down her knitting and looked up at me. Her blue eyes were filled with pain. "You must be missing Nina."

I patted Cheryl's shoulder. "I am, especially since I'm sure she did nothing wrong."

Virginia declared, "We are, too!"

Cheryl sighed. "I heard her apartment was vandalized, but she's the one in trouble."

Virginia didn't stop knitting. "That's because the vandal ended up dead in her apartment."

I didn't admit that I'd been there.

Cheryl hadn't picked up her knitting again, which wasn't unusual. Many days, she did nothing more with her latest project than take it out of her bag and ask the others what she was doing wrong. I hardly ever saw her increase her project by more than a few stitches. She pointed a bare needle at me. I hoped she had finished a row and had not simply pulled the needle out, leaving stitches to unravel. "You tell her that if we can do anything for her, all she has to do is ask."

Virginia looked off into the distance, and then turned to me. "Do you know if anyone has started a legal fund for her?"

I glanced back at the kitchen. "Tom probably wouldn't want me telling people this, but he and a lawyer acquaintance of his are looking after it."

Virginia jutted her chin out. "I won't let on that you told me, but when we leave here, I'm going over to the bank and opening an account for her."

The others said they'd go with her.

I blinked away a threat of tears. "Thank you. How about if I make up a poster we can display here?"

Virginia clapped her hands. "I'll help! We can make flyers, too." She gestured at everyone at the table. "Who wants to help deliver them?"

All of the other Knitpickers said they would.

I thanked them and told them about the day's special coffee, a medium and very flavorful roast from the Dominican Republic. "It will give you a nice jolt of caffeine."

Two of the Knitpickers ordered the Dominican, one ordered a plain Colombian, one wanted a latte made with Colombian beans, and one wanted to experiment with the smoky delight of Lapsang souchong.

As I headed toward the kitchen, Virginia called out to the retired men, "Hey guys, we have a proposal for you!"

Laughter and good-natured teasing broke out behind me.

Beyond the half-wall, Jocelyn was putting fritters and donuts on plates for the retired men. One of them had switched from his usual Colombian coffee to rooibos tea. "On his wife's orders," Jocelyn told me. "I don't think he really wants tea, red or any other color."

"He'll like it when he tastes it."

"I hope so. I'll talk it up."

When I delivered the women's plates, Virginia told me that I didn't have to design and print a poster. The rooibos drinker was a retired graphic designer. He and his wife would design and print posters and flyers.

I went to his table and thanked him.

He set his teacup down. "Hey, we're all in this together. And this stuff is actually good, by the way. No way is it a substitute for coffee." He heaved the sigh of a coffee drinker being deprived of his morning brew. "It's okay."

I pointed out, "It's not really tea. It's called African bush tea, and resembles tea, but isn't. It doesn't have caffeine. No one says you can't also have coffee."

"My wife does. That is, until I go home and become Mr. Grumpy Bear at lunch and all the rest of the day." I smiled at him. I'd never seen him acting remotely grumpy.

One of the other men said they were all going to the bank with the Knitpickers later that morning. "Sorry we'll be leaving here earlier than usual."

The other men joked that by leaving before noon, they would free up tables for people who might want to eat lunch right at noon and would not, for once, have to wait a couple of minutes for the retired men and the Knitpickers to organize themselves and vacate their tables.

I smiled at these wonderful customers. "We're popular,

but not that popular. You're always welcome to stay as long as you want, even if you don't order anything."

One of the men patted his stomach. "Not eating donuts is against my principles."

The front of our shop became chaotic. The Knitpickers and retired men got up from their usual tables and went back and forth to the other table to talk, plot their strategies, map out where to deliver the flyers, and sketch ideas for the poster and flyers.

I refilled coffees and teapots and admired the work they were doing.

The door opened. Looking puzzled by the number of people nearly blocking the front door with their running back and forth between tables, Alf, the tourist I'd met at the carnival, came in without Connie. Maybe she'd had only Friday and the weekend off. Alf sat at the counter and ordered the Dominican coffee. "I like people who understand and appreciate single-origin coffees," he told me. "There are so many distinctive subtleties in their flavors, and I've never tried the Dominican." We discussed our favorites. Both of us loved the mellow coffees grown in Central America and the Caribbean.

The Knitpickers and retired men were still running back and forth between their tables, looking over one another's shoulders, conferring, and laughing. They were never exactly quiet when they teased each other, which was a lot of the time, but at the moment they were more excited and noisier than usual.

Alf glanced over his shoulder. "Is it always this busy in here?"

"Our customers can be lively. It's fun."

"I can see that. You must like working here."

"I do."

I handed him his mug of coffee and his raspberry short-cake donut, a raised donut topped with fresh raspberries and whipped cream and then drizzled with orange liqueur. It was so big we served it in bowls with a fork and a spoon.

Alf did what I often do to test whether a freshly poured hot beverage is cool enough to drink. He touched the outside of his mug with the tips of his fingers. We were always careful to make our coffee with hot but not boiling water to allow the flavors to develop fully without becoming bitter. Alf inhaled deeply and clamped his hand around the mug.

I asked where Connie was.

"She had to work, which is just as well. She nearly wore me out with so much sightseeing."

"What did you see?"

His list was long. I couldn't help smiling. "It sounds like you had a great time. Did you see Fallingbrook Falls? That's one of my favorites."

"I haven't gotten out there yet. I heard it's pretty but involves too much hiking."

He must have heard that from Connie, who seemed fond of sandals and high heels. "It's not too much if your shoes have decent treads."

"Would hiking boots work?"

"Sure. I wear sneakers to hike around the falls."

"How do you get there?"

"Want the scenic route or the direct route?"

"I'm here for the scenery."

I gave him the directions, but I wasn't sure he was listening. He appeared to be counting the freckles on my nose. I sketched a map on the back of a napkin and gave it to him.

He folded it carefully and slid it into the pocket of his tweedy gray golf shirt. The shirt looked brand new and had the sheen of silk combined with fine cotton. "I don't suppose you'd . . . no, I guess you wouldn't."

"Wouldn't what?"

"Like to show me those falls yourself? We could go to dinner afterward."

He was a fast worker. I usually held back more with men I didn't know, but in the comforting safety of Deputy Donut, I couldn't help telling people about my town and the forests, streams, and lakes surrounding it. "I can't. I'm getting together with girlfriends tonight." I guessed he hadn't seen the wedding ring I still wore. Waving it in his face would probably have been too obvious, so I didn't.

"And I guess you don't have time to sit down and have a coffee with me here so we could get to know each other a little. I mean, I don't usually go around inviting women out after barely having met them, but . . ."

You're on vacation. I didn't say it, but I did check his left hand. No ring, and his finger was uniformly tanned, showing that he hadn't recently removed one.

"How long will you be here?" I hoped my question didn't sound like an offer to meet him another time. *And why not?* asked a voice in my head. *Alec has been gone a long time. Do you really want to be alone for the rest of your life? Alf is pleasant, and he's only here on vacation. It wouldn't resemble a commitment. You might even have a good time.* I talked back to the voice in my head. *I like being alone. No one else is ever going to be as right for me as Alec was.* I pushed away a mental image of Brent smiling down at me in his warm and supportive way.

Alf said, "I'll be here for the rest of the week. Here." He pulled a business card from the pocket of his shirt. Alphaeus Chator, I read, Chief Financial Officer, Cornwall Amherst Investments. I was impressed. The large firm was based in New York, with branches around the world. The CFO would have lots of responsibilities, and zillions of people reporting to him.

"I'm Emily," I answered. "Our brochure serves as our business card." I pointed to the stand on the counter next to the donut display case.

"I still have the one from the carnival, thanks."

When he paid me, he said he'd stop in again. "Maybe you'll have time to show me those falls."

I thought of a way of not being alone in the woods on treacherous trails with a man I didn't know. "My parents live in an RV near the falls all summer. They'd be glad to help me show you around." I could go there in my own car.

"Sounds good!" Smiling, he touched the counter and turned to go. At the front, he stopped and held the door for the entire crew of retired men and Knitpickers. When they'd finally all made it through the door, he turned and waved.

I went around the half-wall to the kitchen. "Who was that?" Jocelyn asked. "You were certainly friendly."

"I'm always friendly with customers."

"Especially after you get to know them."

"I do know him, sort of. Yesterday while you were on your break, he came in with a date. I first met them at the Faker's Dozen Carnival. He's visiting from out of town, but she's local and has been taking him sightseeing." I tapped my wedding ring. "I'm not taking this off anytime soon."

She gave me a mischievous smile. "Has he been to Fallingbrook Falls?"

"No. I told him that if he wanted to visit the falls, my parents would help show him around."

"Ooooh," Jocelyn teased. "Taking him to meet your parents already."

"Watch it," I warned her. "I'll recruit you and your parents to join us."

"That'd be fine! We'd come along. I'd be able to keep an eye on you."

Tom read Alf's card and whistled softly. "Next thing you know, we'll have investors from New York clamoring for shares in Deputy Donut." He checked the clock on the kitchen wall. "I need to call my lawyer friend." He went off and shut himself into the office with Dep. I could see him in there talking on the phone.

Frowning, he returned to the kitchen. "Nina got the worst possible judge. She wasn't granted bail."

We all traded looks of frustration. I stomped my foot, gently, since I didn't want to alarm diners. "I still think that the person who killed Zippy Melwyn was really after Nina, and she's safer in jail."

Tom cleared his throat. "Jail is never a safe place, especially if she's transferred out of our local one where she's at least being treated with some respect and compassion." Glowering, he went back to frying. Jocelyn and I served our lunch customers some of the deep-fried veggies, sausages, and cheeses he made. They gobbled them and ordered donuts for dessert. We feasted on the goodies, too.

Despite Brent's and Tom's reminders not to interfere in police investigations, I had to follow every possible lead—the safe ones, at least—that might free Nina and put the actual murderer in prison. When it was my turn for a break, I put a pad of paper and a pen into my backpack and headed down the street toward The Craft Croft.

I would tell Kassandra that she'd given me an address in Michigan and ask her to write down the local address that I assumed she had, since she was working at The Craft Croft. I hoped that by using the word "write," I would make her think of handwriting rather than printing.

At The Craft Croft, Summer was sitting at the reception desk. No one else appeared to be in the gallery. Summer's linen dress was the aqua of the steepest sides of icebergs. With those red curls again piled high on her head, she could have appeared calm and cool. Instead she frowned and shuffled through the contents of a desk drawer.

She lifted her head. "Emily! I was about to call you. Have you seen Kassandra?"

Chapter 23

My smile withered. I told Summer, "I haven't seen Kassandra since yesterday after I left here. She followed me out. Didn't she come back?"

"She did, and she helped me close yesterday at four. I said I'd see her tomorrow—that is today. She mumbled something like, 'Yeah, see you,' so I thought she was coming in. But she didn't. She's not answering her phone, and I can't leave here until another co-op member arrives at three. Otherwise, I'd go down to her apartment and see if she's there. I was going to try Deputy Donut first, to find out if she'd decided to go work for you and had been too shy to tell me." She closed the desk drawer. "Obviously, I won't have to do that."

"No, and I wouldn't have hired her away from you. If she had asked again, I would have called you to find out why she was leaving The Craft Croft or if she'd left without notice. Don't try going to her apartment, though. It doesn't exist."

"What?" Summer glanced toward the front door as if expecting Kassandra to walk in.

I explained.

Summer bounced the eraser end of a pencil on the desk. "Wow." Although Summer and I were the only people in the gallery, she lowered her voice. "Why would she lie about her address?"

I guessed, "Maybe it was because she had to quickly come up with an address in Fallingbrook, and the only one she knew was for where she'd been working, Suds for Buds, but she gave the building a nonexistent second story. Buddy from Suds for Buds has been trying to reach her, too. She left there Friday night for a break and never came back."

"Wait. Wasn't that woman murdered Friday night?"

"Yes, around the time that Kassandra left Suds for Buds. Across the street from Suds for Buds."

Summer's eyes widened. She took a deep breath. "Uh-oh."

Quietly, I told her about the man who'd been at Suds for Buds and had left about the same time Kassandra did. "I don't know if Kassandra was with that guy after he left Suds for Buds."

"We saw her after that, so if he murdered Zippy Melwyn, he didn't murder Kassandra. At least not then."

We stared into each other's eyes. Summer whispered, "He could have done away with her after she left here yesterday afternoon."

I added, only slightly louder, "Maybe he was afraid she suspected him of murder."

"Maybe she helped him do it."

"That's hard to imagine, but . . ."

Summer finished my sentence. "Not impossible." She glanced toward the door again, and I looked too. The door was glass. People were out on the sidewalk, but there was no Kassandra running toward The Craft Croft and apologizing for being late. Summer returned her gaze to me. "Could she be sick, or did something happen to her? Like an accident and the hospital wouldn't know to call me?" Her eyes were aqua like her dress, but about two shades deeper.

"I told my detective friend Brent about her. I suspect that if she'd been arrested or hurt or worse, he might have asked me for more information."

"I might have to report that she's missing, but it seems a

little soon, especially since she seems to make a habit of leaving jobs with no notice."

"She's left at least two nice employers without warning."

"Thanks, I think. She could have run away, like if she knows who the murderer is and saw him following her or something."

I tried to combat my rising unease about whether the man had caught up with Kassandra. "She wrote on our application form that she lived in Lapeer, Michigan. That's sort of near Detroit. If she's commuting to and from there, you can expect her to be late."

Summer let out a sigh that was almost a laugh. "Like a day or two."

"I can tell Brent about our concerns without filing a formal report. I saw both Kassandra and Zippy for the first time on Friday the thirteenth, and Zippy was also from Lapeer." I knew I shouldn't tell anyone that the address Kassandra had given me was also the late Zippy Melwyn's address, so I didn't mention it. Instead, I explained why I'd come. "Aside from worrying about what might have happened to her, I'm sorry that she's not here. I was hoping for a sample of her handwriting."

Summer snapped her fingers. "I have one. I was going to have her compose a letter, but she wanted the exact wording, so I dictated it and she wrote it down. She said her handwriting was faster than her hunt-and-peck keyboarding. She was going to type it for me today. Maybe she was scared to come in and have to use a keyboard." Summer opened the desk drawer again. "It should be in here."

"If you find it, can you handle it by the edges?"

Summer glanced up at me from underneath raised eyebrows. "I'll try." She carefully lifted papers out of the drawer, and then looked through the inbox. "Aha. Here it is. It's not personal, only a letter to a sculpture garden about one of our sculptors." Summer was good at handling things without putting fingerprints on them. She slid the paper onto the desk.

I leaned over and studied it. My heart rate sped. "I'm no expert, but I think this matches the handwriting on another letter. The police should probably see it."

"Unless Kassandra shows up here, I'm the only one who can say for certain that she wrote this letter. Can they get fingerprints off paper?"

"They can if they soak the paper in a chemical called nin-hydrin. The prints show up purple."

"That sounds like an interesting art project, maybe."

"I don't think anyone should spend a lot of time around possibly toxic chemicals."

"Well, there is that. But playing with color is an obses-sion."

I got out my phone and took a picture of the letter. I wanted to compare it right then and there to the photo I'd taken ear-lier of the torn, threatening letter, but I knew I shouldn't tell Summer things that the police and I and possibly no one else—except, perhaps, Kassandra—knew.

Summer again glanced toward the door. "I kind of hope she doesn't come back. I'd be scared to have her around."

I teased, "I'll stay here and protect you while I call Brent. He'll probably want to keep this letter."

"He can have it. I know what it says. I'll type it from mem-ory." She drummed her fingernails on the desk. "Meanwhile, how about if I lock up while you're calling your detective friend? I'll hide in my office and eat lunch."

"Okay."

She locked the glass door, turned her OPEN sign to CLOSED, and went into her office.

I called Brent's personal line.

He answered immediately. "Hi, Em."

I asked him if he'd caught up with Kassandra yet.

"I was just about to look for her at The Craft Croft."

"That's where I am. She was supposed to work here today, but she hasn't shown up. Summer has a sample of Kassandra's handwriting. It's a lot like the handwriting on the torn-off letter I found in the donut car. The letter's here."

"Tell Summer I'd like to talk to her. I'll be there in a few minutes."

I was still in The Craft Croft when he parked an unmarked police car in front. He wore khakis with a matching blazer, a white shirt, and a dark green tie with tan tortoises crawling across it. Despite the whimsical tie, his face was serious and businesslike. I let him in, introduced him to Summer, and left.

Striding up Wisconsin Street, I muttered, "At least he's not with that icy-sharp detective." Luckily, no other pedestrians were close enough to hear. I added, "Summer's tall, gorgeous, and caring. Maybe she'll distract him from Kimberly Gartborg."

Tom went for a short lunch as soon as I returned to Deputy Donut. I fried donuts while Jocelyn waited tables. Tom returned, but Jocelyn refused to go out. The dining room was almost full of kids, and she liked watching them enjoy their milk and donuts. Lots of them ended up with milk mustaches to go with the filling and frosting they couldn't help smearing on their cheeks when they bit into their donuts.

I was drawing espresso for one father when Jocelyn came into the kitchen for Earl Grey tea and glanced toward the front door. "Hey, Emily, is that . . . ?"

Brent? Or Nina, set free, after all?

I whipped around but was disappointed. I turned back to Jocelyn. "It's Marsha Fitchelder, the organizer of the Faker's Dozen Carnival."

Jocelyn giggled and whispered, "She's here to tell you that you can't park the donut car in its garage, and you have to move it."

Tom asked out of the corner of his mouth, "Want me to talk to her?"

I raised my chin. "I can do it."

"That woman's impossible," he muttered. "Signal if you need me."

I grinned and went out to the dining area. Although smaller tables were available, Marsha was settling herself at one of our biggest ones. Today's flowing floral dress, without a black vest over it, was quite pretty. Even seated she was intimidating, though.

I gave her my best customer-service smile and asked cheerfully, "What can I get you?"

She put on her forbidding block-the-entryway-to-the-carnival face. "Nothing. I came to talk to you."

She was sitting with her back to the window. I eased into a chair beside her where I could watch most of the dining area and kitchen in case anyone needed me. "What's up?"

She aimed an index finger, revolver-style, at me. "You need to stop going around telling people that I had an argument with that mime. It was merely a friendly discussion."

She must have been jumping to conclusions based on questions the detectives had asked her. I was certain that other witnesses told them about her argument—or friendly discussion—with Zippy. I kept my jaw from dropping, but I couldn't prevent my eyes from opening wider.

She must have taken my silence and questioning surprise as encouragement. "I know you want that murderer to come back and work here," she claimed, "but I'm warning you. You'll be sorry if you do."

"We . . ." My voice dwindled to nearly nothing. I cleared my throat. "We know her. She's not a murderer. She would never harm anyone."

Marsha gave her index finger several adamant shakes. "She could poison all of your customers and wipe you out financially."

What a bizarre idea. "She wouldn't do that."

"You don't know what I do. Your friend the murderer caught that mime removing a bucket of something from your car and hiding it under a blanket in her car."

At the carnival, I had noticed a lumpy blanket behind the seats of Zippy's car, and later, in an alley near Nina's loft, the blanket had still been in place, but the heap underneath it had shrunk. "Did you see the mime take something from our car and put it into hers?"

"I did."

"And are you telling me that Nina caught her doing it but didn't stop her?" That was hard to believe.

Marsha looked past my donut hat instead of into my eyes. "I did."

"Where was I?"

"You were right in front of your murderous assistant, carrying loads into the carnival, which, if you'd been organized and prepared, you could have avoided by coming the night before when you could have driven to your allotted spot."

I ignored that jab. "Do you mean I had my back to the mime and didn't see her steal from my car?"

"Or you were pretending not to." Marsha squinted toward me, making her dark eyes even smaller. "Maybe it was all arranged beforehand between the three of you."

That suggestion was so ridiculous that I didn't respond. I took my pen out of my apron pocket and pulled one of our printed Deputy Donut paper napkins closer. "I'm trying to picture this." I drew a diagram. "Here's the mime's car and our car, and here's the gap in the fencing, the entryway where you later put turnstiles. Where were you when the mime removed the sugar from our car?"

Marsha grabbed my pen and stabbed it down into the center of the entryway where she'd stood blocking Nina and me from driving into the carnival. The pen went through all four layers of the napkin.

I asked, "Where was I?"

She made a heavy dot that tore through only the top two layers of the napkin. If she was right, I'd been heading toward our tent but had not yet made it to the entryway.

"Where was Nina?"

"Here." She drew an X between me and the donut car. I was pretty sure that Nina and I had walked beside each other. She had certainly never lagged that far behind.

I had another question. "Where was that big black van with no windows?"

She drew a rectangle at the spot where I remembered seeing the van next to the donut car. With a triumphant look on her face, she slapped the pen down onto the glass table.

I grabbed the pen before it could roll off the table. I drew a line between where Marsha had said she was and where our car had been, between the mime's car and the black van. "The van was blocking your view of our car."

"It hadn't arrived yet or had already left. Or I was farther from the entryway than where I put that dot. But I know what I saw. That mime removed a white plastic bucket from your car."

That was the only part of her story that I believed, except that I still wasn't sure that Marsha herself hadn't removed the sugar from our car. She could have put it into Zippy's car. I asked, "Did you see the mime put anything into our car?"

Marsha paused as if wondering how to answer the question to suit her purposes, whatever they were. "I might have, but I didn't particularly notice."

In other words, she hadn't seen Zippy drop that envelope into the donut car, but she was hedging her bets so, if it could help her own case later, she could definitively say that she had or hadn't seen Zippy put something into our car. I went back to the more obvious way of poking holes in Marsha's story. "Are you saying that when the mime took the bucket out of our car, Nina and I were both walking away and had our backs to it?"

"All you had to do was turn your heads, and you'd have seen her. And your car doors aren't exactly silent. Any normal person would have looked toward the sound of their car door slamming. You could have, but according to you, you didn't. And your assistant was even closer. If neither of you looked when your door slammed, do you know what that says about you?"

Probably that we weren't as close as you're claiming. I slipped the pen into my apron pocket. "No."

"It says that you two knew that woman was taking something from your car, but you didn't say anything because you had thought of another way to punish her, later, when your assistant, and maybe you, too, invited her to visit your assistant in her apartment."

"I really don't think Nina heard or saw any of this. I certainly didn't."

"You can deny it all you want. I saw what I saw. And I didn't have an argument with that mime, and no one can say I went to your assistant's apartment that night and killed anyone. Why would I do that? I don't know your assistant. I didn't know the murdered woman. Why would I have wanted to spend time with either one of them?"

I let her ramble on with her denials. Tom peered over the half-height wall. Judging by the concerned look on his face, he was about to come out and prevent Marsha from doing whatever it was he might have thought she was contemplating doing to me. I winked at him with the eye that Marsha couldn't see.

Marsha leaned forward and spoke in a quiet, conspiratorial tone. "What do you know about that murdered mime, besides her name? I know she called herself Zipporah Melwyn, but that name sounds as fake to me as her supposed clown name, Zippy the Mime."

"I don't know her at all. Didn't know her. The first time I saw her was at the Faker's Dozen Carnival. I guess she worked as a mime other places, too, since her car had MIME MOBILE painted on it."

"Those were magnets. I stuck a fingernail underneath one. And that is the only fingerprint I left near her car. If anyone says there are others, that's because they can't tell one fingerprint from another."

I tried not to let my eyes bug out.

Maybe I wasn't succeeding. As if reacting to the faces I was trying to prevent myself from making, Marsha's eyes went beadier. On a long, slow breath, she asked, "Did your assistant kill her for her money?"

"Did she have money?"

"That's what I'm asking you. I mean, her car might have been little, but it was nice. How much money could she make going around to carnivals and acting like a clown, and not a very good one? She must have had a source of income on the side."

I thought, *Like helping a pickpocket steal and then dividing the ill-gotten gains, until the pickpocket decided he wanted it all for himself and killed her to get it.*

"Like family money," Marsha asserted. "That proves I didn't kill her. When they finally get around to reading her will, they'll discover I'm not mentioned."

I opened my mouth and closed it again. The only reply I could think of would have sounded something like, *"Buh, buh, buh."*

Marsha swept her capacious faux leather bag off the table. "No one can say I murdered that woman. I was at the carnival from eight in the morning until midnight that night. People saw me there." She nodded toward Tom. "Your boss saw me there."

I didn't bother to inform her that Tom and I were equal partners.

She stood up and looped the bag's strap over one shoulder. "So, a word to the wise—don't go spreading lies."

She glared at me for a second as if deciding whether the look on my face was guilt.

I was only trying to hide the laughter wanting to bubble up because her threat had sounded like a silly rhyme.

She stomped out.

In black sandals like the ones she'd worn on Friday. The soles were black.

Chapter 24

❧

The sight of the black soles that could have marred Nina's new ladder didn't stop me from wanting to giggle. Attempting to keep a straight face, I rushed back to the kitchen.

Tom asked, "What are you grinning about? It didn't look like you were exactly enjoying that discussion."

I parroted in a sing-song voice, " 'A word to the wise— don't go spreading lies.' She could have added another line. 'About my alibis.' "

Jocelyn put the finishing swirls on a lemon-frosted zesty lemon donut. "What she actually said sounds like a threat."

Jocelyn was too interested in solving crimes for my comfort, so I wanted to dismiss the possibility of a threat. Tom, however, despite always wanting to protect everyone around him, couldn't help going into detective mode. "Did she tell you she had an alibi?"

"She said she couldn't have murdered Zippy because she was at the carnival from eight in the morning until midnight that night, and people saw her. Including you, Tom."

He lifted a basket of golden donuts out of the fryer and shook the basket. "When did you see her at the carnival, Emily?"

"Nina and I saw her several times in the morning between about nine thirty and ten. I saw her again about three thirty when I returned to the carnival after Brent and I toured the parking area. She claimed to have seen Zippy leave the carnival an hour or so before she talked to us, but I don't know if that was true. The uniformed officers Brent called in would know if, when, and where they saw Marsha. When Nina and I left the carnival shortly after nine in the evening, Marsha wasn't at her post in the entryway. I didn't see her again until just now."

Tom turned to Jocelyn. "Did you see her when you took the sugar to the carnival?"

"She was at the turnstiles taking tickets and giving vendors a hard time. She almost didn't let me in, but my hat finally convinced her. She said that no one would wear a hat like these"—she pointed at the fuzzy donut shining like a headlight on the front of her police hat—"unless they had to, so I obviously worked for Deputy Donut. Did you see her, Tom?"

"She was everywhere the night before the carnival, getting in everyone's way and telling us either to do what we were already doing or that what we were doing was wrong. My friends and I made it to the carnival around ten the night of the thirteenth to pack up, and I didn't see or hear her the entire time we were loading or when we drove out around a quarter to eleven."

I summarized, "She could have been gone, even for short periods. She had assistants who could have taken tickets in her absence. Our home addresses were on our vendor application form, so she had Nina's address and might have gone there and thought she was attacking Nina when she was really attacking Zippy. Or she could have somehow known or figured out where Zippy was going, and she went there, too, because she was angry at Zippy for not moving her car." I raised my index finger. "And Marsha has another claim that supposedly proves her innocence. She said that when Zippy's will is read, the police will discover that Marsha had no expectations of inheriting from her."

Tom was good at looking bewildered even when he wasn't. "Why would she bring that up?"

I grinned at the stunned expression on Jocelyn's face. "Marsha seemed to think that Zippy had family money, and that was how she could afford to busk at carnivals and drive a newish car."

Tom choked out a laugh. "That's going from A to Z without bothering with any of the letters in between."

I agreed and added, "Maybe Marsha's not a murderer, but she might have a guilty conscience about other things she doesn't want the police to know about."

Tom lowered his eyebrows like someone faking a severe warning. "Police can be everyone's worst nightmare whether they're guilty or not."

Jocelyn piped up, "I hope the police are paying attention to her. Maybe they'll convince her to be less quarrelsome and threatening. One look at her frown is enough to make anyone keel over."

Tom relaxed his pretend scowl. "In your case, Jocelyn, it would be only to perform a handstand or a backward roll."

In the voice of someone narrating a horror movie, Jocelyn warned, "Don't count on it."

After we closed, Tom suggested I could leave the tidying to him and head to my girls' night out with Misty and Samantha.

I refused. "Tidying hardly takes any time, and Cares Away is only a fifteen-minute drive. Even if we clean this place very slowly, I'll get there before Misty and Samantha do."

It didn't take us long to make the shop ready for the Jolly Cops Cleaning Crew, and then I packaged and paid for Jamaican Blue Mountain Estate coffee beans and Hawaiian Kona beans for our mornings in the cabin at Lake Cares Away. Samantha deserved the expensive specialty coffees.

I harnessed Dep and we walked home. The evening was hot and breezeless, and I could hardly wait to swim in Lake

Cares Away. Despite Nina's problems and my desire to prove that she wasn't guilty of murder, I felt the lightness of anticipation. I hadn't had a real vacation since we'd opened Deputy Donut four years before. This vacation would last only a few days, but except for my worries about Nina, it should be nearly carefree. The only thing I had to do was be ready on time for the ceremony. I could handle that sort of stress.

At home, I opened my suitcase. Dep jumped in. Every time I added another garment, she scrunched down, flattened her ears, peeked at me, and batted at my hand. Packing took longer than I expected. Finally, I lifted her out of the suitcase and carried it downstairs.

She followed me to the kitchen. She didn't interfere while I placed the juice, butter, and jam in my cooler, probably because she was sitting in the cardboard box I'd set out for the coffee and the coffee grinder. Her eyes were huge. I took her out and held her in one arm while I one-handedly packed the coffee and the grinder and closed the box. In her inimitable way, she helped me arrange her special bowls, her cat food, her treats, and a few toys in another box. I had to keep retrieving the toys she removed. With her kitty litter, kitty litter pan, and waterproof mats, she had almost more luggage than I did.

Outside, I couldn't completely open my car's trunk because my kayak's upside-down stern was in the way. I wasn't sure I'd go kayaking on Lake Cares Away, but I kept the kayak on my car during the warmest part of the year in case Brent and I made sudden plans to go kayaking. I could kayak by myself, and sometimes did, but it was more fun with Brent. I carefully slid boxes underneath the lid and into the trunk. Heading back into the house, I sighed. Brent had been at The Craft Croft on business, so he hadn't been as warm as he sometimes could be, but neither had I. Was he considering becoming a DCI agent and moving away? Or was he distracted by memories of the previous evening with Kimberly Gartborg?

Dep never liked riding in her carrier or in the car, but when I returned to the house for my gown in its garment bag, she was sitting on the mahogany-trimmed red velvet armchair in the living room and watching me with one eye. The other eye was closed. I told her, "Don't worry. You're coming along."

I took the garment bag outside, hung it on the hook behind the driver's seat, and returned to the house for Dep.

It was a good thing that I opened the front door carefully. Dep had been waiting beside it. She skittered back a few feet and stood watching me and waving her tail in the air. I picked her up. She purred.

The hated carrier was beside the front door. I toed it closer. Dep stopped purring. "C'mon, sweetie. You're going to spend a few days in a cabin with Misty, Samantha and me." She didn't respond. "It will be fun," I told her. I corralled her feet in one hand, slipped her into the carrier and zipped it.

"Mew."

I asked, "Could you possibly sound more pathetic?"

She could.

I fastened her carrier into the space I'd left for it behind the passenger seat and pulled out of my driveway. "We're off!" I crowed.

Dep only muttered, which was better than the yowling and howling she sometimes did in the car. Maybe knowing that many of her personal belongings were coming with us comforted her.

I drove north on Wisconsin Street past downtown Fallingbrook. Over the years, the town had grown mostly to the south. About five blocks north of downtown Fallingbrook, Wisconsin Street turned into County Road J. After I was certain that 976 Wisconsin Street North, the address that Kassandra might have meant to write on her job application for The Craft Croft, did not exist, I turned east.

I didn't remember much about my childhood visit to Lake Cares Away. I'd spent most of the day filling a bucket with water from the lake, dumping the water on the sandy beach, and wondering how it could disappear so quickly. Samantha and Hooligan had reported that the Cares Away Resort was perfect for their rehearsal dinner, rehearsal, wedding, and reception. And for our mini-vacation.

The route leading to Lake Cares Away wound through woods and past lakes and streams. The woods were still lush and green, with only touches of yellow at the tops of poplars and aspens. I opened the windows a tiny bit and took a deep breath of woodsy air. Dep continued mumbling.

The road narrowed, curving around rocks and ponds and climbing forested knolls before dipping again into valleys.

A rustic sign showed me the beginning of a driveway leading between trees toward the Cares Away Resort. The driveway was long, paved, and barely wide enough for two cars. I took my time, but no one passed me going the other way. The Cares Away Resort was famous for its fine dining, and at this time of late afternoon, more people were probably driving to it than away from it.

I parked the car at the main lodge and stepped out. Tall pines cooled the air. Years of shed needles served as mulch around the parking lot and gave the entire area a deliciously piney fragrance. I pulled Dep in her carrier out of the car. "You'll be quiet in the lodge's office, won't you, Dep?"

The tiniest of mews came from the depths of her carrier.

In the oak-paneled office, the desk clerk told me that neither Misty nor Samantha had arrived. She gave me a key and a map of the grounds, showing cabins placed near twisty roads and cul-de-sacs. Our cabin, Birch, was next to the beach. The drawing showed that, despite Samantha's description of our cabin as "tiny," it was one of the larger ones.

Dep didn't make a sound until I slid her carrier into the car again. "Mew?"

"Soon," I told her. I hopped into the driver's seat.

The road through the resort was barely wider than a single lane of hard-packed gravel. Negotiating its winding curves, I caught sight of cabins tucked away in their own forested enclaves. They looked cozy and private.

I parked in the driveway that ended near Birch cabin's rear wall. Misty and Samantha could park behind me, closer to the access road. They were both supposed to be on call that night. I hoped they wouldn't have to work, but if they needed to leave in a hurry, my car wouldn't be in their way.

I took Dep, still in her carrier, out of the car. "We're here, Dep."

Her answer was an impatient request to be taken out of the carrier.

Like the other cabins I'd glimpsed, this one was made of thick logs with white mortar between them and their cut ends painted forest green. I walked around to the deep front porch, sheltered by a slanting roof. The front door, the shutters, the three rocking chairs, their matching end tables, and the old-fashioned wooden frame surrounding the screen door were all painted the same green as the ends of the logs. The calming dark green plus the braided doormat and the canning jars overflowing with flowers on the tables made the exterior homey and welcoming.

In front of the cottage, beyond a row of maple trees, a sand beach sloped toward a broad expanse of sparkling lake. I took another deep breath, let it out, and felt tension flow out of my body. Lake Cares Away was well named.

I cradled Dep's carrier in one arm.

"Mew?"

"In a few seconds, Dep." I pulled at the screen door and inserted the key into the rustic wooden door's lock. Inside, I shut the solid wood door and set Dep's carrier on the polished floor. "You should feel at home here," I told her. "Pine plank floors. And the smoky smell of a fireplace." Con-

structed of fieldstone, the wood-burning fireplace was between two of the windows overlooking the porch. I unzipped
the carrier and fastened its door back. Dep tucked her front
paws underneath her chest and stared out through the opening. "It's okay," I cooed. "We're staying here for three nights
and most of four days." She didn't budge. I invited her to
look around the cabin with me. That didn't tempt her, either.

The main room was charming and clean. A kitchenette
with pine cabinets and granite countertops ran along the side
farthest from the lodge. The appliances were small—a hot
plate with two burners, a toaster oven, a half-sized fridge, a
microwave oven, and a drip coffeemaker with a conical filter
holder, my preferred shape for drip coffeemakers. A window
over the sink faced the trunks of tall pine trees.

Watching to make certain that Dep, who was still in her
carrier, didn't escape from the cabin, I eased outside. I returned with her luggage. Dep hadn't moved. I filled her food
and water bowls and set them in a corner of the kitchen on
one of her special waterproof mats. Dep watched me but did
not venture into the room. I told her, "I'll figure out where to
put your litter tray next." That didn't tempt her out of her
carrier, either.

As Samantha had warned, all three bedrooms were small,
with tiny attached bathrooms. In the largest bedroom, a
pretty quilt featuring lavender flowers appliqued on white
covered the queen bed. There was just enough room near the
bed for a chair, a dresser, and a bedside table. The teensy
middle room had a dresser, a chair, and bunk beds covered by
similar quilts except the flowers were pale blue. The third
room was also teensy, with yellow-flowered quilts on the
bunks.

I figured that Samantha deserved the largest room. I chose
the middle one. I didn't need to clamber up and down ladders
to the upper bunk, but Dep could sleep up there if she wanted

to. I tucked her litter tray on the other waterproof mat in a corner behind the door of my well-equipped little bathroom.

In the main room, Dep was still inside her carrier. I placed a catnip-filled dinosaur just beyond her reach in front of her doorway. She opened one eye.

I brought my garment bag inside, removed the lovely pale blue bridesmaid's gown from it, and hung the dress in the closet in my room. I put my suitcase on a folding rack. Finally, I went back out to my car and brought in my cooler and the coffee and coffee grinder.

I unpacked and then investigated the kitchen drawers and cabinets. Everything was organized, leaving me very little to do besides take the emptied cartons, cooler, and garment bag out and store them in my car.

I returned, apologizing to Dep for not having space to leave a carton in the cabin for her to use as a toy or another bed. She tentatively extended one paw out of her carrier but couldn't quite reach the toy. She tucked her foot underneath her chest with the other one again and closed her eyes.

The dining table was in the middle of the room, with another glass jar of wildflowers centered on an orange and yellow handwoven table runner. Four chairs surrounded the table. Even though only three of us would be staying in the cabin, I found placemats and cloth napkins that matched the runner and set them at the four places.

On the opposite side of the room from the kitchen, a love seat and two chairs faced a TV on a set of shelves containing books, games, and jigsaw puzzles. As long as the coffee held out, I could be happy in this cabin for weeks.

Tires crunched on gravel behind Misty's bedroom. Car doors slammed, and I heard Misty's and Samantha's laughter-filled voices.

Chapter 25

✻

Footsteps thumped on the wooden porch. Samantha sang out, "Anybody home?"

I flung the door open. Carrying sheet-swathed garments on hangers, Misty and Samantha looked down through the screen door toward the floor near my feet. Misty asked, "Where's Dep?" They obviously weren't about to open the screen door if there was a chance that Dep might escape.

I glanced back into the room. "She's in her carrier. It's open, but she apparently prefers it to a big, scary new space."

Misty and Samantha came into the cabin, and we gave one another the sorts of hugs three people can give when two of them are holding hangers high to keep long gowns from brushing the floor.

Misty glanced around the cabin. "I was afraid this resort would be too primitive, but it's not. You chose well, Samantha."

"Hooligan helped."

I deadpanned, "And you chose well there, too." I pointed toward the larger corner bedroom. "I hope you can find a place to hang your gown in there, Samantha."

We all trooped into her room. Samantha opened the closet door and carefully hung her gown.

Misty's gown was too long for the closet in her room. She hung it on a hook on the back of her bathroom door.

We all returned to the main room. With the tips of her claws, Dep dragged the catnip-filled dinosaur into her carrier.

It took us several trips to retrieve everything Samantha and Misty needed from their cars. When we were all inside again, Dep's front half eased out of her carrier. She rolled around, rubbing her face and shoulders against the catnip toy.

Samantha glanced toward the woods outside the cabin. "Our dinner reservations aren't until eight. I'm sorry. I didn't realize how popular the restaurant here is."

After teasing her that she wasn't as organized as we'd believed, Misty and I said we didn't mind waiting.

Samantha asked, "What shall we do until then? I'd say we should get into the wine, but Misty and I are on call tonight."

Beyond the cabin's porch, the beach and water beckoned. Misty and I said, "Beach!"

By the time we had changed into bikinis, Dep was sitting in front of her carrier. She ran to the screen door and peered out.

"Yes," I told her, "there are probably birds, chipmunks, and creepy-crawlies out there, but you're not going to pounce on any of them." I draped my beach towel around my shoulders, fastened Dep's harness around her, snapped on her leash, and took her into the fresh-smelling outdoors.

The shoreline was lovely, with sand sloping down to clear water. At the end of the beach near the lodge, kayaks and canoes were overturned on the sand in a colorful row.

We put our towels on Adirondack chairs and our water bottles on tables between them. Reminding me of my childhood visit here, children and their parents built castles and dug moats. In the roped-off swimming area, a father and son played catch, a mother pulled a little girl around on an inflated unicorn, and a woman swam laps.

I spread my towel on my lap and lifted Dep onto the towel She stretched out in the early evening sunshine. Stroking the warm, purring cat, I watched Misty and Samantha wade into the lake and do some serious swimming.

After our first meeting in junior high, Misty, Samantha, and I had laughed together, daydreamed together, cried together, grown together, and stayed close even when we went our separate ways to college. We'd all returned to Fallingbrook, though, and it was like we'd never been apart.

In two days, Samantha was getting married. I knew that her marriage would not diminish our friendship. My much-too-short marriage had strengthened it. We were lucky to have one another, and Hooligan was a welcome addition, just as Alec had been. Sentimental tears pricked at the backs of my eyes. "I will not cry when she walks down the aisle," I whispered to Dep. She curled into a tight ball and immediately stretched out again.

Dripping, Samantha came back and wrapped herself in her towel. I looked up at her wet head and teased, "You can swim because you didn't put any interesting colors in your hair that might have washed out in the lake."

"I have lots of time to swim before I need to decide what temporary dye to use."

"What color?" Knowing she would keep it a secret, I tried to sound innocent.

"Whatever I feel like at the moment." She sat in the chair next to mine and patted her towel-covered legs. "Here, give Dep to me so you can swim."

I placed Dep gently in Samantha's lap. The rhythm of Dep's purrs went on unbroken.

I padded barefoot across the sand. It was soft and retained some of the day's earlier heat.

The water was a different story, although it was probably as warm as small lakes ever got in northern Wisconsin. I waded in, dunked myself, and tried not to gasp. Within seconds, I was used to the temperature. I swam beside Misty. At the end of the laps nearest our cottage, I checked the beach. In sunglasses, wrapped in a towel, and stroking the cat on her lap, Samantha faced the lake, no doubt keeping an eye on everyone in the water and ready to spring into action if any of us needed help.

Increasing my speed, I reassured myself that the charges against Nina would be dropped and she'd be freed. Samantha and Hooligan would have a beautiful wedding and head to their secret honeymoon location. Nina would repair her painting and have it shipped to the Arthur C. Arthurs Gallery in time for the show. Samantha and Hooligan would live happily ever after. Misty and Scott would, too. Nina would become so famous that she'd be able to paint full-time, but she wouldn't move away, and we'd see her often. She'd walk to Deputy Donut for breaks.

Dripping, Misty and I made our way back to the sun-warmed sand, walked across it, wrapped our towels around ourselves, and settled into our chairs. Dep clambered into my lap, closed her eyes, and purred loudly.

The other three of us sat quietly enjoying one another's company. I almost dozed.

Something to my left jingled. With a joyful bark, a half-grown but very large puppy bounded toward us, his tongue lolling out the side of his mouth, which was stretched in a happy smile. He was mostly white with large black splotches. A lopsided white streak snaked up from his nose to the top of his fluffy black head. His ears flopped and his paws were about the size of teacups. Despite his speed, he wore an adorably bewildered expression.

Dep leaped up and dug her claws into the towel—and into my legs. Arching her back, she made herself about twice her usual size. In case that wasn't enough, she twitched her tail, flattened her ears, and hissed.

Spraying sand, the puppy put on the brakes exactly like a dog in a cartoon. A whistle sounded in the distance. The puppy turned around and scooted back toward the lodge. At first, his giant white plume of a tail was down near his back legs, but by the time I lost sight of him, his tail was high again and waving proudly.

We three humans laughed. The puppy had been very cute. "I guess you showed him, Dep," I said. Still puffed up, she stared toward where he'd disappeared among trees. I had a feeling that, unlike us, Dep hadn't found him either funny or cute. I wondered who had blown the whistle and if the puppy had returned to his owner.

Samantha's smile was almost motherly. "I love the way puppies run."

I agreed. "There's a weird sort of grace in their roly-poly clumsiness."

Misty was still smiling, too. "They look completely happy and free."

Dep settled back into my lap, but she continued watching where we'd last seen the puppy as if she expected him to return and only she could fend him off. "Free," I said a little sadly. "I wish Nina was free and the actual killer wasn't."

Misty seemed to choose her words carefully. "We always hope we catch the right person. Sometimes, we don't, though. And I agree with you that Nina is an unlikely killer. Maybe that's because I hate to believe that you've had one working with you at Deputy Donut, and maybe it's because, as you've pointed out, she seems too nice. But murderers can fool people, and often do."

I went over all the reasons I believed that Nina had been the target of the murderer. Samantha and Dep both seemed to be catnapping.

Misty agreed with me. "Those are all valid. I've seen photos of Zippy Melwyn when she was alive and not wearing mime makeup. She and Nina could have been sisters."

"Is Nina still denying that they're distant cousins?"

"Yes, but Kim Gartborg and Brent don't believe her. They're

sure that Nina is the person who reported her locket stolen when she was eight."

"Do they know Nina's real name yet?"

"I think so, but they haven't made it public. I don't know what it is."

I suggested, "Maybe they have to keep it secret to protect her."

"I suspect it's something like that."

"Did they search her phone yet?"

"She's had it for a couple of years and has made hardly any calls."

"Did she ever call or get a call from Zippy?"

"Not on that phone. We have no evidence of their ever having been in touch except for the anecdote from the resort owner where they attended that family reunion when Nina was eight. The call history shows that you called her at 9:43 the night of Friday the thirteenth, and that the call wasn't answered, but your message was picked up at nine minutes after ten."

"Which is what Nina and I told Brent."

"Yes." Misty tilted her head. "If Nina didn't kill Zippy, who do you think did?" Because of Misty's sunglasses, I couldn't see her eyes. I saw only my reflection.

Smoothing my rowdy curls, I repeated the clues I'd found pointing to the magician, also known as Marv the Marvelous and Marvin Oarhill.

Misty took off her sunglasses and pointed them toward me. "He couldn't have done it."

I spluttered, "But a man fitting his description was sitting in the pub watching Nina's apartment all afternoon and evening until shortly before I found Zippy."

"If Buddy told the truth the second time that Brent and Kim interviewed him, a man was in Suds for Buds watching all afternoon and evening, but the man wasn't Oarhill."

Chapter 26

✻

I argued, "How can the man not be Marvin Oarhill? Both Kassandra Pyerson and Buddy described him." I sat up straighter. "Brent has a video showing him leaving the pub and starting across the street toward Nina's apartment at about the right time."

"Oarhill couldn't have been there then." Not wanting to believe her, I gave my head a little shake, but Misty went on. "A witness saw Oarhill removing the magnetic signs from his van doors right after he stole money from your cash drawer. Then he drove out of the carnival parking lot."

I raised my index finger in an *aha!* gesture.

"But he couldn't have spent the afternoon and the evening in Suds for Buds. New evidence came in this morning. An hour after Oarhill stole from you, he used his credit card to buy gas fifty miles from Fallingbrook."

"He could have turned around and driven back those fifty miles."

"Granted, but he was pulled over for a burned-out head-light at ten that evening in Des Moines. Those officers didn't know he was wanted for anything else, so they let him go."

"Then he attacked Zippy before he left Fallingbrook." Even before Misty gave me her you've-got-to-be-kidding look, I saw the error in my logic and admitted, "Zippy was seen in Nina's neighborhood around the time that Oarhill was stopped in Des Moines."

"Right. He was caught this morning in Minneapolis and charged."

"Minneapolis, and he'd been in Des Moines. Does that mean he was coming back here?"

"He claimed he was on his way to Duluth."

I let sarcasm creep into my voice. "That's where he was pickpocketing before he came to Fallingbrook. They must have lots of fairs in Duluth."

"It's possible."

"What did they charge him with?"

"Something to do with his fraudulent websites and his activities as a pickpocket. And it's largely due to you that he was stopped this morning. You're the one who photographed his license plate, and you're also the one who confirmed that the magician who stole from you was Marvin Oarhill."

"Is he in jail?"

"He was released on bail. They don't consider him a danger to society."

I continued my stubborn arguments. "Someone is, especially to Nina if she's released, which she should be." I was in a bikini, wrapped in a towel, sitting on a beach with my cat on my lap, but I had a police officer to talk to, and I wasn't about to give up my attempts to figure out who had killed Zippy. I argued, "It seems like too much of a coincidence that a man was looking out toward Nina's street door all afternoon and evening, and then left shortly before Zippy was killed."

"Coincidences happen," Misty said.

"There was another man, Rodeo Rod, at the carnival who I believe drives a windowless van. I told Brent about him, and that when I was walking home yesterday, he might have been trying to follow me. Maybe he was heading to wherever he thought Nina might go if she was freed, like her apartment or my house."

Samantha wasn't sleeping, after all. She suggested, "Maybe he was looking for you because he likes you."

I admitted, "He was a little flirtatious, but at first, at least, he seemed more interested in Nina than in me. And I still wear my wedding ring."

Samantha touched the engagement ring on her finger. "That doesn't stop everyone."

Misty asked me, "Do you know of any reason why this rodeo performer might have wanted to kill Zippy?"

"No, but he was at the carnival the same time she was." I knew it sounded childish and could not have been considered as evidence in a murder.

Misty put her sunglasses on top of her head. "So were you."

I fidgeted with the corner of my towel. "So were a lot of people. Marsha Fitchelder, the carnival organizer, didn't like Nina, plus she had an argument with Zippy about where Zippy should park her car. Zippy used her miming talents to mock Marsha, which obviously annoyed Marsha. Later, Zippy refused to move her car, and Marsha called you guys to tow it. The responding officers refused. I'm sure that made Marsha even angrier. She visited Deputy Donut this afternoon." I recited her rhyming warning.

Misty grinned. Samantha laughed.

I added, "After Marsha left Deputy Donut, Tom and I discussed her so-called alibis. Marsha claimed she'd been at the carnival all day and evening on Friday. Nina and I didn't see her at the carnival when we left shortly after nine. Tom was there from about ten until about quarter to eleven Friday night. He didn't see Marsha at all during that time although she'd been around the night before when they were setting up."

Misty tapped her neatly trimmed fingernails against the wooden arm of her chair. "We don't have anyone who has reported seeing her at the carnival between about nine and eleven fifteen on the thirteenth. Someone saw her arrive at the carnival in her car around midnight, however."

"That explains why she's warning me about talking to the police about her supposed alibis. She doesn't have any for when Zippy was probably killed. And she's big and muscular. She could subdue just about anyone, even Zippy, who didn't weigh much considering her height. But if the man who was watching Nina's apartment didn't murder Zippy, there's another suspect besides Marsha who is more likely than Rodeo Rod."

"Who?"

"Kassandra Pyerson, the woman who told me about the man in Suds for Buds. She could have described him to cover the fact that she left Suds for Buds shortly before Zippy was attacked. She told me that she returned to work that night after a break, but Buddy said she never came back. Also, I caught her peering into our donut car at the carnival. Her hand was on the handle of the driver's door. I called to her, but she skulked away."

"Skulked," Samantha repeated. "I love that word, Emily."

"It fits," I said. "And she did something else that makes me suspect her." I described the two different addresses, one that was actually Zippy's address in Lapeer, Michigan, and one that didn't exist in Fallingbrook.

Misty let out a big sigh. "I heard about that, and you know I would love it if Nina proved to be innocent. Brent and Kim have collected evidence that points to Nina, except for one little chink in the case."

If I hadn't been holding a sleeping cat in my lap, I might have jumped out of my chair. "What?"

"I'm probably not supposed to tell you this, but Zippy Melwyn and Kassandra Pyerson were roommates in that Lapeer apartment. They signed a lease together."

I crowed, "I knew it!" Dep stood, stretched, gave me a disgruntled but sleepy look, turned around, and settled in my lap again. For Samantha's benefit, I described the torn letter I'd found in my car.

Misty smiled at Dep. "Kim and Brent agree with you that the handwriting on that fragment of a letter could be Kassandra's, but they're calling in a handwriting expert."

I couldn't help giving Misty a smug look. "Brent told me that Zippy's apartment key looked new. If she changed the locks and kicked Kassandra out, Kassandra had a grudge. And Kassandra showed Summer Peabody-Smith and me photos of paintings that she said were hers. Arthur C. Arthurs said that Zippy had been in contact with him about those same paintings. Zippy had said that she, Zippy, painted them. Brent told me that Zippy signed all of the paintings in the apartment that Zippy and Kassandra once shared. Maybe Kassandra wants to be known as an artist and killed Zippy to take over her identity." Although the evening was still warm, I shivered.

Samantha leaned forward and brushed sand off one shin. "Wouldn't that be killing the goose that laid the golden egg?"

I frowned out at the lake, blue with silvery sparkles. "Maybe she thought she could paint as well as Zippy did, and the gallery wouldn't notice."

Misty demanded, "How could she pass the paintings off as hers if Zippy already showed them to Mr. Arthurs?"

I guessed, "Kassandra must not have known that Zippy had been trying to find a gallery. Kassandra could have planned to paint her signature over Zippy's, but Zippy changed their apartment lock. Kassandra had a motive. She had the opportunity. And after she followed Zippy into Nina's loft, she conveniently found the means. Kassandra is small, but she could have knocked over the ladder while Zippy was on it. Zippy's wrists and ankle broke when she fell. After that, Kassandra might not have had much trouble dragging her out of sight of the door, restraining her, and putting the bucket of confectioners' sugar over her head. But I'm afraid that Detective Gartborg can't be bothered considering anyone besides Nina."

Misty was silent for a moment. "She can, actually. I believe she and Brent want to talk to Kassandra Pyerson again, but . . . and I probably shouldn't tell you this, either. They don't know where she is."

I said, "I know she didn't show up at The Craft Croft today. Do you mean that Kassandra Pyerson is officially missing?"

"I'm not sure I'd word it that way. Brent doesn't know where she is."

I crossed my arms. "She killed Zippy, and she's hiding from the police."

Misty took her sunglasses off the top of her head and ran fingers through her long blond hair as if to hurry its drying. "Or she herself has met with foul play. I'm not saying that's what happened, but we have to be open to all possibilities."

I retorted, "We know that Nina didn't hurt Kassandra. Nina's been incarcerated since before I last saw Kassandra."

Misty agreed and added, "That doesn't mean that Nina didn't kill Zippy. And just because we don't know where Kassandra is doesn't mean that anything has happened to her."

"Well," I grumbled, "since I know that Nina didn't kill Zippy and you're saying that Marvin Oarhill didn't, either, that leaves Rodeo Rod, Marsha Fitchelder, and Kassandra Pyerson, and I'm betting it has to be Kassandra. Rodeo Rod could be merely flirtatious, and Marsha is caustic and annoying, but Kassandra's the one with the strongest motive. She was nearby shortly before Zippy was attacked, and she appears to have run away."

"Maybe the other two have run away by now, too." Although Misty's tone was gentle, I thought I heard sympathy in it. "Brent will look into all of it."

Samantha sat up as straight as she could in the relaxing Adirondack chair. "You'll have to talk to him again, Emily, and convince him to look further into this Kassandra person."

"I'm not good at convincing him of anything."

"Not police work," Misty said, "but you could wrap him around your little finger if you wanted to."

It must have been my evening to be stubborn. "Maybe I don't want to. Brent and I are not like Samantha and Hooligan."

Looking at me, Samantha tilted her head. "Alec's been gone a long time, Emily. Do you want to be alone for the rest of your life?"

"Yes." Flustered, I admitted, "I don't know. I don't want to be disloyal to his memory."

Misty threw me a sympathetic glance. "I can imagine what Alec would say about your being loyal to his memory and turning into a dried-up old prune."

I repeated in mock horror, "Old prune!" My outburst caused Dep to leap off my lap into the sand. I managed to hang on to her leash.

Samantha eased out of her chair. "Alec would say he wanted you to be happy."

I stood, too. "He did say that."

Samantha picked up her water bottle. "It wouldn't have to be Brent, but you two always seem to have such fun to-gether—"

I flung my towel over one shoulder. "Not when we're ar-guing about his cases."

Misty accused, "Ha. You like doing that. And he does, too. You should see his face when he has to go talk to you. He looks happy and eager."

I argued, "That was probably before Kim Gartborg came into his life."

Misty pointed her water bottle at me. "And after, too. She's not right for him. The least you can do for Alec's best friend is save him from Detective Kimberly Gartborg."

Samantha shot me a mischievous grin. "Save him from her, and then dump him if you have to." She grabbed her towel. "We should probably get ready for dinner."

Misty sprang to her feet without touching the chair's armrests with her hands. "Thanks for finding us a cottage with a bathroom for each of us, Samantha. We can get ready quickly."

"You two always can," I said.

Misty twisted her hair into a ponytail. "Only when we're heading to work. Getting ready for dinner in a restaurant at a resort might take more time. And we don't have wash-and-wear curls like you do, Emily. We have only about forty-five minutes until it's time to walk over to the restaurant."

We gathered the rest of our things and returned to our cottage. I carefully shut the door to keep Dep inside.

The shower in my bathroom was one of those easy-to-adjust ones that quickly reached and maintained a comfy temperature. Shutting it off, I heard voices and footsteps as if Misty and Samantha were in the main room. A door slammed, shaking the cottage. Car doors closed, engines started, tires rolled on gravel, and then everything was quiet.

Chapter 27

✺

Wondering if it was later than I thought, I wrapped my towel around myself and padded out into the main room.

A note was propped against the jar of wildflowers on the table runner.

Called to a collision between here and Fallingbrook. Go to dinner without us. We'll join you as soon as we can. Misty

Muttering, I set the note on the table. Misty and Samantha were on call only until ten, and then Misty had the next two days off. Samantha and Hooligan would be able to enjoy two whole weeks away from work. They loved their professions and handled it all with grace, and I was probably more upset than Samantha and Misty were about their being called out during what was supposed to be our relaxing girls' night out. They always rushed off to do whatever they could. Alec had been the same way. Scott, Hooligan, and Brent were, too. They served people in need of help.

I served people in need of donuts, coffee, and tea. "But that's not bad, right?" I asked Dep.

She didn't answer or move from her perch on the arm of the love seat.

I returned to my room and put on a yellow sundress sprinkled with tiny blue flowers and strapped on a pair of pretty flat-heeled sandals.

In the main room, Dep hadn't moved. I told her, "You and I might as well explore the resort during the fifteen minutes before I need to claim our table in the restaurant." She paid me no attention. I picked up her harness. She leaped off the love seat and rubbed against my ankles. I leashed her, followed her out onto the porch, and locked the door.

I wasn't keen on collecting sand in my open shoes, so we walked around to the back of the cabin. My car was the only one there. At the end of the driveway, Dep and I turned left, toward the part of the resort I hadn't driven through on my way to the cabin. Tall pines, oaks, and maples shaded the gravel road. Oak leaves pattered in that recognizable pre-autumn, slightly leathery sound. My sandals hardly made any noise. Dep walked silently.

Farther on, newer cabins were close to the lane winding through the woods and not as secluded as in the older section of the resort. The cabins on the lake side of the road were almost on the shore and faced the lake. The cabins across the road faced the road and the backs of the shore-front cabins. Like Birch, they were constructed of large logs with their cut ends painted deep green. The porches I could see were broad, with homey rocking chairs beside tables where canning jars held fresh bouquets.

This time, I recognized the jingling rapidly approaching from behind, now accompanied by the thumping of teacup-sized paws. I turned around. Tongue hanging from his grinning mouth, the big fluffy puppy galloped toward us. He must have forgotten that Dep did not want to join his games.

She reminded him.

He leaped straight up, landed on all four of those fuzzy paws, and veered toward the porch of the nearest cottage. At the last second, he avoided a bulging black briefcase on the bottom step by scrambling up to the second step. His back legs tangled with each other and knocked the briefcase down. It fell on its side on the ground. The zipper across its top wasn't zipped. Papers spilled out.

One of the sheets of paper fluttered in the puppy's mini-whirlwind. The puppy regained his footing, whipped around, grabbed that sheet of paper in his mouth, and dashed toward us as if presenting Dep with a treasure that would make her want to play with him. The paper hanging from his mouth appeared to be the printout of a family tree. Reading upside down, I made out the name Seaster at the top of the page. I'd heard of only one Seaster family, the founders and owners of Seaster Enterprises.

I didn't have a chance to find out if this was the same family.

Dep again reminded the big fluffy puppy that he was not allowed near her.

The puppy spun around. Waving his banner of a tail and proudly shaking the piece of paper, he bounded away.

Somewhere behind us, a whistle blew. With his plunder in his mouth, the puppy galumphed away from us and farther from the whistle.

Still enormous, Dep shook one paw as if to show off her dainty grace and remind me that when she knocked things off steps or shelves, it was never an accident.

No one came out of the cottage.

Feeling at least partially responsible for the mess and afraid that the puppy would return to complete his job, whatever it was, I picked up my temporarily supersized cat and plunked her down next to the briefcase.

I told myself that lots of briefcases resembled the one that Marvin Oarhill had carried at the carnival.

I set the briefcase on the step and shoved papers into it. How had they all originally fit?

Inside the cottage, a man spoke. I jumped almost as high

as the puppy had when he encountered the force of Dep's disdain. "Sweetheart," the man cooed. "I can't wait to get home to you so we can go on with the plans for our wedding."

Obviously, he wasn't talking to me, and Sweetheart wasn't in the cabin with him. He must have been on a phone. I ducked my head and picked up another piece of paper.

"This business trip has lasted longer than I expected." His voice was so syrupy that I wouldn't have been surprised if Sweetheart told him not to return unless he learned to talk like a normal person. However, he went on in the same coaxing voice, "I've had to recycle some of my dirty clothes."

Ewwww.

Sweetheart didn't have time to reply. He informed her in more of those sugary tones, "But your ironing is so perfect that my shirts aren't very wrinkled."

Double ewwww.

I almost expected that when she heard that, his fiancée would dump him in the middle of their conversation, and he would come storming out of his cottage to confront the woman stuffing papers back into his briefcase. He didn't. He added, "I changed hotels. Out here in the wilderness, hotels don't launder shirts." His tone was still fake-romantic, but it was also patronizing. And possibly familiar? I couldn't connect it to anyone.

I glanced down at the sheet of paper in my hand. It was a list of addresses. I did a double take and focused.

Nina's address was the first one.

Deputy Donut was next.

The Craft Croft was the third.

The fourth one was for the Arthur C. Arthurs Gallery in Madison.

Those addresses were all typed. Below them, someone had scrawled my home address, which just happened to be the address that Nina and I had been approaching when the gray car nearly hit us.

As if flames were engulfing the paper, I shoved it into the briefcase.

I grabbed Dep, held her against me, and hurried off in the direction the puppy had gone.

A black windowless van was parked on the far side of the cabin, between it and the next one.

I didn't remember Marvin Oarhill's license number, but I was almost certain that this one was different, which wasn't too surprising. Brent had told me that Oarhill had varied his vehicle descriptions and license numbers when he registered at carnivals. Hurrying to get myself and Dep out of sight, I didn't take a good look at the number.

Misty had told me that Marvin Oarhill had been released, but she hadn't said when. If it had been before four that afternoon, he could have already driven, with the black briefcase he'd carried at the Faker's Dozen Carnival, to Lake Cares Away.

I had never heard Oarhill's voice. He had removed four-leaf clovers from people's ears and had stolen cash from our till, but he'd done it all as silently as Zippy Melwyn had performed her miming acts.

I had definitely heard Rodeo Rod's voice, both at the carnival and in Deputy Donut. According to Jocelyn, he also drove a van. Could Rod be the man on the phone? I chided myself for not checking the back of the van for a white silhouette of a galloping horse. Maybe Rod's drawl was only for a folksy effect, and he tried for a different—and to me, yucky—effect when talking to his fiancée.

Behind us, that whistle blew again. I walked faster. Before the puppy returned to his owner, I was going to gently remind him to give me the piece of paper, and then . . . well, I probably wouldn't return it. I suspected I was going to fold it and keep it hidden in my palm until I was back in our cottage and could read it in privacy. Maybe I could figure out possible connections between the man in the cabin and Nina, our donut shop, Arthur C. Arthurs, The Craft Croft, and me.

The road through the resort twisted. I hoped it would double back past another row of cabins, but it ended in a turnaround. Maybe the puppy had run back to its owner through the woods or along the beach. Even if he hadn't, by now the family tree I'd hoped to study was probably a soggy, chewed-up, unreadable mess. I didn't have time to continue searching for the puppy. I needed to claim our table at the restaurant.

Dep and I started back toward our cabin. Between other cabins, I caught glimpses of the lake. It now reflected the brilliant orange sunset.

The black van hadn't moved. Behind it, a pine branch hid where the right rear window would be if it had rear windows, and I couldn't tell if the galloping horse was there. The left side was plain black. Glancing at the license plate, I noticed a trailer hitch. I didn't remember seeing one on Oarhill's van or in the picture I'd taken of his rear license plate.

I walked faster.

The overfilled briefcase was still upright on the cottage's bottom step. I was about to avert my face in hopes of not being recognized despite the leashed cat prancing ahead of me when I heard the door of the next cottage open.

I couldn't help looking toward it.

With a swish of a long purple skirt, Kassandra Pyerson glanced toward me and then turned on the heels of her clunky black boots, slipped inside, and closed the door. I heard it lock.

My first thought was relief that Kassandra seemed to be okay. My second thought was that she was apparently hiding, and I was one of the people she feared might spot her. Was she afraid of being caught by a murderer, or was she a murderer, afraid of being seen and reported to the police?

Was it a coincidence that she was staying in the cottage

next to the one where the man had been sweet-talking a woman who ironed so well that wrinkles didn't show on the shirts he was forced to wear more than once between washings?

A gray sedan was tucked between the two cottages, so far up the driveway that I didn't see it until one of the day's last sunbeams angled between trees and spotlit it. I couldn't tell if that driveway belonged to the cottage where Kassandra was staying or the one where the dirty-shirt man was staying.

Marvin Oarhill had carried a black briefcase and had driven a black windowless van. Rod had driven a black windowless van. I had never seen Rod carrying a briefcase, but the van and the briefcase probably belonged to one of those two men.

That meant that the gray sedan probably belonged to Kassandra. The trunk was open, and a suitcase was inside it. The license number was shining in that beam of sunlight. It was a Wisconsin plate and ended in the numbers that Nina and I had remembered from the car that had almost hit her. I'd seen the two fives. Nina had seen one of the fives and a four. Leaf shadows blotted out the sunbeam, leaving the car in the gloom of the forest again.

Chapter 28

On Saturday, had Kassandra nearly rammed that car into Nina? And had Kassandra done it on purpose because she had mistakenly attacked Zippy when she'd meant to kill Nina? And why would she have wanted to kill Nina? Not to create a job vacancy, surely, and she'd told me about the man in Suds for Buds supposedly to help me prove Nina's innocence. But as Misty had said, it could have been a coincidence that the man left Suds for Buds and headed across the street toward Nina's apartment around the time that Zippy was attacked.

Kassandra had also been in the vicinity at the time.

I needed to rush away from Kassandra's cabin, and not at the pace that Dep might choose. I swept her up into my arms. I desperately wanted to run but didn't want to call more attention to myself in case Kassandra was watching me from inside.

She and the man who had to recycle his dirty shirts were staying in adjacent cabins. Did they know each other? Had they been working together to harm Nina? Was either one of them a threat to the other? And who was the dirty-shirt man—Marvin Oarhill, who had me to thank for his recent arrest, or Rodeo Rod?

Any of them could have been a threat to me. Carrying my

warm and wriggling kitty, I rounded a curve and ducked between two of the shorefront cabins. I immediately regretted my decision. There was no packed-down pathway in front of these cabins, and the soft sand slowed me. Besides, I was making footprints. If Rod, Marvin Oarhill, or Kassandra wanted to follow me, I had just made it easier.

Lights were on inside the first two cabins I passed, and people were laughing, talking, and clinking glassware. At the third cabin, a woman was sitting on the front porch in the sunset's glow. She called out, "Are you okay, honey?"

I squeaked out, "Yes."

"Is that a cat you're carrying?"

"Yes."

"Is the cat okay?"

"She's fine. I like hugging her."

The woman laughed softly. "I can understand that."

I hurried past the next cabin and plowed between young spruces to the driveway beside it. I couldn't hear anyone on the road, either on foot or in a vehicle.

Dep squirmed. I was afraid she was about to start yowling.

"Just a few more minutes," I whispered before I eased out onto the shoulder of the road. Jogging along the weedy and pebbly shoulder in sandals wasn't easy, but it was better than trying to move quickly in soft sand.

Dep's complaints about being held tightly and jounced became louder. I kept running. Finally, I saw the driveway for Birch cabin. My breath in jagged gasps, I ran to my car. I stopped and turned around. The driveway wasn't completely straight, and from the back of my car, I could see only a tiny bit of the road.

Struggling to keep Dep from jumping out of my arms, I hurried to the front of Birch cabin, unlocked the door, and took Dep inside. As soon as I unlatched her harness, she jumped up to the arm of the love seat, apparently ready to resume her self-appointed job of staring at the view beyond that side of the cottage. Dusk crept from the woods toward the still-pale lake.

Shivering, I threw a cornflower-blue cardigan over my dress, and then I speed-dialed Brent's personal number.

He answered right away.

I blurted, "Kassandra Pyerson is here, at the Cares Away Resort." I hadn't noticed a name on the cottage where I'd seen her, so I described how to find it. "A gray car is between her cabin and the next one. Based on some of the numbers on its license plate, I think it's the car that almost hit Nina. The trunk was open as if Kassandra has just arrived and is unpacking or she's about to leave."

"It's a strange time of evening for someone to check out."

"Not if she's hiding from someone and about to change locations. Which she might be doing. I think that Marvin Oarhill or Rodeo Rod is staying in the cabin next to hers. Could Oarhill have gotten back here by now?"

He didn't ask how I knew of Oarhill's whereabouts. He acknowledged, "He could have." Brent sounded like he was talking through clenched teeth.

"A van and a briefcase like his are beside the cabin next to Kassandra's. The van has a different license plate than the one I photographed at the carnival."

"What is the number?"

"Sorry, I didn't have a good look, but there was an S or a five and an F. Could that be Rodeo Rod's license number?"

"I'll check with the rodeo organizers again. They were going to try to dig up his real name."

Afraid that Brent might disconnect before I told him everything I should, I spoke quickly. "I heard the man in the cottage between the gray car and the black van tell someone, over the phone, I guess, that he was about to be home from what he called a 'business trip.' I didn't see the man I heard talking, so I could be wrong about him being either Marvin Oarhill or Rodeo Rod."

"I don't know that any of the people you mentioned could be a danger to you, but I'm concerned about the coincidence of them being where you are."

"It might not be a coincidence." I described the list of addresses and told him how I'd gotten hold of it. "I also caught a glimpse of the name at the top of a family tree that had also been in the briefcase. It was Seaster, as in Seaster Enterprises."

He repeated, "Someone has been carrying your address around." His voice became urgent. "Where exactly at Cares Away are you, Em?"

"I'm in the cabin I'm sharing with Misty and Samantha. It's called Birch. Misty and Samantha were called away to a collision. We have dinner reservations, so I'm heading for the restaurant."

"Driving? The person who added your address to that list has probably seen your car, and your car is recognizable, especially if your kayak is still on it."

"It is, but my car is mostly hidden from the road, so I think it should stay where it is. The restaurant is a short walk, and I won't have to pass the cabins where those three people might be staying. I think the dirty-shirt man might have been packing to leave, also, or his briefcase wouldn't have been on the porch step. Maybe he's already left. I'll feel safer in the restaurant among other people than I'd feel alone in this cabin."

"Okay, but take care, and text me when you get to the restaurant. You caught me just in time. I have to attend the collision where Samantha and Misty are. There were serious injuries. I need to work on the collision reconstruction to determine what happened and if anyone should be charged. Then I'll come down there and find Kassandra Pyerson. I'll have a talk with her about where she's been and why she took off from her job at The Craft Croft and doesn't answer her phone. I'll have a talk with the man in the cabin next to

Kassandra's, too. I might see you in a while, but Misty will probably get there before I do."

"If we've already left the restaurant, come to Birch cabin and give Dep a pat."

"I don't want to interrupt your bachelorette party."

"Dep insists. And so do the rest of us."

"Okay." The smile was back in his voice. "See you later."

In case the cabin was too warm for Dep, I raised one of the front windows a few inches and fastened it in place to prevent anyone from opening it farther. I tucked my phone into my cute little yellow purse, told Dep goodbye, went out to the porch, and locked her inside.

I stood still and listened. Dep was quiet. Teenagers swam and shouted in the lake that now resembled rippling liquid copper. Someone played a guitar. A man crooned the sort of ballad my parents liked singing at their campfires.

Although I would have enjoyed hearing more of the music, I walked cautiously down the steps, around to the back of the cottage, and to the end of the driveway. No one was on the road. It was only a few minutes past eight. I hoped the Cares Away restaurant would hold our table.

I was only a little out of breath when I arrived at the restaurant entrance of the lodge. The heavy oak door looked like it belonged to a castle, complete with a high rectangular window protected by wrought iron bars and curlicues. I tugged the door open. Candle-like sconces cast a warm glow on the room's honey-gold oak walls, the spotless rock maple floors, the rustic chairs and love seats, and their dark red leather cushions. Made from peeled and twisty tree branches, no two pieces of furniture were quite the same. Side tables supported by gnarled legs displayed books and magazines. This woodsy resort was for all seasons and weathers. To make everything even more perfect, the food was supposed to be excellent. I couldn't help smiling.

I stood in line behind a gray-haired couple at the hostess's station. The hostess looked past them and told me, "I'll be with you in a moment."

I sent Brent a text that I had arrived at the restaurant.

Brent texted back, asking me to stay where I was and wait for Misty. Which was exactly what I planned to do.

Behind me, the door opened. A shoe squeaked against the polished maple floor.

"Emily?" The man sounded tentative and surprised.

I turned around. The tourist who had asked me out earlier that day was dressed almost like he'd been when I'd first seen him at the Faker's Dozen Carnival, in black slacks and a white shirt. He wasn't wearing a straw hat at this time of night, and his sleeves were rolled up. Alf, that was his name. Alphaeus Chator, Chief Financial Officer of Cornwall Amherst Investments. I immediately wondered if Alf was the man from the cabin where I'd seen a list of addresses connected to Nina.

Maybe I was obsessing too much about it.

First, I'd thought the man talking on the phone in the cabin was Marvin Oarhill, then I'd wondered if he was Rodeo Rod, and now I was trying to fit Alf to the syrupy voice. "Hi, Alf. You've found another of the great sites around Fallingbrook."

He returned my smile. "This restaurant comes highly recommended. So, is this where you're out with your girlfriends tonight?"

"You got it, only—"

The hostess interrupted me, "Do you have reservations?"

I faced her. "Yes, for three of us at eight o'clock, and I'm sorry I'm late. My friends should be along soon."

"Name?" she asked me.

"Samantha Andersen made the reservation."

The hostess gushed, "Samantha! Our soon-to-be-bride!"

The hostess looked past me at Alf. No longer gushing, she asked politely, "How many are in your party, sir?"

"Just me. For dinner."

"We should have a table available in about fifteen minutes if you don't mind waiting. The kitchen closes at nine."

"I'll wait," he promised.

The hostess was a little too enthusiastic about trying to make everyone happy. "If you two are both here for the wedding, maybe you wouldn't mind if your friend"—she nodded at Alf—"sat at the extra place at your table?"

He shook his head. "I'm not here for the wedding."

He was honest about that. Maybe he wasn't the man from the cabin with the briefcase on the porch step. But if he was, it was probably safest to let him sit with me where I could keep an eye on him. If I learned anything connecting him to Zippy's murder, I could tell Misty and Brent when they arrived. I offered, "Why don't you sit with me, anyway? We can continue our discussion about the things you haven't yet seen around Fallingbrook." Great. The next thing I knew, I'd have to rope my parents into helping me give him a tour of Fallingbrook Falls.

Alf was polite. "I don't want to intrude. What about when your friends arrive?"

"They won't mind." I'd have to endure a lot of teasing from them afterward, though. "It would be a shame for you to miss dinner if another table isn't ready in time."

He threw me a smile. "Since you insist."

The hostess led us to the only empty table in the room, one almost beside her station, and removed the RESERVED placard. In keeping with the resort's rustic theme, the fumed oak table was not covered, but even without a tablecloth, it was elegant, set with white cloth napkins and sparkling china, cutlery, and glasses. Alf and I sat across from each other and picked up our menus. The candle on the table cast flickering shadows. I hoped the shadows didn't make me look like a monster. Alf looked okay, though, except for one thing made more obvious from the table-height lighting.

When I'd first seen Alf on Friday the thirteenth at the Faker's Dozen Carnival, his white shirt had been freshly and neatly pressed.

Now, it wasn't, and the wrinkles were haphazard, not like the creases in a clean shirt that had been carefully folded and packed in a suitcase.

Chapter 29

❧

Maybe I wasn't obsessing too much. Maybe Alf really was the man I'd heard in the cabin next to Kassandra's.

Even though he was still studying his menu, I didn't want him to look up and recognize the apprehension that had to be dawning on my face. I bent my head toward my menu.

I thought back to my short discussions with Alf. Even when he'd been with Connie, I hadn't heard him lower his voice in the phony sexy way that the man who needed clean shirts had used with his fiancée. But the voice of the man in the cabin had sounded familiar. That voice could have been Alf's.

I didn't think I'd ever seen Alf driving anything, and I didn't know if he'd driven here from wherever he lived or if he'd flown to, say, Duluth and rented a vehicle.

I wanted to haul my phone out of my bag again and tell Brent that I might have identified the dirty-shirt man and that Marvin Oarhill and Rodeo Rod might not be at Cares Away, but I couldn't call Brent if Alf was the dirty-shirt man, and I didn't want Alf to see me texting, either.

"What are you having?" Alf's question from across the table startled me.

I pointed blindly at the menu. "Um. Sherried mushroom

soup to start." I quickly skimmed the list of entrées. "And the spinach and ricotta ravioli looks good."

He set his menu on the table. "Are you a vegetarian?"

"No. Are you?"

"No, but I'll order the same thing. I figure that the people who live in an area know what's best there."

"Donuts," I joked.

The waiter asked what we'd like to drink. Alf ordered a scotch on the rocks. I ordered freshly squeezed lemonade.

"Not a drinker?" he asked.

"Maybe later." Knowing the kitchen was closing at nine, I told the waiter we were ready to order our meals.

Alf chimed in and ordered for both of us. The waiter left. Alf folded his hands on the table in front of him. "I just noticed your wedding ring. Are you and your friends having a bachelorette party, and that's why your husband let you out for the evening?"

Let me out? Alec would have been horrified at the thought of deciding when and where I was allowed to go. For one thing, we'd both worked shifts. "No, he's . . ." I ran the thumb and forefinger of my right hand over the ring. "I'm a widow. This ring is like part of me."

He lowered his head as if examining his clasped hands. "I'm so sorry. I had no idea." He raised his head, looked at me again, and asked, "Are you seeing anyone?"

"Sort of." I pictured Brent. Having a close male friend was often handy. As far as I knew, Brent and I would both be at the wedding and reception on Wednesday. If Alf was still at Cares Away, he might see Brent and me together. I felt warmly proud at the thought of being seen with a man as tall, handsome, and gentle as Brent. I liked being with him. I liked him. I . . . my face heated, and I decided I wasn't going to finish that thought until I was alone and could ponder it. "How about you?" I asked. "Are you married, engaged, seeing anyone?"

"Free as a bird."

Right, I thought, *until you need clean laundry and freshly pressed shirts*. Besides, I'd heard him say that after he returned to this phenomenal ironer, they would continue planning their wedding. Maybe Alf wasn't the dirty-shirt man, but I strongly suspected that he was.

He must have noticed my skepticism and, fortunately, misinterpreted it. "And no, I'm not dating the woman I met at the carnival. She wanted to spend all of her free time showing me around, which was nice of her. I'm sure she'll find a man who doesn't mind being controlled."

This was the man who seemed to think that husbands allowed their wives out. I put on an empathetic face. "I see where that could be a problem."

Alf gave me an admiring look. "It was."

The waiter brought our drinks. Alf and I clinked glasses. "To your friend the bride," he said, "wherever she is."

By the time our soup arrived, I had enjoyed a few sips of delicious lemonade and Alf was not only ready for another scotch, his nose had turned red and his voice had lowered to confiding tones similar to the ones I'd overheard when I was repacking the overflowing briefcase outside his cabin.

If Alf was the dirty-shirt man, he was the man who had been carrying around addresses for Nina's apartment, for where she worked, for where she'd exhibited her paintings in Fallingbrook, for her new gallery, and for where she'd been staying temporarily, which also happened to be my home.

The first four addresses on his list had been typed. My address had been scrawled beneath the others, as if he'd found out where Nina was staying after Zippy's murder, after he'd had the other addresses printed. A logical conclusion could be that Alf had come to Fallingbrook specifically to find Nina and harm her, and if he'd been unsuccessful, he had another plan involving possibly following her to the Arthur C. Arthurs Gallery in Madison.

But after Zippy's name was announced, he'd come up with a third plan, hitting Nina with his car in my neighborhood. The gray car had been as close to Alf's cabin as the van had been. What might he have done to Nina, either inside my home or at Deputy Donut, after he missed her with the car if she hadn't been incarcerated? I felt like my curls were straightening themselves and sticking out all over my head.

The soup was delicious. I should have wanted to stay and enjoy it.

I really wanted to shove my chair back and flee. *Wait for Misty.*

Alf was what my parents would call a male chauvinist. That was annoying, but now I believed he was also a murderer. And a danger to Nina if she was freed.

While I spooned up more soup and tried to make comments that weren't completely inane, I thought about the speckly video Brent had told me about. A man in dark pants and a pale shirt had left the pub and started across the street toward Nina's apartment. Alf was dressed that way now, he had also been dressed that way when I'd seen him on Friday at the Faker's Dozen Carnival, and Buddy and Kassandra had seen him take off the suit jacket he'd worn in Suds for Buds.

I began asking questions that would sound innocent but might cause him to describe the vehicle he'd been driving in and around Fallingbrook. "Do you work at Cornwall Amherst's head office in New York City?"

Beaming, he signaled the waiter for another scotch. "I do."

"How do you like living in New York?"

"It's the only place to live, really, but coming here and meeting people like you is a breath of fresh air."

"Why did you choose northern Wisconsin?"

"A complete change in scenery is invigorating. I heard that it's beautiful." He leaned toward me and brought out his phony sexy tones. "It is."

"Did you drive here?"

He seemed to find my Northwoods naïveté charming, if a little laughable. "I don't own a car. My job comes with a driver, and if I want to go outside the city, I fly."

"Company jet?"

"Only when it's company business."

"Do you bring your driver with you on vacations?" I glanced around as if checking the restaurant for someone in a chauffeur's uniform.

Alf laughed as if I were the cutest little backwoods girl he'd ever met. "I rent a car. I like driving, but at home, I need to spend commuting time working."

"I don't think I've ever met anyone as high in the corporate world as you." It was true, and I had no trouble looking impressed.

He seemed to like it.

The waiter brought Alf's second scotch and took away our empty soup plates. "Your dinners will be out shortly," he told us.

After he left, I gave Alf another admiring look. "You're young to have the position you have. How did you rise so fast in the corporate world?"

A flicker of something like anger crossed his face.

Chapter 30

Why had my question about Alf's rapid rise in his career caused that spark of anger in his eyes?

Maybe I'd only imagined it. When he answered, he sounded proud. "I excelled in school and worked hard all my life." Despite the pride, I heard a note of bitterness in his reply that was as odd as the anger I'd glimpsed.

The waiter set a plate of steaming ravioli in front of me. I thanked him, and he served Alf.

Alf's second scotch was already half gone. He asked for another one and then gestured at his plate and continued his answer to my question. "Most people expect to have everything handed to them on a silver platter, and I was no different from everyone else. Fresh out of college, I applied to Seaster Enterprises."

I'd seen the name Seaster at the top of the family tree that I hadn't been able to rescue from the outsized, fluffy puppy. And had Brent recognized the name when I told him about the family tree I'd glimpsed? Brent had become very serious, but that could have been because of the addresses I'd listed.

Alf leaned forward. "I'm sure you've heard of Seaster Enterprises."

"Hasn't everyone?"

He aimed another approving smile at me. "Yes. Thinking I'd have a better chance of getting the job, I brashly let the interviewer know that I was a direct descendent of the original founder of the entire conglomerate, which is true."

I tried to look suitably impressed. "What happened?" At the rate he was drinking, Alf might tell me his entire life history before the meal ended. Maybe he'd even confess to murder. *Sure*, I thought.

Alf took another sip. "What I didn't know was that the man interviewing me was also a descendent of Zebadiah Seaster."

Zebadiah Seaster. I couldn't remember hearing much about Seaster Enterprises except that it was huge, but the founder's name sounded familiar, as if I'd heard it recently. I didn't think I had, and the puppy had whisked the family tree away too quickly for me to register more than the surname, Seaster. Maybe some part of my brain had caught the full name of Zebadiah Seaster and the rest of my brain hadn't noticed.

Alf looked at me over the rim of his glass. "If the receptionist had told me what my interviewer's last name was, I might have been cautious. I had no idea that his last name, unlike mine, was Seaster. I'm descended from one of old Zebadiah's daughters, but Nick Seaster was descended from the male line, all the way down. So, you know how they ask where you see yourself twenty years from now?"

I shook my head. Except for summer and part-time jobs when I was a kid, my only job interview had been with 911, and I didn't remember being asked anything like that.

Alf set down his empty glass and picked up his third scotch. "No, I suppose that's the advantage of being a waitress. Good for you."

I tried to appreciate the delicious ravioli. "What did you say when this Seaster guy asked where you saw yourself in twenty years?" The feeling of almost recognizing something about the name Zebadiah Seaster needled at my subconscious.

I didn't remember reading it. I felt like I'd heard it, but not on the news. It was more like someone had said it to me personally. Who?

Alf swirled the amber liquid in his glass. "Remember, I was young. I said I planned to be head of Seaster Enterprises."

Some people telling a story like that on themselves would see the humor and smile. Alf didn't, so I kept a straight face, too. "Did you get the job?"

"No. Nick Seaster obviously felt threatened by the possibility of another direct descendent of old Zebadiah Seaster joining the firm. Soon afterward, I was offered a job at Cornwall Amherst, and there's no looking back, only forward." He set his glass down with a thump, nearly spilling some of the scotch. "And I'm still looking forward. I still intend to head Seaster Enterprises. I have five years to meet that twenty-year goal. Nick Seaster, who is now CEO of Seaster Enterprises, will have to retire one of these days."

"You don't hear the name Zebadiah much."

"He was christened a long time ago, but the family is still fond of old-fashioned names. Look at me. There aren't a lot of Alphaeuses around."

"Alf's a great name, though, and Alphaeus sounds very executive, don't you think?"

He gave me a slightly tipsy smile. "I hope so."

"Be glad they didn't name you Methuselah." Or whatever name was so embarrassing or horrible that Hooligan preferred being called Hooligan. "What are some of the other strange names in your family?"

"Nick's real name is Nicodemus. I don't remember any others at the moment." He looked off into the distance. "Wait, I think there was also a Nehemiah."

Biting into another little pillow of ricotta and spinach goodness, I realized why the name Zebadiah Seaster had sounded familiar.

I had heard Zippy Melwyn say something that I'd decided

was "a die a seized her" or "I die. I seized her." Could she
have been trying to tell me that her attacker was connected to
Zebadiah Seaster? I hadn't made out all of the syllables, but
she could have said something about her attacker being descended from Zebadiah Seaster. Had Alf been bragging about
his ancestors when he attacked her? He seemed proud enough
of his lineage to have done such a thing.

But maybe he'd had another, more sinister reason for mentioning Zebadiah Seaster to her. Zippy's real name was Zipporah. Was she connected to the Seaster family and their
penchant for old-fashioned names? Had Alf intentionally attacked a relative and told his victim about their relationship
while he was trying to kill her?

Nina had told me that the old gentleman whose photo had
been in the locket had been one of Nina's ancestors. Alf
could have intentionally killed a relative, but maybe he
thought she was Nina.

The ravioli that had tasted marvelous only minutes before
was now revolting.

Alf gulped at his scotch and nearly finished it. "It's not just
wishful thinking that I can take over Seaster Enterprises. I'm
the right guy to make the best decisions. Nick Seaster and his
wife are likely to topple their entire empire. They wanted to
pass all of their companies down through the family, but they
disinherited their only child."

"What did he do that got him disinherited?" Maybe he'd
been a murderer.

"She. Their daughter refused to join the family firm, so
they disinherited her."

I pictured Zippy and her career as a mime. Her smile had
been only painted on, but she'd thrown a lot of enthusiasm
into her performances. "Forcing someone to run a company
when they don't want to or don't have enough experience
doesn't make sense."

He fingered his glass. "You understand."

"Not completely. Do you mean they cut her out of their wills entirely?"

"You got it."

"If she doesn't want to work for the family firm, why not simply choose the best person for the job? Cutting her out of their wills seems gothic and extreme."

"That's how they tried to coerce her. They could still change their minds. She might do something that would make them decide she was worthy of inheriting after all."

He was talking about Nick Seaster's daughter as if she were still alive. Zippy must not have been the disinherited daughter. "What kind of thing?"

"Become very successful in another field, perhaps."

"But then for sure she wouldn't want to head the corporation. Being successful in one field doesn't guarantee she'd automatically do well in another, does it?"

"It certainly does not. They probably would let her continue in her chosen field if she became very well-known. She hasn't. She might never. For now, the Seasters are willing their entire fortune to a ranch for rescued horses and dogs. I'm sure their daughter can dispute that when the time comes, if she has a brain in her head. I would."

Zippy and Nina were probably distant cousins, and if the old gentleman in the locket was Zebadiah Seaster, he could have been the ancestor of both women. Which would mean they were both related to the man across the table from me. If Alf disputed a will giving a fortune to a ranch for stray dogs and horses, and if he successfully argued that he was the Seasters' closest living and nonincarcerated relative, he could possibly gain the wealth he needed to increase the earnings of Seaster Enterprises. And his own net worth, too, no doubt.

Alf didn't seem to notice that I was lost in conjectures about him and his possible motives for killing someone he had believed was Nina, or for killing Zippy in Nina's apartment, causing Nina to appear guilty of the murder. He took a deep breath that expanded his chest and made the wrinkles in his shirt less obvious. "Are you having dessert, Emily?"

My smile had become about as wooden as the table. A large silver platter of dessert samples was perched on a small table beside ours, between us and the door to the restaurant. "The choice looks impossible." That was true. "I probably want one of each." That was not true. I'd lost my appetite. I went on with my lies. "But I'd better not, so I'll go take a good long look at all of them."

"You're the expert on sweets." His smile bordered on lecherous, and I liked him even less than I had moments before, if that was possible. "Let me know which one you choose. I'll have the same thing."

I stood up. I wanted to go past the desserts and out into the night, but that would have been obvious. Besides, I was safest where I was, surrounded by strangers. I stood staring down at the desserts.

It was hard to believe that the disinherited heir could be Nina, but it seemed to fit. It could explain why Nina never talked about her family. She must have been so hurt by her parents' actions that she'd changed her name in a sort of reverse disinheritance. She could have chosen the new last name of Lapeer, consciously or unconsciously, because of the slightly older distant cousin who lived in a city called Lapeer.

Alf could have learned Nina's new surname. She'd once told me she'd tried dating sites. Had he recognized her on one of them? It seemed more likely that he'd found out from her parents or from gossip that she'd chosen art over commerce, and then all he had to do was follow news in the art world. He could have seen her photo on the Arthur C. Arthurs website or in an art magazine. Knowing he was searching for a woman whose first name was Nina, Alf could have recognized a family resemblance between that photo and some of his own relatives.

And then, discovering that the prestigious art connoisseur

Arthur C. Arthurs was promoting Nina, Alf could have feared that she might become so famous that her parents would reinstate her, and he had decided to prevent that. He had taken a couple of weeks for a visit to Fallingbrook, giving him plenty of time to finalize his plans and carry them out. He had brought addresses of where Nina might be. He had watched her front door and had followed the woman he thought was Nina up to Nina's loft, and his attack on the woman had caused her death and Nina's arrest. I was sure he'd have gone to Madison for Nina's opening gala if he hadn't achieved his goal in Fallingbrook.

Eliminating the wrong woman wouldn't have mattered as long as Alf wasn't caught. If Nina was in jail for murder, her parents weren't likely to reinstate her. As a bonus, he'd conveniently knocked Zippy out of the line of heirs. If Nina or another human stood to inherit the Seaster fortune, it would probably be impossible for him to overturn the will. He might have thought he had a chance of taking the money from the horses and dogs. He could have been wrong, but believing that he could successfully contest the Seasters' wills might have emboldened him to try, and he'd started the process by attempting to kill the Seasters' only child, Nina.

Meanwhile, I was annoyed by his cavalier attitude toward animals, and also by his flirtatiousness when I was certain he had a fiancée, one whose laundering skills surpassed mine.

I stared down at the desserts. How had Zippy learned Nina's new surname?

Maybe it had been easy.

Zippy had been in touch with Arthur C. Arthurs. She must have paid attention to his gallery's website. She could have seen the photo of Nina Lapeer of Fallingbrook, Wisconsin. Even if Zippy hadn't recognized Nina as the distant cousin whose locket she'd stolen, she would have noticed how closely Nina resembled her. Zippy had come to Fallingbrook, probably with the hope of destroying Nina's budding art career and giving herself a better chance at an art show of her own at the Arthurs Gallery. She must have thought she was lucky when she discovered Nina's street address on Marsha's clipboard. Then, after we left the sugar behind the passenger seat and hadn't locked the car, Zippy had hidden an encrypted form of the address in Nina's locket and had stolen the sugar and, accidentally or not, left the envelope with the fragment of the letter and the 1890s woman's photo in the car.

Later that night, Zippy had taken the sugar to Nina's apartment and vandalized Nina's painting. And what Zippy might have thought was the best of luck turned out to be the very worst, for her.

Again, Alf's voice startled me. He called from the table, "Which do you think looks best, Emily? Is there anything with chocolate?"

I took a better look. "No chocolate." Ordinarily, I'd have had a terrible time choosing between sugar cookies, lemon meringue pie, pecan pie, raspberry cheesecake, peach tarts, and crème brûlée, and I was having a terrible time at the moment, but for a different reason. I couldn't concentrate on anything besides Alf, what he must have done, and how I could prove it without putting myself in danger.

I returned to the table. "They all look good," I lied, "but I have a slight preference for crème brûlée because I never make it."

"Then that's what we'll have."

"And I think I should come up with a recipe for crème brûlée donuts."

"Definitely."

When the desserts came, along with another scotch for Alf, his eyes were almost as glassy as the crème brûlée's golden melted-sugar coating. Despite my concern for Nina's safety if Alf ever found her and my anxiety about dining with a possible murderer, I managed to eat my dessert.

The waiter approached.

I didn't want Alf to pay for my meal. I put my hand out for the folder containing the bill, and the waiter gave it to me.

Alf protested, "You shouldn't."

I gripped the folder tightly. "It's Wisconsin hospitality. If I'm ever in New York, it'll be your turn." I didn't add that there was exactly zero chance of my contacting him if I ever went to New York.

"Done." He rolled down his sleeves as if he'd accomplished an important job.

White powder spilled out of one of his sleeves.

Chapter 31

It was only a sprinkling, but I had seen the white powder fall directly from Alf's sleeve. Had he recycled the shirt he'd worn when he attacked Zippy on Friday? He'd told his fiancée that he'd lengthened his "business trip" and changed hotels. Was that true? If it was, had he done it to give himself more time and a better chance at killing someone else?

He could have chosen to stay at the Lake Cares Away Resort because Samantha and Hooligan were holding their wedding here. One of their friends and relatives could be next on Alf's list. Me, for instance, if he feared I had recognized him driving the car that almost hit Nina.

I wasn't sure I could breathe.

Kassandra had described the man in the pub as having a roundish or squarish face, a large and reddish nose, and as being old, and I'd pictured Marv the Marvelous. Alf's nose was rather long and had reddened while he'd been drinking scotch. Although I wouldn't say that Alf was old, Kassandra, who seemed to be in her early twenties, might.

Brushing the powder off the table and onto the floor, he gave me an assessing look.

I tried to act like I hadn't noticed the powder, what he'd done to it, or his expression. As innocently as possible, I slid my gaze past him to the window. It was dark outside. Wavy glass distorted the reflection of the homey candlelit restaurant. My face above the cornflower blue sweater looked oddly stretched and pale. And frightened.

My phone rang. I grabbed it out of my purse and hid my fear by looking down at the display.

"It's the other bridesmaid," I told Alf without looking up. "I should answer."

"By all means. Do."

"Hi, Misty," I said. "The restaurant kitchen closes in five minutes. I hope you can make it."

"I'll drive fast."

I tried to put a little doubt into "answering" a question she hadn't asked. "Sure, it's okay if you bring Brent."

As always, Misty understood my ploy. She asked quietly, "Do you need him for official reasons?"

"Yes. You, too!" I threw about a ton of enthusiasm into my answer.

"We'll be right there." She stated each word firmly.

"Great." She had disconnected.

I looked across the table at Alf. He was frowning.

I gave him my best smile. "They might make it before the restaurant closes."

"Who's Brent?"

I twirled my wedding ring around my finger. "The guy I'm seeing. She said he hasn't eaten yet, either."

"You're letting him crash your bachelorette party?"

That was rich, coming from someone I'd invited to share part of our evening with us. "Only for dinner." Anyone who knew me well would be able to tell that my smile was false. "I'll wait here for them and try to keep the kitchen open a little longer."

"Okay. See you later." He stood. He probably didn't realize that white powder dotted his black trousers, and I wasn't about to tell him. He patted my shoulder as he passed. I tried not to shrink away.

Again, I heard a shoe squeak against the hard maple floor. This time I was sure it was his shoe. The front door opened and closed.

My knuckles were white. I loosened my grip on my phone and called Misty back. "Bring Brent and drive fast. You're not looking for Marvin Oarhill, Rodeo Rod, or Kassandra Pyerson. I believe that another distant cousin of Zippy's, Alphaeus Chator, killed her, and is probably driving the gray car I told Brent about. I suspect he's about to leave Cares Away."

Her answer was terse. "I'll pass that along."

We disconnected, and I searched the internet for images of Zebadiah Seaster. I found one that was identical to the photo in Nina's locket. As I'd guessed, Zebadiah's wife was the Victorian lady in the black dress in the photo that undoubtedly fit into the other side of the locket.

I typed Nicodemus Seaster into a search engine and found him mentioned in an obituary for his father, Nehemiah Seaster. In addition to his son, Nehemiah had been survived by his daughter-in-law Jane Ellen Seaster, and his granddaughter Nina Seaster.

The hostess came to my table. "Is Samantha still coming?"

"She and the other bridesmaid will be here soon." I didn't tell the hostess that I had already enlisted the other bridesmaid in police duties. I hoped Misty wouldn't end up pursuing Alf to an airport. I didn't want her missing any more of our girls' night out.

"Our chef thinks Samantha is sweeter and kinder than any other bride he's ever worked with. He loved helping her plan her rehearsal dinner and reception menus. When he found out she might be late, he promised to stay as long as necessary to cook for her and the other person in your party."

"Thank you! And thank the chef for me. Samantha is on her way with the other bridesmaid and a friend of ours."

"Not the guy that just left?"

"A different guy. One who hasn't eaten." I also didn't tell the hostess that Brent might end up missing dinner.

"That's fine. We're happy to feed them all." She pointed back toward the crowded room behind her. "As you can see, lots of people are still here, so several of us will be staying for a while, anyway."

I straightened my napkin and placed it on the table. "Please don't let anyone clear the table or clean the floor near it yet."

"We don't usually sweep around diners, but the table . . ." She tilted her head in question.

"I can't explain, but there's something I want my friends to see before the table's cleared." She was going to think I was really strange.

Apparently she didn't. Nodding vigorously, she smiled. "We get lots of bachelorette parties with all sorts of games and pranks. We'll do whatever we can to help Samantha live happily ever after!"

She went off toward the kitchen. I put my phone in my bag, left my bag on the table, and walked toward the front door.

Two black marks marred the rock maple floor. They were about where I'd heard Alf's shoes squeak, once when he was arriving, and the second time when he was leaving.

I bent down for a closer look. Only a forensic investigator would be certain, but I thought that both scuff marks resembled the one near the base of the ladder Zippy must have been on when she fell.

I stood up and glanced warily toward the door.

Usually, when I'm afraid someone might have been watching me do something I don't want to be seen doing, no one's there.

This time, through the door's high window with its wrought iron curlicues and bars, I saw the top half of Alf's face.

He was staring straight at me.

Pretending I hadn't noticed, I turned and headed toward the table I'd vacated.

I heard the door open.

I didn't look back. A shoe squeaked against the floor, and then it seemed that he stopped walking. Judging by the sounds he made, he was brushing at the floor with the sole of his shoe as if he could wipe off the scuff marks I'd examined.

I didn't look, even when I heard footsteps coming closer to where I'd suddenly halted as if frozen beside the platter of desserts.

"Did you lose something, Emily?" His voice was pitched low, his mouth almost against my ear.

I stood still, blocking him from getting past me and perhaps cleaning the remnants of sugar off the table and the floor. I repeated inanely, "Lose something?" I stared at my bag and the napkin I'd left on our table.

"Why were you bending over and looking at the floor?"

Quickly, I made up a likely story. "I thought I kicked something, and I checked to see if it might be someone's earring, but all I saw was a piece of . . . I think it was a nut or a crumb." I still didn't meet his gaze.

"The moon's up. Come for a walk on the beach with me."

The moon had been up for hours. "I promised my friends I'd wait here."

"You'll be nearby. You'll hear their cars arrive. Besides, you've already eaten and the kitchen's closing."

"The kitchen is staying open for my friends."

"Why are you lying?"

Finally, I turned to look him in the eye. "I'm not. After you left, the hostess came and told me they'd wait. They like Samantha. The bride."

"Come with me." His cajoling tone sent shivers up my spine.

"I can't."

He gripped my arm just above the elbow. "You can, and you are." He squeezed so hard he was pinching a nerve.

Chapter 32

I didn't want to disturb the other diners or the staff. I kept my voice as quiet as Alf's. "Ouch. Let me go."

He repeated, "You're coming with me." He pulled at my arm.

Locking my knees, I resisted, but he was bigger and probably stronger. The rubbery black soles of his shoes had good treads. The soles of my sandals were flat leather. As if I were wearing skis, I slid unwillingly behind him.

It was time to stop trying not to make a scene. I yelled, "Let me go!"

Diners and waitstaff turned their heads toward me. With my free hand, I grabbed the nearest thing, the platter of desserts.

It was heavy. I couldn't hang on to it with only one hand. It tipped. The sample desserts started sliding downward. I tightened my grasp and hurled the entire thing at Alf. It slammed into his upper chest.

He lost his grip on me and fell flat on his back on the floor. The platter landed upside down on his face.

People ran toward us. Hoping for help, I turned toward them.

Two elderly men grabbed my arms.

Their female companions arrived only seconds later. "Why

are you holding her?" one of the women demanded. "That man had his hand on her."

The other woman agreed.

The two men didn't let go of me. One insisted, "She attacked him. See? She's standing up and he's . . ."

The hostess and a couple of waiters knelt beside Alf. The hostess lifted the tray. Alf's face was covered with meringue, lemon and pecan pie filling, crème brûlée, and cheesecake, complete with gobs of bright red cherry topping.

I wanted to giggle about giving Alf everything on a silver platter, but I managed to restrain myself. "Serves him right," I muttered.

The men tightened their hands around my arms.

The restaurant staff swabbed some of the goo off Alf's face. As soon as his eyes were uncovered, he glared at me.

One of the men holding me announced, "You assaulted that man. I'm placing you under citizen's arrest."

One of the women snapped, "That's ridiculous. No man should be able to force his date out of a restaurant if she doesn't want to go."

The other woman, however, pointed out, "She ruined a lot of perfectly good desserts."

The two men's grasp became painful. Apparently, the loss of baked goods was enough to turn the tide against me.

The restaurant staff helped Alf to his feet.

"Let's all wait here calmly," I suggested. "The police are on their way."

The woman who had complained about the ruined desserts ordered, "Don't clean anything up yet. It's evidence against her."

I'd definitely lost her support, but I agreed. "Right. Don't change anything." Hoping the hostess would fulfill her promise of not cleaning the table and the floor around it until after my friends arrived, I sent her a pleading look. She smiled and nodded as if all of this was bachelorette party fun.

Alf leaped to his feet, dashed to the door, shoved it open, and ran out into the night.

His departure must have stunned my captors. They relaxed their hands.

Knowing that Brent and Misty would arrive soon and might be pulling into the parking lot that very moment, I wrenched myself free and tore outside after Alf. I told myself that I wouldn't get close to him. I just needed to see which way he went so I could tell Brent and Misty.

"Catch her!" one of the men behind me yelled.

"I'll be back!" I called over my shoulder. "Watch my purse."

The door shut behind me.

Alf had been right that the moon was up, but it was only about half full and was not yet reflecting on the lake. A walk on the beach would have been less than romantic. I didn't think that walking on the beach had been Alf's goal, however. His goal was probably more like dragging me into the water and attempting to hold me down or pushing me into the gray sedan and driving me to a spot where he could stop me, forever, from telling the police what I had pieced together about him.

Although the resort didn't seem to have any lights on its road or paths, the moonlight was enough for me to see Alf's white shirt bobbing along. He was running down the resort's road toward his cabin.

My cornflower blue sweater might have blended with the shadows, but my yellow dress was almost as pale as Alf's white shirt. Afraid that diners and resort staff might chase me and prevent me from finding out where Alf was heading, I ran, but I stayed far behind him and hoped that the sound of his feet hitting the gravel would prevent him from hearing mine. And that he wouldn't turn around.

Hanging back wasn't entirely successful. I was almost at the driveway to Birch cabin when the road curved, and I lost sight of him. If he understood that I knew he'd killed Zippy, he would probably jump into that gray sedan and flee.

I did not want to be on or near the resort's narrow road when he raced past in the car. He might do a better job of hitting me than he had on Saturday when Dep's sudden action had saved Nina and me. I didn't dare continue in the direction Alf had been going. Turning back toward the restaurant where I could meet Brent and Misty wouldn't be safe, either.

Hoping to conceal myself, I stepped into a thicket of bushes and small trees at the side of the road. The moonlight didn't penetrate well between the branches of trees above me.

I heard footsteps on Birch's wooden porch. There was a sound like a screen tearing, the yowl of a highly annoyed cat, a crash, and then a muffled curse.

Alf's voice. Not the phony sexy one, but the angry one.

A window rattled as if Alf were trying to shake it out of its frame.

The rattling stopped.

Hard shoes hit the wooden steps leading down from Birch cabin's porch. I thought I heard someone running down the gravel driveway, someone who was trying to be quiet.

Something rustled in the brush beside me.

Ears flat against her head, and the rest of her body double its usual size, Dep streaked out of the woods and into the road.

Chapter 33

Dep galloped toward the lodge. All sorts of terrible things could happen to a kitty in the woods at night. She was used to the safe confines of our yard, our house, and Deputy Donut.

Ignoring the need for stealth, I dashed after her down the moonlight-speckled road.

Joyful barking erupted. Dog tags jingled.

Barely slowing, I looked over my shoulder. The big fluffy puppy galumphed down the road from the direction of Alf's and Kassandra's cabins, and toward Dep and me. In the darkness I could barely see more than the white patches in the puppy's fur. He did not appear to be carrying sheets of paper.

I hoped that Dep would stop, arch her back, and allow me to capture her, but she seemed to have forgotten the tricks she'd used to scare the dog twice before. She also seemed to forget that she had never learned how to back down trees. She scooted up the broad trunk of a tall pine tree. Its lowest branches were about thirty feet up. She stopped about two feet beyond where I'd be able to reach her, clung to the trunk with her claws, and looked down at me.

I whispered up toward her, "Dep! Come down." I held my arms out to encourage her to jump into them.

The giant puppy was no help. Sniffing, he ran around the base of the tree.

"Mew." Fortunately, Dep didn't attempt to climb higher.

Whimpering and wagging that giant plume of a tail, the dog stood on his hind legs, placed his front paws as high as he could on the tree trunk, and let out a muted *woof*.

Looking down at his puppy face, I muttered, "If I can't reach her, you can't, either. And if you keep doing that, she might keep climbing away from me. She could be up there all night!"

Far behind me, a whistle sounded.

I added to the puppy, "And I think you're being called."

The puppy paid me and the whistle no attention. He kept whimpering and jumping as if he could climb the tree as easily as Dep could.

In my fear for Dep, I'd almost forgotten about Alf.

He must have been following me almost silently. He pounced out of the darkness and grabbed my arm again. "I said you're coming with me."

The puppy turned around, stood up, and plopped his front paws on Alf's far-from-clean shirt. Between the dog's enthusiastic greeting and my attempts to jerk myself out of Alf's grip, Alf lost his balance and fell on his back on the road.

Wagging his tail, the puppy held Alf down with those big front paws while he licked desserts off Alf's neck and shirt. The puppy was not only huge, he was enthusiastic and thorough.

Alf flailed his arms ineffectively. "Get him off me! He's trying to kill me!"

I couldn't help it. I stated calmly, "No, he's only washing your dirty shirt for you." If the desserts had contained chocolate, raisins, or nutmeg, I would have pulled the puppy away from Alf, not for Alf's protection, but for the dog's. Thanks to the restaurant staff, the puppy couldn't find much besides raspberries, cherries, sugar, and dairy products, none of which should harm him in such small quantities.

Alf yelled, "He's going to bite my neck and sever an artery! He's going to tear open the wound on my arm where that cat scratched me!"

I was certain the playful puppy was not hunting for blood. He was merely enjoying the unexpected sweet treats he'd found. I asked Alf, "Are you Nina Seaster's and Zippy Melwyn's cousin?"

Alf batted at the puppy's front legs. "Zippy had no business disguising herself as Nina, but she got what she deserved, and now both she and Nina are out of the way of the inheritance that should be mine. And you're next."

A shy and very feminine voice spoke out of the woods on the other side of the road. "Zippy claimed she was almost an heir to the Seaster fortune. She also kicked me out of our apartment, wouldn't let me have the pictures I'd been painting for months, and changed the locks."

Alf turned his head toward the newcomer, who was staying out of reach of all of us. "Who are you? I know. You're the waitress in the pub across from Nina Seaster's, I mean Nina Lapeer's, apartment. You must have worked with Nina to kill my dear cousin Zipporah."

"I never hurt anyone." Kassandra's voice was farther away, as if she were backing into the woods.

I called to her, "Don't go away. Do you recognize this man?"

She had stayed nearby. I could still understand her quiet words. "He's the one I told you about, the man who spent Friday afternoon and evening looking out the window of Suds for Buds."

Alf hollered, "No, I'm not. Get this mutt off me!"

I listened for the sounds of Brent, Misty, and Samantha driving up to the lodge, but footsteps pounded toward us from the opposite direction. "Havin' trouble here?" a man asked. "Can you ladies use some help?" I recognized the drawl.

Kassandra and I both answered, "Yes."

The puppy jumped away from Alf and would have headed toward Rodeo Rod if I hadn't grabbed a handful of fur at the back of the puppy's neck.

Alf sat up.

"Stay where you are!" Rodeo Rod shouted.

I froze, and so did the puppy. I still couldn't see Kassandra.

Alf jumped to his feet.

There was a whoosh and a zinging noise and then a loud thump as Alf fell on his back on the road again, this time with a rope around his ankles.

"I told you to stay where you were," Rodeo Rod drawled.

Chapter 34

✻

"Untie me!" Alf sounded short of breath.

As if expecting more desserts to materialize, the puppy investigated Alf's face again. I didn't stop him, but Alf flapped his hands between his face and the dog's eager tongue.

I was still hoping to hear my friends coming from near the lodge, but beyond Rodeo Rod, someone ran toward us. A flashlight blinded me. "Stay, Ivan," a woman commanded. Bewilderment made me almost woozy. What was Detective Gartborg doing here?

I felt around the puppy's neck and discovered a collar underneath all that fur. Grasping the collar, I asked Detective Gartborg, "Is this puppy yours?"

"Yes. Thanks for catching him. Good boy, Ivan." She handed me a soggy piece of paper and clipped a leash onto Ivan's collar. I hadn't pulled him away from Alf, and neither did Gartborg. She asked, "What's going on, Emily?"

I pointed at the man on the ground. "This is Alf Chator. I think you just gave me his family tree."

Alf accused, "Emily chased me and tripped me."

From bushes at the side of the road, Kassandra said, barely above a whisper, "No, she didn't."

I continued my introductions. "And that is Kassandra Pyerson."

"Come out where I can see you, Kassandra," Detective Gartborg ordered. "No one's going to bite you."

Arms up and looking about to faint from fright, Kassandra stepped into the glow of Detective Gartborg's flashlight.

"You can put your arms down, Kassandra." I'd never heard Gartborg sound so gentle before. "The police have been looking for you."

Blinking, Kassandra raised her hands higher and stepped back.

Gartborg repeated, "Put your arms down. Forensics experts examined the paintings in the apartment where Zipporah Melwyn illegally locked you out. Zipporah painted over your signature and replaced it with hers. We'll be returning the paintings and the apartment key to you."

Wearing that long skirt, Kassandra appeared to almost curtsy. "Thank you." She covered her face. Her shoulders shook.

"Don't go away," Gartborg told her.

Her face still covered and her voice coming out between sobs, Kassandra agreed.

I pointed beyond the circle of Detective Gartborg's light. "And that's Rodeo Rod."

Rodeo Rod strode into the light. "Evenin', ma'am, nice to see you again. This man seemed to be botherin' these two ladies, so I lassoed him. Just give me the word, and I'll untie him."

Gartborg shook her head. I wasn't sure I'd ever before seen her so completely at a loss for words. "I . . . um . . . everyone, stay where you are."

I didn't move. Kassandra didn't move.

Alf pushed at the puppy's inquisitive muzzle. "I wasn't bothering anyone. These two so-called ladies were bothering me. I was on the ground. They were standing over me. With this vicious animal."

"He just wants to play," Detective Gartborg told him. She still didn't pull Ivan away from Alf.

Alf flapped his hands at the happy-go-lucky puppy again. "Well, I don't want to play. And then some cowboy came along, endangering life and limb."

"I told you to stay where you were," Rod said mildly. "I wouldn't have roped you, but you got up."

"You've all had your fun," Alf whined. "Now call off your dog, whoever's dog this is. Ugh. His tongue is slimy."

Gartborg shined her light on the paper in my hand. "So, you're Alphaeus Chator?"

"Of course I am. I'm CFO of Cornwall Amherst and I demand to be released. You're all going to hear from our corporate lawyers."

Gartborg ignored the threat and went on with her questions. "And are you descended from Zebadiah Seaster?"

"If you say so. I don't know."

I spluttered, "He told me he was."

Gartborg pointed at the family tree I was still holding where she and I could both see it. "According to this, he is." I read as much as I could of the damp and tooth-marked page as Gartborg recited the ancestry of Alphaeus Chator and of his fourth cousins Zipporah Melwyn and Nina Seaster, whose last name had been crossed out and replaced, in handwriting, with Lapeer. Gartborg concluded, "If both Zipporah Melwyn and Nina Seaster were eliminated, you would be the heir to the Seaster fortune."

"The Seasters are willing everything to a ranch for rescued horses and dogs."

Gartborg answered, "Well, yes, except for that important fact. I'm surprised you know the details of the wills of Nicodemus and Jane Ellen Seaster, considering that they're both alive."

"It's common knowledge. And Nina is the Seasters' daughter. Zipporah's only a cousin."

"Zipporah is, or was, exactly as close to Nina's parents as you are."

That seemed to surprise Alf, but he didn't confirm or deny it. "I didn't mean to kill *her*." The way he put the emphasis on the word "her" gave me chills. He muttered, "I should have left Fallingbrook sooner, but I thought you were cute, Emily. Besides, leaving before I told you I was would have made me look guilty."

I stomped my sandal down on the gravel road. "You are guilty, and you meant to kill Nina, but when you discovered you'd killed Zippy instead, you tried again."

Gartborg didn't take her eyes off Alf. "I'll handle this, Emily. Mr. Chator, earlier this evening when Ivan got away and I was looking for him, I became curious about who was renting a particular gray sedan parked beside a nearby cabin. I called the rental company. It's rented in your name."

"So?" Alf asked.

"So, your name was also on the family tree that Ivan brought me, showing your connection to Zipporah Melwyn and to Nina Lapeer, who has told us she was previously known as Nina Seaster. The police have been wanting to talk to the driver of that car after reports of some dangerous driving. I called the local detective. He was already on his way. He'd received a message that Emily was in trouble here. I see that she was."

"Thank you," I managed.

Alf scoffed, "Emily has a wild imagination. I always drive carefully. I never tried to hit her." Alf must have heard me suck in my breath. He quickly added, "Or anyone else. Ever. The sun was in my eyes one night and I might have hit a curb, but I didn't crash into anyone. And then tonight, Emily invited me to have dinner with her, and after a few drinks, she decided that my acceptance was causing some sort of trouble for her. That's utter nonsense. She's not all that at-tract—" Ivan's big sloppy tongue prevented him from finishing the word. He pushed Ivan's face away, but the irrepressible big dog put those teacup-sized paws on Alf's chest again. "Can't you get this mutt off me?"

"I can," Gartborg answered, "but I won't until backup arrives."

Rod offered, "I have more rope. I can hogtie him."

Alf complained, "This mutt's heavy."

"He's still a puppy." Detective Gartborg scratched Ivan's ears and told him what a very fine boy he was. I was beginning to change my mind about the detective. Maybe she was good enough for Brent, after all.

I hadn't forgotten that Dep was in the tree above us, but I had been distracted. I heard noises above my head and then Dep landed with a thump on Alf's chest, between Ivan's front paws.

As if spring-loaded, Ivan leaped straight up into the air. When he hit the ground, he backed as far as his leash would let him and sniffed in Dep's direction. Dep arched her back and puffed up her fur and her tail.

And, apparently, extended her claws.

"Ouch!" Alf yelled. "What is this, bring-your-pet-to-meet-the-top-executive day?"

"Could be." Gartborg seemed to enjoy sarcasm even when it might be directed at her.

Kassandra removed her hands from her face and stared at us.

Still holding the end of his lasso, Rod moved protectively toward her.

A quavering male voice shouted, "There she is! She must have knocked that man down again. And now she has accomplices!"

Chapter 35

❧

I heard the welcome sound of Misty's voice. "Thank you. We'll take it from here. You four people can go back to the parking lot. We'll talk to you there."

A woman shouted in a shrill voice, "I still say he started it. He was dragging her out of the restaurant!"

Three flashlights bobbed toward us. Four others headed back toward the lodge.

Brent reached us first, but Misty and Samantha weren't far behind. None of them were out of breath.

Alf focused on Misty, the one wearing a police uniform. "Arrest these women. They attacked me and sicced their vicious pets on me."

Gartborg said quietly to Brent, "He admitted to killing Zipporah Melwyn."

Alf shouted, "Did not!"

I contributed, "I heard him, too. He said he didn't mean to kill *her*." I accented the word "her" the same way he had. "He also threatened that I was next."

Kassandra found her voice. "I heard that, too."

"So'd I," Rod concurred.

Alf argued, "That's not saying that I killed anyone."

Gartborg handed Ivan's leash to Samantha and turned to

me. "Emily, I don't think our friend here on the ground quite caught my name when you were introducing everyone."

"Alphaeus Chator," I said in a singsong voice, "meet Detective Gartborg of the Wisconsin Division of Criminal Investigation."

Alf muttered, "I didn't kill anyone. Or hurt anyone, either."

Brent detached Dep's claws from Alf's shirt and handed her to me. She was still puffed up. I cuddled her. She wriggled, but I was not about to let her go in case she decided to climb more trees. Warily, Ivan stared up at the tree trunk where Dep had been as if wondering how many more cats might be about to fling themselves down on him.

Telling Alf he was under arrest for the murder of Zipporah Melwyn, Gartborg flipped him over and handcuffed him. She rolled him onto his back again and called to Rod, "You can untie him now."

Rod loosened his lasso and removed it from Alf's ankles. Rod was deft and quick, but I sensed that he was a little reluctant to end his role in the capture of a murderer.

Misty and Brent helped Alf to his feet. "You're coming with us, sir," Misty said in even icier tones than she might have used for other murderers. Either Brent had told her, or she'd figured out that Alf was the driver who had aimed a rented car at Nina, Dep, and me.

Together, Misty and Brent marched Alf down the gravel road toward the parking lot. I asked Samantha, "Did Brent drive a cruiser here?" I knew that Misty probably hadn't switched her own car for a cruiser at the scene of the collision.

"Yes, he did."

I asked Gartborg, "Can they lock Alf inside it while I show you and Brent the white powder that spilled out of one of Alf's shirtsleeves?"

With a low whistle of something like astonishment, she took Ivan's leash from Samantha. "They sure can. Where's this powder?"

"In the restaurant."

Gartborg asked Samantha, "Do you mind coming along and hanging on to Ivan while I'm in the restaurant?"

"Not at all, especially if I can eat afterward. Emily, Misty said they were keeping the kitchen open for us."

"They are. For some reason, you made a good impression on them."

She pretended to swat at me.

With the help of Gartborg's and Samantha's flashlights, we started toward the lodge. I corralled Dep's feet before she could scramble up onto my shoulders or head and make it almost impossible for me to keep her from charging off into the woods and climbing trees. "I hope they haven't cleaned up the white powder while we were gone, but despite everything that happened to Alf this evening, he might still have some up his sleeve." I imitated him telling Sweetheart about recycling his dirty shirts.

When Gartborg finished laughing, she commented, "He seemed to be wearing a lot of desserts."

"That was my fault," I admitted. "I knocked him down with a platter of them."

Hearing Kassandra giggle, I looked over my shoulder. She and Rod were following us. Rod, who seemed prepared for nearly anything, had a flashlight.

Gartborg told them they could go back to their cabins and give her their statements later.

Kassandra offered, "I could hold the kitty while Emily goes into the restaurant."

"I'll help you, Kassandra," Rod drawled. "I like kitties and dogs."

I asked them, "How did you both happen to be at the resort where Samantha's wedding preparations are going on and Alf Chator was staying?"

Kassandra answered first. "I didn't know about the wedding or that it had anything to do with you, Emily. I arrived in Fallingbrook in July and have been staying here while I look for a place to rent. When I filled in my permanent addresses on job applications, I put my old address—that's the one I gave you, Emily—or the pub's address because, well, staying in a resort might have looked fishy. Mr. Chator wasn't here until today. A nice retired couple was staying in that cottage. After I saw Mr. Chator here and recognized him as the man who'd been in Suds for Buds, I didn't know what to do. I hid in my cabin. Then I saw you near his cabin, and that really scared me. I was afraid that you and he were part of a gang out to get Zippy and me."

I suggested gently, "You could have called the police."

Kassandra whispered, "I was too afraid."

Gartborg said something like, "Oof," but maybe the grunt was only a comment about the way Ivan was pulling. She added, "I wish you had called the police, Kassandra. I'm staying at the end of the cul-de-sac. And the only thing scary about me is my teenage boys and this monster that they were supposed to be looking after. Cool it, Ivan."

He didn't.

Rod corroborated that an older couple had been staying in the cabin between his and Kassandra's until that day, and then Alf had moved in. "I've been here for a week, between rodeos. They have a stable, so I can keep Lucky nearby, look after him, and ride him."

I asked Kassandra, "Why did you come to Fallingbrook? Were you following Zippy?"

"I knew where she planned to perform as a mime. I was desperate to get my paintings back, so I tried to meet her here, but I didn't succeed. If only I had also seen her go into Nina's loft, I might have recognized her and run across the street to talk to her, and she might still be alive, but I didn't."

And Alf would have found a different way to try to prevent Nina from ever inheriting from her folks, and he might have continued trying until he succeeded. I didn't say it. I asked Kassandra, "Why did you leave the two jobs you had in Fallingbrook without giving notice?"

"Like I told you, I was afraid that the man I'd talked to in Suds for Buds was a murderer, and he might come back there and find me. Then, my last afternoon at The Craft Croft, I saw him looking through the window, and I was afraid he recognized me. But I wasn't careful enough when I drove back here. I think he followed me, and then he moved in today, right next door to me. I'm . . . I'm glad you caught him."

Gartborg said drily, "So am I."

I agreed, and then asked Rod, "Will you be performing evenings this weekend? I have to work during the days."

"Yep. Both Friday and Saturday nights."

"I'm coming to cheer you on. Want to go with me, Kassandra? The Craft Croft closes at six on Saturdays."

"That would be nice, but I'm not sure that Summer will take me back."

"She will," I stated, "after we explain."

In the parking lot, the four seniors watched Misty and Brent put Alf into the back of an unmarked cruiser. The woman who had championed my cause, off and on, crowed to the other three, "See? I told you!"

Ivan apparently found all of this activity very exciting. In my arms, Dep lifted her head and stared toward the puppy. She was obviously scornful of his undignified and uncatlike behavior.

Misty stood beside the locked cruiser where she could prevent Alf from even thinking about trying to open doors that

couldn't be opened from the inside. She called to the four seniors, "Come give me your contact information. We'll get
your statements in the morning." She removed her pen and
notebook from pockets in her armored vest and asked Gartborg, "Would you like me to take Kassandra's and Rod's
statements if you have other things you need to do?"

Gartborg nodded. "We do, but I've had dinner. I'll come
out as soon as we're done inside, and then I'll take over the
interviews so you can eat."

Misty smiled and thanked her.

Gartborg and Brent both made phone calls and asked
someone to pick up a fugitive. In Gartborg's case, the fugitive
was Ivan. In Brent's, the fugitive was Alf. Brent also asked for
a team of crime scene investigators.

Kassandra and Rod didn't need to hold my cat. Gartborg
took Ivan's leash while Samantha helped me put Dep into
Samantha's car. "It's only for a little while," I told Dep. The
night air was soft and warm but not hot. Dep should be
comfy.

Samantha, Kassandra, and Rod stayed outside with Ivan
while Brent and Gartborg went with me to the restaurant.

The hostess was too short to see out the high window in
the front door. She was holding the door ajar and peeking
through the opening. She let us in. "We didn't touch a thing,"
she told me proudly. "Where's Samantha?"

I pointed. "In the parking lot. You probably don't recognize her in her EMT uniform. She's the one hanging on to the
dog." Ivan was trying to pull Samantha into the restaurant,
but Samantha was strong. Rod looked ready and eager to
help her.

Gartborg and Brent showed the hostess their badges. Gartborg asked, "Mind if we have a look around?"

The hostess stepped back. "Of course not." She shot me a
perplexed look. "You mean all of that wasn't some kind of

bachelorette prank? Was that man really trying to drag you out of the restaurant?"

"Yes. And I'm sorry I made a mess, but I didn't dare let him take me with him."

"I should hope not! But then you went outside after he did, so it all seemed like part of the game."

Brent studied my face. He did not look happy.

Chapter 36

I showed Brent and Detective Gartborg the black scuff marks and the spilled sugar. Brent seemed to understand that I had not purposely put myself in danger. He let me remove my cute little yellow purse from the table.

He taped off the area around where Alf and I had sat. He and Gartborg decided we could sit at a table on the other side of the restaurant, and then Gartborg went back to the parking lot to take Kassandra's and Rod's statements. The chef brought out delicacies for Brent, Misty, and Samantha.

I answered Brent's questions. He confirmed that Nina would be released and that her loft was still a crime scene.

I handed him my house key. "I want to stay here at the resort, but tell her she's welcome to go back to my place."

Gartborg came back inside and told us she'd sent forensics investigators to check out Birch cabin before they investigated the restaurant. Gartborg questioned the restaurant staff.

White-suited investigators came into the restaurant. After conferring with them, Brent and Gartborg headed off to police headquarters to question Alf Chator. I hoped that Brent had gotten enough to eat.

Misty and Samantha finished their meal, and we trooped outside. Rod, Kassandra, and Ivan had all left the parking lot.

Samantha drove Dep and me to Birch cabin while Misty

followed in her car. Hugging Dep on the cabin's porch, I shined my phone's light on the window I'd left slightly open. Despite all his cursing and rattling, Alf hadn't managed to open it farther. There was a hole in the screen.

Misty commented, "Alphaeus Chator made a habit of punching holes in screens. I think you solved the case, Emily."

"With help from Kassandra Pyerson, Rodeo Rod, Ivan the puppy, and Dep. And of course, Brent and Detective Gartborg. She mentioned her kids. Do you know if she's married, Misty?"

"She's a single mom. She has twin sixteen-year-old boys that she raised alone. I don't know if their father ever helped or if she's divorced, widowed, or never married."

I had to admit, "She's a lot nicer than I thought at first."

"She's okay," Misty agreed, "but not for Brent."

I asked her, "What are the boys like?"

"I've met them only once, but they seemed genuinely nice and mature for their age. I hear they win all sorts of prizes in school, in both sports and academics. And they're obviously responsible enough for her to let them stay alone in the resort and look after the dog while she's working."

In other words, although the twins might have had problems preventing their dog from escaping, they were kids that Brent would undoubtedly enjoy being around. With Detective Gartborg, they could be a ready-made family for Brent, complete with a loveable if slightly bumptious dog.

I carried Dep inside and set her down near her carrier. She jumped onto what seemed to be her favorite perch in the cabin, the arm of the love seat. All she would be able to see in the window at the moment would be her own reflection. Maybe Samantha and Misty felt the same way I did about the possibility of anyone outside peering in at us. We pulled the curtains across the windows. I made certain that the one with the broken screen was again firmly closed and locked.

The cabin did not appear to have been disturbed except

for fingerprint powder on the window frame that Alf touched while trying to open the window.

"Why did he do that?" Samantha asked. "Was he trying to get inside?"

Misty's answer was terse. "He was probably planning to hide in here and ambush Emily. He must have reasoned that she'd return here."

"How did he know which cabin?" I asked.

"Your car. Plus, he followed you to the restaurant to-night."

"He wasn't on the road behind me. I kept checking."

"He was walking between the cabins and the beach and keeping track of you."

Samantha asked, "How do you know all of this already?"

"Brent got it out of Alf when we were escorting him to the parking lot."

I commented, "Alf didn't seem particularly willing to admit to his crimes."

Misty gave us an impish smile. "Alf made it sound like he was following you because he was worried about you alone in the woods."

I shuddered. "Ugh. Let's forget about him." I picked up the note propped against the jar of flowers and waved it at them. "How was the collision?"

Misty shrugged. "Not as bad as it could have been. A couple of people will be in the hospital for a while."

Samantha added, "I wasn't needed. Other EMTs took care of nearly everything, including transporting the injured people to the hospital."

Misty glanced toward the fridge. "Let's forget all that, too. I don't know about Samantha, but now that both of us are no longer on duty or even on call, I want to get out of this uniform and start on the wine."

Chapter 37

❧

At the rehearsal the next afternoon, Hooligan and Samantha practiced everything except reciting their actual vows. I listened carefully. The minister didn't say Hooligan's and Samantha's full names.

Misty's, Samantha's, and my parents attended the rehearsal dinner. Scott was there, but Brent wasn't, and Hooligan had no family present. The food was delicious, and the restaurant staff were wonderful. Downplaying my part, I filled my parents in on the capture of Zippy Melwyn's murderer. My parents didn't seem surprised that I had come through the experience unscathed except for a few bruises on my arms, courtesy of Alf and the two elderly gentlemen who had tried to protect Alf from wayward silver-platter-wielding women.

My mother was understandably more concerned about Nina than about me. "Will Nina be freed?"

"I hope she already has been." Nina hadn't called me, though. I pictured her falling into my guest bed and staying there for days. Or, knowing her, she'd gone to work with Tom and Jocelyn. And then she'd fallen into bed.

The weather the next day was everything that Hooligan and Samantha could have wanted. It was sunny and warm without being hot. Misty, Samantha, and I dressed in shorts and T-shirts, ate brunch, and sat on the front porch savoring our Kona coffee. Dep stayed inside the cabin. She seemed to have decided it was nice and homey, after all.

In a large, open-sided white tent on the lawn sloping down toward the beach in front of us, people from the chair-rental company were setting up chairs facing the lake. They were leaving a nice, wide aisle between the two sections. A woman set a podium in front of the aisle.

Another woman carried an armful of flowers toward the tent. She was tall and thin, and wearing the Deputy Donut uniform of black jeans and a white polo shirt.

Samantha, Misty, and I shouted, "Nina!"

We plunked our mugs down on the wide arms of our Adirondack chairs and raced barefoot toward the tent. Nina set the flowers down and met us halfway. There was a lot of whooping and hugging.

Nina looked thinner than ever. I asked her, "Are you okay?"

"Sure. Brent took me to your place. I made myself at home. It was just what I needed. Thank you."

I asked, "How did you get here?"

"Brent offered to bring me, but I caught a ride with the florist. Let me go finish the decorating, then I'll come up and help you all get ready. Is it still okay if I change in your cabin? My dress is in the florist's van."

Samantha gave her another hug. "Of course it's okay."

Misty added, "We're happy you're here!"

I brushed tears out of my eyes.

Nina was almost her old, bubbly self. "Samantha, don't you dare look toward that tent again until you're ready to walk down the aisle."

"Okay."

After she finished with the flowers, Nina brought her dress and shoes into the cabin, and we all did each other's hair and makeup. Samantha had left her hair its natural shiny brown. I asked Nina, "Did you call Mr. Arthurs?"

"Yes, and the show will go on as planned. Not only that, Mr. Arthurs said it could be the most successful show he's ever mounted. Art museums and collectors around the world are asking about me and my work. And no one has even seen a picture of the big painting, which is my favorite ever, or was before sugar landed on it. Brent says I can go back to my loft in a couple of days. I'll get that painting finished in time to ship it."

We all congratulated her.

Samantha nearly bubbled over. "We'll celebrate your big success today, too."

Nina made a regretful face. "I should have waited to tell you. This is your day, Samantha, and Hooligan's, not mine. And maybe none of those collectors will end up buying. We'll celebrate when they do."

I slid my feet into my shoes. "We sure will! Nina, at the carnival, did you know who the mime was?"

"No. I didn't recognize her until I saw you trying to save her in my apartment. I hadn't seen her since she was about thirteen, and I had decided then that I never wanted to see her again. I'm sorry I implied that she'd stolen that locket on Friday. She must have taken it when she was a teenager and I was still a kid."

Misty asked her, "Why didn't you tell us that at first?"

Nina let out a tremulous breath. "I was so shaken up by the whole thing, her showing up and causing me trouble again, that I just didn't think about making everything clear, and then it seemed too late and maybe like it didn't matter."

I pinned a flower in Misty's hair. "Who wrote that coded address that I found in your locket?"

"She must have. I'm sorry to say that both times I encountered her, she was not a nice person."

Misty told Nina, "We figured that out. She kicked her much younger roommate out of their shared apartment. Her ex-roommate is an artist. Zippy painted over the roommate's name, signed the paintings herself, and tried to interest the Arthurs Gallery in them."

Nina released the last of Samantha's curls from the curling iron. "That all sounds like her."

Misty asked her, "Did you ever meet another cousin named Alphaeus Chator, Alf for short?"

Nina settled Samantha's veil over Samantha's curls. "Not until early yesterday morning. I didn't exactly meet him. I saw him being taken to another cell, and I heard him shouting. He's going to sue all of you Fallingbrook police officers, plus Detective Gartborg, Emily, and even Rodeo Rod, that rodeo performer we met at the carnival."

"Rodeo Rod came to Deputy Donut looking for you," I told her.

She blushed.

I added, "But don't get excited about it. He has since met the artist who was Zippy's roommate."

Nina twitched Samantha's veil into place. "I'm not excited about it. He probably has a sweetheart in every town."

"Thanks to Alf, we found out your real name," I told her. "Are you going to invite your parents to your opening?"

"No. I'm Nina Lapeer, and I'm happy the way I am, working at Deputy Donut, making friends in Fallingbrook, and painting."

"What if you become really famous?"

She didn't look up from buckling her sparkly sandals. "I'll be proud that I made it on my own and not because of my parents' famous last name. I'll be the person I want to be. And now that person is about to go to the wedding of the world's best bride and groom." She picked Dep up, held her away from her pretty green silk dress, gave the cat a kiss on the nose, and set her down. "See you all in a few minutes." She ran outside, followed by our shouted thanks.

Carrying the bouquets that Nina had designed and wearing the powder blue gowns that Samantha had chosen to go with our eyes, Misty and I went out onto the porch and held the doors open for Samantha. Her parents were waiting for her on the front porch. Samantha was so radiant in her white gown and her parents were so solicitous, loving, and close to tears that my own eyes filmed over.

In front of us, guests sat facing the water, and the aisle seats were decorated with beribboned swags of flowers.

The string quartet started the processional. I carefully made my way down the steps, past the row of trees, and across the grassy space to the tent. Hooligan and the minister and Hooligan's groomsmen were all smiling. People turned around in their seats, and I smiled, too.

I arrived in front, turned around, and watched Misty. I hoped that Scott, on the other side of the podium, noticed how perfectly elegant, despite the damply sparkling eyes, she was.

Samantha walked down the aisle between her parents. As far as I could tell, she never took her eyes off Hooligan.

Misty's and my parents sat together near the front. My mother passed Misty's mother a box of tissues. Misty's mother took one and handed the box back to my mother. I scanned the audience. I saw plenty of Hooligan's friends, but again, it seemed that none of his family had attended, and I wondered if he, like Nina, had a sad story he was hiding.

When I thought it was time for the minister to say Hooligan's name, I leaned slightly toward the couple.

The minister smiled at the congregation. "I've known Hooligan Houlihan since we were in first grade. I made the mistake, way back then, of announcing his real name in public. I earned a broken nose and two black eyes. Hooligan earned his nickname, and I learned a lesson. Hooligan and I have been good friends ever since. I have not spoken his birth name in public from that day to this. And now we come to one of the most important days in my good friend's life. Today . . ." He paused dramatically.

I held my breath.

"Today," he went on, "is no different. While I know that my longtime friend will not punch me in the face, I will continue to keep my promise to a scrappy six-year-old. I assure you all, and especially Samantha, that Hooligan is not an interloper. He is who he says he is." The minister held a card in front of Hooligan and Samantha where only they could see it. "Do you, Hooligan Houlihan, also known as"—the minister pointed at the card—"take Samantha Quinn Andersen to be your lawfully wedded wife?"

Hooligan's voice rang out. "I do."

The minister tucked the card into his shirt pocket. When it was time to ask Samantha a similar question, the minister referred to Hooligan as "this man."

"I do," she said.

I glanced out over the congregation. Brent was peering around the man in front of him. His eyes warm, he focused on me. Nina was sitting beside him.

I wasn't sure I had ever smiled a bigger smile.

Brent winked and echoed the look on my face.

I decided to keep my eyes open for a match for the beautiful detective with the perfect teenaged sons and the perfectly goofy puppy. She deserved someone wonderful.

But not quite as wonderful as Brent.

He and I kept smiling at each other as I followed Hooligan and Samantha toward the back of the congregation.

Some day, I promised myself, we would discover Hooligan's first name.

I wasn't the only one.

When Nina reached me in the receiving line, she hugged me, and then backed up and pointed at the minister, whose shirt pocket might still contain the card with Hooligan's real name on it. With a perfectly straight face, she asked me, "Where's a pickpocket when we really need one?"

RECIPES

Corny Fritters

1 cup all-purpose flour
1 teaspoon baking powder
½ teaspoon salt
2 eggs, beaten
¼ cup less 1 tablespoon milk
½ cup corn kernels—fresh, frozen, or canned. If using
    frozen, thaw first, then drain and pat dry on paper tow-
    els. If using canned, drain and pat dry with paper towels.
1 teaspoon (or to taste) sweet smoked paprika for regular
    corny fritters
or
1 teaspoon (or to taste) whole black peppercorns for pepper-
    corny fritters
or
¼ teaspoon (or to taste) powdered ancho or other hot chiles
    for turbo-charged spicy corny fritters

Vegetable oil with a smoke point of 400 degrees F or higher
    (or follow your deep fryer's instruction manual)

Optional:
Granulated sugar
or
Confectioners' sugar

   Sift the flour with the baking powder and salt.
   Stir in eggs, milk, corn kernels, and paprika, peppercorns,
or powdered chile until blended.

When oil reaches 370 degrees F, drop batter by spoonfuls into the oil without crowding them. Fry until both sides are golden, approximately 1 minute per side, turning once. Lift basket to drain, then drain fritters on paper towels.

While still warm, roll in sugar (if desired) and serve with guacamole (below) and/or sour cream.